James Monkres is a new author from Texas. While this is his first novel, he has written as a hobby for years. He recalls reading an interview with Stephen King in which Mr King said that when he was writing, he felt like he had found the button that started the bulldozer that was taking up so much space in his head. This is one story that Mr Monkres finally got out of his head.

To Cynthia for staying by my side. To my mother, Linda, for always encouraging me to write.

James Monkres

NIKODEMUS

AUSTIN MACAULEY PUBLISHERS™
LONDON * CAMBRIDGE * NEW YORK * SHARJAH

Copyright © James Monkres 2021

The right of James Monkres to be identified as author of this work has been asserted by the author in accordance with section 77 and 78 of the Copyright, Designs and Patents Act 1988.

All rights reserved. No part of this publication may be reproduced, stored in a retrieval system, or transmitted in any form or by any means, electronic, mechanical, photocopying, recording, or otherwise, without the prior permission of the publishers.

Any person who commits any unauthorised act in relation to this publication may be liable to criminal prosecution and civil claims for damages.

This is a work of fiction. Names, characters, businesses, places, events, locales, and incidents are either the products of the author's imagination or used in a fictitious manner. Any resemblance to actual persons, living or dead, or actual events is purely coincidental.

A CIP catalogue record for this title is available from the British Library.

ISBN 9781528989060 (Paperback)
ISBN 9781528989077 (ePub e-book)

www.austinmacauley.com

First Published 2021
Austin Macauley Publishers Ltd®
1 Canada Square
Canary Wharf
London
E14 5AA

Prologue

Her scream shattered an otherwise idyllic Fort Worth, Texas, afternoon. Elizabeth Rollins was the daughter of Senator Mike Rollins, and as such, she had a driver. Ray Brooks was an ex-Navy Seal and had been with the family for almost five years. He had seen Elizabeth leave the west-side faculty entrance to John Phillips High School with two of her friends right on time as usual. Brooks thought of it as the VIP entrance to the school.

The school was in an affluent part of Fort Worth, Texas, and had more than a few children of influential couples. Her friend, Sheila Richardson, was the daughter of Mark and Karen Richardson. Richardson owned oil production over "hell and half of Georgia" as the old saying went. Janet Ledbetter, Elizabeth's closest friend, was the daughter of Mayor Thomas "Tommy" Ledbetter. By arrangement, Brooks was picking up all three girls for a trip to Grapevine Mills mall.

Brooks was getting out to open the door when it happened. A bearded guy in coveralls stained with grease like a mechanic jumped out of the hedge, right in front of the three. With no hesitation, he grabbed Elizabeth by the arm and yanked her into the hedge with him. Brooks sprinted towards the hedge. Her friends were staring in shock as Brooks reached the hedge in maybe ten seconds. He heard a pop as he get there. Out the other side. Nothing. Nobody. Bill Harris and Allen King came through the hedge further down. The two football stars had heard the scream.

"Where is she? Elizabeth?"

No answer to Brooks' yell.

"You two, check towards the parking lot!"

Without a word, Bill and Allen streaked across the lawn and hurdled a parked Lincoln Town Car. Brooks was checking under and in cars near the hedge. There hadn't been time for them to get anywhere far. He pulled out his phone while he was looking.

"Siri, Dial 911!"

Allen and Bill showed up empty-handed. Brooks ignored them.

"John Phillips High School. West faculty parking lot. Senator Mike Rollins' daughter Elizabeth has just been abducted. White female, seventeen years old, five feet eight inches, one hundred five pounds, blonde hair, blue eyes, blue dress, blue shoes. Abductor. White male, forties, six feet, two hundred pounds, dark long hair, dark long beard, unkempt appearance, stained mechanic-type uniform, grey in colour. Get somebody here now! Confirm!"

Brooks listened to the dispatcher list the information back to him and sat down on the grass. Allen and Bill sat down next to him. They didn't speak or move until Sheila and Janet sat down next to them. Both were crying. Allen finally asked Brooks, "What the fuck?"

Chapter 1

FBI Special Agent Charles Bone had worked more abduction cases than anyone else in his division. That was why he was the agent in charge for this one. Something was off about this case, though. Senator Mike Rollins' daughter had a driver who was an ex-Navy Seal. His name was Ray Brooks, and he was at a loss. Bone was going over his account of the event for the fifth time.

Elizabeth had seen the car and waved. She was in front of her high school in an affluent area of Fort Worth, Texas. She was walking towards the car on a sidewalk that was bordered by a hedge with several walkways through it that led to the faculty parking lot. A man had jumped out, grabbed Elizabeth and pulled her through an opening. Brooks was out of the car and at the hedge by his account in less than ten seconds. He burst through ready to deal death to whoever the bearded low life was. Nobody there. No screams. No answers to his calls. Something didn't add up.

Bone pulled up to the carport that could house ten or twelve vehicles. The six federal cars plus a sheriff's sedan fit in easily. The house was a large sprawling two-storey affair. The carport was situated so that the swarm of official vehicles weren't visible from the street. The door was opened for him as he ascended the steps in the front of the house.

The mood amongst the agents was of utter hopelessness. These never turned out good. The fact that the father was Senator Mike Rollins, a Republican from Texas, meant something. Hence the five special agents in the house. The mother, Mary, could be heard crying from the bedroom. Figured it wasn't a ransom case. The picture of the seventeen-year-old Elizabeth showed that she was already a knockout. Sexual predators didn't usually return them alive.

There was a sound that started coming from the living room. Kind of like tearing paper. Everyone went towards it. They stopped, though, once they saw the source. In the centre of the living room, in front of the fireplace, it looked like glitter was falling from nowhere. Then there was a pop, and out of nowhere, a cell phone dropped to the carpet and started ringing.

For a second, no one did anything but looked at it. Then the closest agent, a mean-looking Hispanic named Miguel Torrez picked it up and answered it. It was on speakerphone. A male voice broadcasted out.

"I'm going to come through the same way the phone did. I'm coming to assist you. If anybody shoots me, I'll peel them like an apple."

The voice paused.

"Do you understand me?"

Agent Torrez hesitated and then said, "I hear you. What do you mean by coming through?"

The voice on the phone sounded irritated, "The same way you got the phone."

Torrez said nothing.

"Just stand clear of where it dropped, and I'll explain everything when I'm there. Fair warning, one minute."

Torrez stood there dazed until the Agent in Charge Charles Bone barked at him, "Step back. I don't know how the phone popped in but it sounds like we're getting a company the same way."

He looked at two agents.

"Smith, Ringer, weapons drawn, safeties on, stand in the foyer. If I say it, you pop in. Got it?"

They nodded their assent. Senator Rollins spoke for the first time in hours, "He said he was going to assist us."

Agent Bone looked at the Senator and then his watch.

"We're going to find out, I guess, in about thirty seconds. Ringer, Smith, stay out of sight. Everyone else, leave your weapons in your holsters."

The door to the master bedroom opened, and Mary Rollins came out. Eyes swollen, hair askew.

"What's happening?"

Senator Rollins was staring at the spot by the fireplace that was starting to look like glitter falling again. Then he said, "Someone made a phone appear out of nowhere and said he's going to help."

He nodded towards the glitter falling.

"It looks like he's arriving."

The tearing sound was louder this time. Loud enough that everyone winced Then it popped, and a man stepped out of the falling glitter and was standing in front of the fireplace. He was dressed in blue jeans and a buttoned-up, long-sleeved white shirt. His hair was salt and pepper, and he wore light green-tinted sunglasses. He looked around intently. Waiting for something apparently. Then he relaxed and looked at Agent Torrez.

"My phone, please."

Agent Torrez handed it to him. The man stood there a second before asking, "Who's the agent in charge?"

Agent Bone snapped out of his reverie and stepped forward.

"Special Agent in Charge Charles Bone. And you are?"

The man came forward and shook his hand answering, "Call me Nikodemus."

Agent Bone answered, "Do you have a last name?"

Nikodemus grinned and looked around as he answered, "Not for the purposes of this event, no. Nikodemus is it. May I sit?"

Nikodemus was indicating a chair. Without waiting for an answer, he seated himself.

"I work for a consortium. Different members have different…duties. For want of a better word. Anyway it has been decided that we are going to intervene on your behalf. It was decided by the…well, the higher-ups."

He kept hesitating in different parts of his dialogue. Agent Bone interjected, "You seemed unsure of your wording on duties and whatever. Any reason for that?"

Nikodemus answered unaffected by the interruption, "I'm just trying to word things so you'll understand. Look, I'm a Level 7 Magic User. A Seeker. I know when you hear magic, you think rabbits out of hats. It isn't. I can seek. I can make. I can do many things such as going between like I did to get here."

Nikodemus stood up without waiting for a comment. He looked at Mary Rollins. His tone softened as he went up to her. She was sitting on the couch, and he knelt in front of her.

"I'm going to bring Elizabeth back to you."

Mary sobbed and grasped his hands.

"I need something she has worn that hasn't been washed. If not clothing, then a pair of shoes. Run a bath for her. I'm going to bring her back between, and she will be sort of unconscious. She'll be naked. I'm going to drop her in the tub and step out of the bathroom. You, Mary, will then open the door and say something to her, anything. The sound of your voice will wake her, and she won't remember anything that happened today."

Senator Rollins stepped forward raising his voice, "What's going on? Who are you? What have you done to my daughter?"

Nikodemus looked up and was about to speak when he started staring at the Senator incredulously. Bone got nervous and stepped between them unsure of what was happening. Then Nikodemus muttered, "Holy shit, you're the real thing."

The Senator was taken aback by this. He asked, "What do you mean?"

Nikodemus spoke as he drew his cell phone from his pocket, "I mean you're in politics to make a difference, to help people. You want to make the world a better place. You're not in it for the money or the power. You're a man who is actually righteous without being self-righteous. I didn't know any existed. Now I know why I'm here."

He then spoke into his cell phone, "Holy shit! I didn't know why you sent me until I saw him. His soul shines like a beacon. I'll have Elizabeth back here in a few minutes. What do you want me to do with whoever has her?"

He paused, listening. Then spoke again, "Really, take an agent between to arrest them? That'll be expensive as hell."

An agent named Moore interrupted the conversation.

"Money is not an issue here."

Nikodemus glanced at the agent as he hung up his phone. He looked at Moore and asked, "Tell me, junior. Do you remember when you were a little kid, like five or six, when your mom or dad bought something with a credit card or a check?"

He didn't wait for an answer before continuing, "It seemed like they were just showing them something, and it was buying it. Later you came to know that these were transactions that would require real money to change hands, right?"

Agent Moore nodded.

"Well, let me assure you that your understanding of your mommy's credit card at age five far exceeds your understanding of what it costs to appear like I did. At least at age five, you knew what money was. What a dollar was. You have no concept of what the cost is and where I'm going."

Nikodemus looked up impatiently and said, "Mary! The clothing or shoes now! Time is getting short."

Mary jumped up and ran up the stairs towards Elizabeth's room.

"Don't forget the bath! It's important."

Nikodemus turned to the Senator, "Where is the bathroom she bathes in?"

The Senator pointed upstairs. Water could be heard running. Nikodemus started up the stairs and then stopped. He looked at Bone.

"You need to pick someone for me to take with me when I return. One of the two holding their guns in the foyer will do. Or any one of you. I would suggest more than one gun. Something bigger than a pistol wouldn't be a bad idea."

Nikodemus ran up the stairs looking at his watch. He shouted up, "Now Mary! Shoes or clothes! Quick!"

They met in the hall. A door into the bathroom with water running was behind her.

"We'll meet right here in about one or two minutes. I'll have Elizabeth. Remember, I'm going to drop her in the tub, and then you speak to rouse her from the glamour. She won't remember anything. Act like you heard her fall or something."

Nikodemus took the pair of offered shoes and bellowed in a voice that seemed to rock the entire house as the glitter falling started, "Once I drop her, I'll come down the stairs and take an agent back to where she was. We'll bring whoever is there to the Sheriff's Station over on Riverdale. We'll step between and be in the main holding tank. It's empty now. See it stays that way. Later."

Then the tearing sound started, and he was gone.

Chapter 2

The pop of his departure was so loud that pictures by the stairs vibrated. One fell off the wall and bounced on the carpet. Bone stared at where Nikodemus had been for a second and then started barking orders.

"Smith! Get a riot gun and a vest from your car and wait on the stairs. Torrez, you and your partner get to the Sheriff's Station."

Bone paused for a second and breathed before getting out his cell phone.

"This is getting weirder by the minute."

The statement was to no one. Then he dialled and reported what had happened. He hung up and looked at the Senator.

"They knew. The office knew he was coming. Said they'd been called from an untraceable number and informed that they were intervening in our behalf."

The sound of the faucets being turned off in the tub upstairs caused everyone to look up. Mary was shaking. Her voice broke, and she had to start again as she spoke.

"Rea… Ready, I guess."

Then the tearing sound started again. Agent Torrez's car could be heard screeching out of the driveway. Then the pop again. Everyone expected it now, and no one was startled by it.

There he was. He was holding a naked girl. Presumably Elizabeth in his arms. Mary started to speak, but Nikodemus interrupted her.

"Don't speak! Wait till I put her in the tub. She'll wake up at the sound of your voice."

Nikodemus looked at Smith, in a vest and holding a riot gun.

"Get ready."

He turned to Mary.

"Actually, you should wait till we're gone. The sound of our departure will be hard to explain."

Then he went into the bathroom and dropped Elizabeth in the tub. He walked out and came down the stairs towards Smith.

"What's your name?"

Smith answered, "Smith."

"Your first name?"

This was said almost tenderly.

"Bill."

"Well, Bill, this is kind of like diving into a lake in January. It'll seem painfully cold for a second and then boom, you're there."

Then Nikodemus took Bill's arm, and they vanished. The pop made Mary scream. Then Elizabeth could be heard screaming. Mary shut the door, and they could be heard crying and talking. Bone looked at the Senator.

"We're heading to the Sheriff's Station. Want to come?"

The Senator said nothing but rose and started for the door.

Chapter 3

Smith felt like he had barely survived the transit. His fingers were numb with cold. The riot gun felt like it had been in a deep freeze. He looked around and saw bare concrete walls, a bed in the centre of the room and men. Successful-looking men. Two were in suits, and one was stripped to his boxers. They were standing staring, not moving. Nikodemus' voice startled Bill.

"They're in a glamour. They'll stay that way until I lift it. Let's look around a little before I do."

Bill moved towards a table with the boxer shorts guy's clothes on it.

"What is this place?"

He was picking up a wallet as Nikodemus answered, "I don't know. It's underground. These guys don't seem like the typical sexual predator types. Do they?"

Bill held up a business card.

"No, they don't. This guy's a lawyer. My guess is they all are."

Nikodemus indicated a guy Bill hadn't noticed who was on the floor.

"This guy wasn't. He looked at me like he knew what I was. I knew the glamour wouldn't hold on him so I killed him."

Bill looked at a bearded man in torn mechanic's clothes. He looked like he had been stepped on by several elephants.

"What did you do to him?"

Nikodemus went to the boxer shorts guy. He answered Bill absently, "I hit him hard. Let's see what this guy knows. I'm going to wake them all at the same time. As soon as they wake up, introduce yourself as a federal agent. Have a gun in your hand. Then let me do the talking."

Without waiting for assent, Nikodemus snapped his finger. Only the sound of it rattled Bill's teeth. Then, like a switch was turned on the two dressed guys started talking in mid-sentence.

"I can't wait."

This from the taller of the two. The short, fat one started to speak and then noticed Bill and Nikodemus. His eyes widened, and the tall guy whirled on them.

"This is a private property."

Nikodemus didn't even look at them. He just said, "Bill?"

Bill snapped out of his reverie. He had his credentials in one hand and his gun in the other.

"FBI! Put your hands on your heads and face the wall!"

He was louder than he had meant to be. It startled everyone. Not Nikodemus, though. He was looking at the boxer shorts guy. The boxer shorts guy was staring back, mesmerised. Like he was picking up a date Nikodemus spoke.

"And you are?"

The guy in shorts answered dreamily, "Pete, Pete Ringo."

Nikodemus' tone stayed the same. "What is your occupation?"

Before he could answer the short guy barked, "Don't say another word, Pete. They're here obviously without a warrant. We'll have their asses."

Pete lost the dreamy look as his associate yelled at him. Nikodemus turned and glared at him.

"What's your fucking name, fat boy?"

The man looked at Nikodemus haughtily.

"Nobody is going to say another word until I see a warrant."

Nikodemus grinned and started sauntering over to the guy. Something about the grin scared Bill. It was about then that the guy noticed the flattened body of the bearded, dead guy. His eyes widened.

"Holy shit! What happened to him?"

Nikodemus was starting to invade the guy's personal space.

"I did. I made it happen to him. I guess you're not gonna tell me his name either, are you?"

The retort was not as forceful as before. He was backing away as Nikodemus moved closer to him.

"I am not saying another word. If you touch me, I'll sue you for assault."

Nikodemus laughed, and the last few chuckles seemed impossibly loud. He grinned at him and casually asked:

"Have you ever been on fire?"

Nikodemus paused and then continued.

"I'm talking about flames consuming your flesh all over. Feeling the nerve endings reach the absolute maximum pain possible and then going numb? Smelling your skin cook?"

Nikodemus started rubbing his index finger against his thumb in a circular motion. The guy was getting pale but said nothing.

"I can tell by looking that you haven't. Well, next time somebody asks you that question, you'll be able to answer yes."

Nikodemus rubbed his thumb and index finger a little longer and then softly snapped them. As he did, he quietly said one word, "Burn."

The guy hit the ground screaming louder than Bill had ever heard anybody scream. You could tell it was torturing his vocal cords. He was writhing and rolling and clawing at his face and then his chest. He voided his bladder and his bowels as he continued to writhe in obvious agony. Pete, Bill and nameless watched, spellbound. After about twenty or thirty seconds, Nikodemus put his hand out and then brought it towards himself as he closed his fingers like he was squeezing something.

The guy stopped screaming and flopping and lay there gasping. Nikodemus softly said, "I didn't touch you, did I?"

The man tried to speak but his voice was gone. Screamed out. He collapsed, weeping. Nikodemus looked at the other guy.

"You want some of that?"

The guy shook his head and turned white.

"What's your name?"

Nikodemus was advancing on the guy, and the guy was looking at him like he was Satan, walking the earth.

"Scott, Scott Peterson. You know he's Pete Ringo."

Scott indicated Pete as he said this and then looked at the guy on the ground who was still lying there weeping.

"That's Walter Richardson. He's a senior partner at our firm."

Nikodemus waited till he stopped and then asked him, "What are the three of you doing here?"

Only then did Scott and Bill look towards the bed. They looked at each other quizzically. Then at Nikodemus. Pete spoke first.

"I don't exactly remember coming here. I remember there was a girl here. I mean a woman here. A prostitute."

Nikodemus looked at Bill and shook his head.

"Scott, do you recognise the guy pancaked over there?"

Nikodemus indicated the bearded corpse. Scott spoke hesitantly.

"I kind of recognise him, but I can't exactly recall his name. Believe me, I'd tell you."

This last was spoken fervently as Scott and Pete started to sit Walter up. The master of the universe look was gone from him now. He looked at Nikodemus like a whipped puppy.

Nikodemus started barking orders.

"Pete, get dressed. Steve, get Walter here upright. We're leaving."

Bill went over to Nikodemus and whispered, "Do you want me to cuff them?"

Nikodemus shook his head negative as he went to the centre of the room.

"Everybody, front and centre."

As soon as they had Walter upright, the tearing sound started. The three lawyers looked terrified but noticed that Bill was calmly looking at them. Then Bill spoke. "Don't freak out but in about ten seconds you're going between."

Pete looked at him with a weird expression. "Between?"

Bill's answer was lost as they entered the darkest, coldest space for a second and then were in a brightly lit holding tank at the Sheriff's Station. Bill looked out and saw the Agent in Charge Bone along with several deputies and a couple of plain-clothed onlookers who were wide-eyed and staring.

Nikodemus took one look at the crowd and then nudged Bill.

"Later."

Poof, he was gone. Walter collapsed on the floor weeping, and Bill just shook his head.

Chapter 4

Bill, Agent in Charge Bone, and Deputy Director Allen Perkins were looking through the glass into the interrogation room with Scott Peterson and Pete Ringo. They weren't speaking at all. Their lawyer instincts had kicked in once everything was normal. Well, sort of normal. Walter Richardson had been taken by ambulance to All Saints Hospital.

He was having trouble speaking. Vocal cords or something. Deputy Director Perkins addressed Bill without taking his eyes off the two lawyers.

"So, this Nikodemus guy never touched Richardson?"

Bill answered, "No, sir. Not a finger."

Now Perkins looked at Bill. Which necessarily meant Bill looked at him as he spoke.

"Your statement is… I don't know what it is."

"It's the truth, sir. Richardson can't speak because he screamed louder than I have ever heard a human scream. Nikodemus snapped his fingers and said "Burn," and Richardson was screaming, shitting and pissing himself, and flopping around like he was on fire. Then Nikodemus turned it off. Like he flipped a switch."

Bone spoke for the first time.

"Interesting interrogation technique. Not a mark on the guy. Wonder what he'll say happened?"

This was the interesting part. The lawyers were in Fort Worth now. They had woken up that morning outside of Pittsburgh, Pennsylvania. Bill said what they were all thinking.

"How is anybody going to explain them suddenly being in Texas? I asked Nikodemus where we were when we went between. He said, 'I don't know. It's underground.' I don't think he knew where we were."

Deputy Director Perkins had taken a phone call during this exchange and started to open the door.

"I suggest we let these gentlemen call their office and then we'll see. We have no legal reason to deny them access to their phones. Should be interesting."

Bone snorted and followed him out. The door closed behind them leaving Bill alone in the room watching as Bone and Perkins entered the interrogation room. They started talking to them, and Bill's phone rang. He looked at his phone. Caller ID blocked. He didn't usually answer those but today... He wasn't surprised to hear Nikodemus' voice.

"What's happening?"

Bill activated the recorder on his phone and answered.

"Looking at two lawyers; the other is in the hospital. Trying to figure out how they're not in Pennsylvania. You?"

Nikodemus chuckled and said something to somebody in the background and then was back on the phone.

"Chilling out. Just wanted to make sure you were okay. I was going to give you my number, but I've been told not to."

Bill was watching the lawyers through the glass as they were given their cell phones. He could hear them saying they wanted to leave the interrogation room to make their calls. Perkins informed them that they were, at the moment, not at liberty to do so.

"Who told you not to?"

Nikodemus again said something to somebody else and answered, "Same guys who sent me. This apparently is contained. The bearded guy. You know the dead one. He's been very helpful in nipping this whole thing in the bud."

Bill turned away from the glass and asked, "Isn't he dead?"

Nikodemus' voice changed. He sounded like he had sounded after he did whatever he did to Walter Richardson.

"He was, and he will be again. You really don't want to know more than that believe me. Anyway who knows? I might see you again sometime. Regrettably, I'm not doing any depositions or any shit like that. If those maggots start telling people what happened, they'll be in straitjackets in about two days. The less you tell them, the better."

Nikodemus paused and somebody else got on the phone.

"Agent, I will be contacting your superiors with a glowing report of your behaviour during a situation that some people would not have been able to perform in. Nikodemus says you stayed cool-headed and all business. We'll ask for you by name if there are any further moves involved."

Before Bill could reply, the unidentified man hung up. He looked at his phone and walked out of the room looking for Deputy Director Perkins.

Chapter 5

Deputy Director Perkins looked over the table at the Intelligence Committee. As the recording of the phone call to Agent Bill Smith ended. N.S.A., D.H.S. and other members of the alphabet soup gang. No one said anything for a minute. Then Perkins addressed the POTUS Chief of Staff.

"We don't have anything on how to find Nikodemus. The short time he was in the holding tank, the camera blanked out. The GPS on the lawyers' phones placed them in an underground bunker about seventy miles outside of Pittsburgh, Pennsylvania. They had no recollection of driving there. Their memory ended at breakfast. In the bunker, we found hair that DNA matched to the Senator's daughter. The so-called bearded guy's dead body was not there. The owner of the property is a holding company in the Cayman Islands."

Somebody at the other end of the table commented, "I've been waiting for the story to break on the news, or National Enquirer. Nothing. Probably won't if it hasn't by now. What's the guy… Richardson's condition?"

Chief of Staff William Riley interjected.

"I've heard he'll never speak normally again. They're keeping tight-lipped about it, though. No pun intended."

Chuckles sounded from around the table. Perkins continued.

"The GPS on Agent Smith's phone showed him in Fort Worth at 2:17 p.m. Then reacquired outside of Pittsburgh at 2:19 p.m. Then reacquired in Fort Worth at 2:32 p.m. So Agent Smith… Well, he travelled around one thousand two hundred miles in less than two minutes. Then returned in the same time frame. This really happened. There were five or six agents who saw Nikodemus arrive, leave, arrive holding the daughter and leave with Agent Smith. Then there were several agents and a couple of deputies that saw Smith, Nikodemus and the three lawyers arrive in the holding tank. Then Nikodemus left."

The NSA (National Security Agency) director Whatshisname addressed Perkins.

"I would like to interview Agent Smith. I've got something that he might shed some light on. Had to do with the 'Between' thing."

There was sudden quiet at the table as Perkins answered. "I have no objection. You can see him now if you want. He's waiting outside. He could come in now."

The NSA guy shook his head.

"I'd rather do it one on one. I've got some photos, and some unusual eyewitness accounts I'd like to run by him. He's the first agent to go 'between' that we're aware of. However, we've heard of it before."

Perkins realised the gasp he heard came from himself.

"You've heard of it before? Why haven't I been told?"

There were several small noises of agreement with Perkins from around the table.

"I didn't want to end up in a psych ward. Nobody would have believed it. We've got video but special effects can do damn near anything. It was two years ago and involved somebody escaping custody. Never found him. I'd like to show his mugshot to Smith. The guy was dirty and bearded and had a thing about looking like a mechanic."

Chapter 6

"That's him. No question."

Agent Smith was looking at a mugshot from the NSA.

"That's the dead guy at the bunker."

One of the three NSA agents, Walker, was asking the questions.

"You say he was dead. Could you tell the cause of death?"

Bill remembered the scene vividly. He's been unable to think of anything else in the three weeks since the incident.

"I remember thinking he looked like he'd been stepped on by more than one elephant. I asked Nikodemus what had happened to him, and he said, 'I hit him hard.' Later when he was asked by the lawyer, I think Ringo, he referred to the dead guy as "pancaked"."

Walker looked at his two colleagues and then back at Bill.

"Let's talk about the transit. To and from Pennsylvania. Tell us again about it. Try to remember the actual travel thing itself. We've heard about the 'falling glitter.' You said it was cold?"

Something else Bill had been unable to quit thinking about.

"It took less than one breath to go from a living room in south Fort Worth to what looked like a concrete basement in Pennsylvania. I didn't realise where I'd gone to at the time. I felt like you do when you come into your warm house from a freezing snowstorm outside. The riot gun was still cold when we got back to Fort Worth. It was so cold when I was in Pennsylvania that I thought it would take away skin if I put it down."

Bill paused and took a drink of water. He looked at Walker and then focussed on the mirror behind him. Wondering how many people are watching.

"Sorry, it was weird. Dark, cold then bam! It's over. Same thing coming back. If you look at the video from the holding tank, you can see steam coming off our skin."

Walker started gathering his notes and nodded to his associates.

"Thank you, Agent Smith. We'll contact you if we need anything further."

Bill looked at the mirror and smiled.

"Anything you need, sir. Anytime."

Chapter 7

Nikodemus didn't look happy. "Well, so much for contained."

He poured whiskey from an ornate crystal decanter into an equally ornate tumbler. The ice cubes tinkled almost musically against the rim as he dropped three in. One by one. Hitting the rim each time.

He looked up at the tapestries on the walls of the Scottish Castle whose main hall he was in. This was what passed for the High Council of Magic. The four figures seated at the ancient, long table were indistinct in the lighting. Torches were burning on the walls. Not real flame. Wereflame… Produced by the oldest, Myron. All four had red hair. Myron, Lydia, Ethan, and Morgaine.

Morgaine looked beautiful. She could also be terrifying. Nikodemus had little experience with the other three. It was she who addressed him.

"We had hopes. Markmor isn't giving up. He's planning something else. The Senator must be the next president. Or…"

"Or what?"

Myron interrupted. His deep bass voice sounding like a creature from the deep.

"Nothing good, I assure you. You are going to have to join the FBI or the Secret Service to keep it from happening."

Nikodemus downed his drink in one gulp and glared at Morgaine. She showed her same emotionless grin he had seen before she blasted a guy's soul from his body.

"Fine, I don't have a choice anyway. I exist only to serve."

The sarcasm dripping from every word wasn't lost on the assembly.

"Why can't we just kill Markmor?"

Nikodemus' question hung in the air unanswered as Myron, and Ethan vanished. Leaving Nikodemus alone with the two women. Morgaine and Lydia both smiled as they got up and came around to Nikodemus. They took his hands and pulled him towards the bedroom.

Lydia whispered in his ear as Morgaine undid his belt. "Because he's my brother."

Chapter 8

The front of the Fort Worth FBI building was brick and steel and glass. Huge windows. The building housed several federal agencies and occupied an entire block of downtown. Nikodemus looked up from the street and wondered what thirty stories of federal government employees would think of him.

He entered the main door and went to the information desk. There were two armoured guards with MP4's slung low standing in two corners of the lobby. Nikodemus addressed the twenty-something black man who occupied the desk.

"I need to speak to Agent Bill Smith or Charles Bone. Tell them Nikodemus is here."

The man nodded absently and picked up his phone.

"Last name?"

"Trust me, they know who I am."

Agent Charles Bone was at his desk with Bill Smith sitting in front of it when the phone rang. He pushed the speakerphone button.

"Bone"

"Sir, I have a Nikodemus here at the information desk wanting to talk to you or Agent Smith."

Bill sat up straight as Bone answered, "Tell him Agent Smith will be down in a moment."

Bone got up and dialled a number on his cell phone at the same time.

"Bring him to interrogation one." Then into the phone, "We've got Nikodemus headed to interrogation one if you're interested."

He hung up without waiting for a reply. Smith was already out the door.

Interrogation room one was closest to the elevator on the seventeenth floor. Nikodemus had said almost nothing to Bill's enquiries. His only statement being, "Let's wait till we're upstairs. Then I won't have to repeat everything."

They entered the interrogation room, and Nikodemus pulled out a chair and leaned it back on two legs against the wall. He put his feet on the table crossing his legs. Then he looked at the mirror.

"Well, Bill, the only guy I recognise back there is Agent Bone. Hey, Charles." Nikodemus waved at the mirror.

"The other four guys I haven't met."

Bill sat down with a clipboard and a pen.

"You can see through the mirror?"

"Yep."

"How?"

Nikodemus stretched, dropped the chair back level and laid his head on the table. He mumbled through his crossed arms, "Does it really matter?"

He then sat up and looked at the mirror. Behind the mirror, Agent Bone felt like Nikodemus was looking him directly in the eye.

"The real questions should be, why did I come here? Why now?"

Nikodemus stood up and walked to the mirror. Again, Bone felt like he was looking right at him.

"Agent Bone, I'd rather talk to you in here. The other guys can stay there and analyse."

The door opened and Agent Bone entered and sat down next to Agent Smith.

"Okay, Nikodemus, I'm in here. Why did you come in?"

Nikodemus kept looking at the mirror. He looked at Agent Bone before he replied. "The senator isn't out of the woods apparently. I guess since I'm here I can give you more details. One of my superiors can predict future events. He is the one who sent me the first time."

Agent Bone started to speak, but Nikodemus interrupted him.

"Before you ask, I'm not telling you his name. I will tell you that the name of our adversary is Markmor. I've never seen him, have no clues about his appearance. But, he has somehow concealed his intentions, even from our soothsayer. The senator is in danger. I've been sent to assist in his protection."

Behind the mirror, Deputy Director Glenn had been on the phone. His request of two armed and armoured agents was granted in the form of four armed and armoured agents. They entered the observation room and observed Nikodemus through the glass.

Nikodemus saw them too.

"Bone. I don't know if you know this, but four men with armour and MP5 submachine guns are in the booth now with the old guys."

The occupants of the booth looked at each other, and Deputy Director Glenn gave the detailed instructions.

"Go in there and cuff him. I want his fingerprints, and I want his DNA. Facial recognition software shows nothing. I want to know who he is. Now!"

Nikodemus glanced at Bone and Smith and smirked.

"Yeah, I know Smith here has seen what I can do. These yahoos coming in apparently don't read or don't believe reports. I'm not gonna hurt any of them, but all of you together couldn't get those cuffs on me."

As he said this, the door burst open, and the lead agent pointed his weapon at Nikodemus and yelled, "Hands on your head! Get down on your knees!"

He was going to yell something else, but as he got closer, Nikodemus flickered like a flame being blown out and suddenly wasn't there.

The armed agents all gasped and looked around. Bone looked at Smith.

"He didn't go between, did he?"

"Didn't seem like it."

The agents were kind of milling around as Deputy Director Glenn entered the room.

"Where is he, Bone?"

Bone calm replied to the screamed question brought the whole thing down a notch.

"I don't know. Why did you do that? He's here voluntarily. He wants to be integrated into our detail. I say let him."

Glenn's retort was condescending in its delivery. Made Bone want to bounce his head off of something.

"I'm not giving that weirdo a badge."

Glenn started to walk out of the room. As he got near the door, Nikodemus suddenly reappeared. He was inches away from Glenn. Leaning casually in the door frame. Blocking it.

"I don't want a fucking badge. I want to remove all threats from one man's life. So the council will leave me alone."

He flickered out again and reappeared in the lead armoured agent's face. The agent had been moving forward and was forced to stop.

"You need to back off. That gun doesn't scare me. I realise you're following orders. However, this won't end well for you."

He flickered out again and reappeared seated next to Agent Smith.

"Bill." Nikodemus nudged Agent Smith.

"I think these guys need a demonstration. By the way, Bill, you noticed that there wasn't any dimensional pop or warning when I did my little disappearing act, didn't you?"

Nikodemus flickered out again and was standing in Deputy Director Glenn's face.

"I didn't go between. Wanna know how I do my little disappearing act, Mr Deputy Director?"

Nikodemus waited a moment for an answer. Then continued before Glenn could reply.

"It's simple really. I project myself 180 degrees out of phase with this plane of existence. This is Plane 1. So I project myself to Negative 1. That, my friends, is towards hell!"

The last two words of his sentence resonated throughout the building. The word "hell" felt like a wrecking ball hitting the room. The mirror on the wall broke and several ceiling tiles fell. Nikodemus' face was impassive. Calmly gazing into Glenn's eyes.

"Smith, is there a firing range here anywhere?"

Smith was as shaken as anyone. The fire alarm was going off, and every floor of the building was panicking. It had felt like a bomb going off.

"Bone, you should call security and tell them that there isn't anything to worry about. The building isn't coming down or anything."

Agent Bone was already on his cell phone saying something to security about a minor accidental detonation and that there was no further danger to the facility. He hung up as Nikodemus again addressed Deputy Director Glenn.

"You want my prints? Fine, ask me. If you try any of that shit again, I'll show you things you've barely glimpsed even in your worst nightmares."

Nikodemus smiled and walked over to Agent Bone ignoring the startled faces in the now-revealed observation room. There were close to twenty people in it now. Standing room only.

"Bone, buddy. Let's go photograph and print me. Then I wanna show you something at the firing range."

Chapter 9

The indoor firing range for the federal building was in the basement. There were several training areas set up like interiors of houses, some long hallways. The ten-lane target range extended to hundred yards.

Deputy Director Glenn had opted not to witness the demonstration. He was with the IT guys processing the prints and running Nikodemus' picture through facial recognition software. The entire breach team plus Bone, Smith and the range warden were present.

There was also another windowed observation room. Full of top brass and aides. The "accidental detonation" had drawn a crowd apparently.

Nikodemus was conversing with the range warden.

"If I fire a gun into this material here."

Indicating a wall in a training area.

"You can pull the slug and tell what the calibre is and do ballistics, right?"

The warden nodded. Nikodemus leaned against the wall with his legs spread and his palms on the wall over his head.

"Search me and see if I'm armed."

The warden patted Nikodemus down from wrists to ankles.

"You are unarmed."

Nikodemus stood up. Smoothed his clothing and backed away from the wall.

"Step back. What was your name again, Jantzen?"

Warden Jantzen nodded and stepped back. Nikodemus looked at Bone, grinned and gestured at the wall. There was a loud almost ripping sound, and something hit the wall.

"Pull that and tell me what it is."

Over the next ten minutes, Jantzen and another agent dug into the wall and removed a slug. Jantzen looked at it closely and declared, "This is a .44 magnum hollow point."

There were gasps from the breach team. Nikodemus motioned for Jantzen to move over and gestured several times. There were rips and popping sounds as several slugs hit the wall again and then a louder one as what looked like a shotgun pattern appeared next to the closely placed slugs.

"You can analyse those but you will find another .44 magnum, a .50 calibre Teflon-coated sniper round and a .00 buckshot round."

Nikodemus' cell phone rang. He frowned and pulled it out looking at it. Then his eyes widened, and he addressed Bone. "We need to go to Divide, Colorado, now. You, Smith and I. Now. You guys are both armed, aren't you?"

They both nodded.

"Jantzen, suit both of them up now. Armour and assault rifles."

Bone started removing his jacket and shoulder holster. Smith did the same.

"What's going on?"

This from Smith as he was pulling on Kevlar.

"The senator is fishing, and something bad is going to happen if we aren't there within ten minutes."

Chapter 10

Markmor was a pale, red-haired wisp of a man. He looked frail and weak. He also looked rich with his necklace, visible diamonds, and Rolex watch. His appearance had sometimes drawn predators that would try to rob him. As their last act.

The son of Myron. Leader of the council. Renegade. He revelled in this role and sowed destruction and chaos whenever, and however, he could. Today was no different. He had no doubt that his father would stop this attempt also. It would, however, be fun to watch.

He was seated on a rock with a five-hundred-pound grizzly bear in front of him. The bear was in a glamour. It was staring dreamily into Markmor's eyes as he placed a compulsion upon it. It lumbered off with Senator Rollins scent in its nostrils. An insatiable hunger mixed with rage started to infuse its body as it ranged in a circle. Sniffing the wind.

Markmor felt his father summon him. He blocked it as always. He could feel Morgaine and Lydia trying to locate him. He brushed them off as he watched the bear nearing the edge of the heavily wooded area. Soon he would catch Senator Rollins' scent.

The dimensional pop of Nikodemus, Bone and Smith travelling between sounded. There was a fluttering of birds and animals that ran from it. The bear, however, headed towards it. Senator Rollins was standing in the middle of a stream wearing thigh-high waders. His fly-fishing rod was in mid-cast when Nikodemus, Smith and Bone appeared twenty yards away.

The Senator shook his head and looked away casting again. It looked almost like cracking a whip. Then he pulled the line and moved his rod drawing the fly across the shallows. His voice was disgusted as he addressed them.

"This is the first time in almost four months that I've been alone. My Secret Service detail is down at the county road. Sitting in their suburbans."

He reeled in and then cast again. Repeating the previous actions.

"But. If you're here."

Indicating Nikodemus.

"Something is very wrong. What is it this time?"

Nikodemus wasn't looking at the Senator. He was moving his head left to right sensing. His voice sounded distracted.

"Bone, it's a bear. A big one. Coming from that direction." Nikodemus pointed to the right.

"Markmor is here. I'm going after him. Think you can handle the bear?"

Without waiting for a reply, Nikodemus sprinted across the stream and into the trees. He could hear the bear crashing through the trees. He could feel Markmor looking at him. Then he wasn't. Cursing, Nikodemus started back towards the sound of gunshots as Bone and Smith were shooting the bear. Something was wrong. Nikodemus could see the glamour on the bear and also a shield. The bullets were bouncing off him.

The bear was ignoring the shooters and was going for the Senator. Senator Rollins was still in the stream. Frozen in fear. The bear seemed impossibly big. As it raised up, Nikodemus was suddenly between them. He gestured, and it sounded like the sky ripped open. There was a smoking hole where the bear had been. On trees fifty yards away, blood and gore were splattered.

Bone and Smith were on the ground holding their ears as the Senator's Secret Service detail rolled up. Not knowing who Nikodemus was, seeing two uniformed men on the ground. They drew their weapons and fired at Nikodemus. The air in front of Nikodemus shimmered as the shots were absorbed. Rollins screamed at them.

"Stop goddammit! He saved me! This is the guy. The magician."

They both holstered their weapons as Smith stumbled up.

"What the fuck was that, Nick?"

Nikodemus smiled at the familiar shortening of his name.

"That was a 105-mm sabot round."

Smith gasped.

"No, shit? I'm beyond asking how you do anything. What next?"

Nikodemus smoothed his shirt and assisted the Senator out of the stream.

"Now, we see if the Senator will give us a ride. We have a great deal to discuss."

Then he went up to the two Secret Service agents who had shot at him.

"You two. Don't ever fucking shoot at me again. You get a pass this once. Here're your bullets back."

He gestured and two shots ricocheted off the hood of their Suburban.

"In recent years, every single person who has shot at me has died."

Without another word, he got into the back seat.

Chapter 11

Markmor popped back into his house in the Alps just as Nikodemus destroyed the bear. He was impressed. Nikodemus could "make." One of the hardest things to master. Anything that had ever been used against him was waiting with him to be unleashed on someone. Still, a Level 7 Seeker wasn't going to be able to track a Level 12 Mage.

But, Markmor realised that he wouldn't be able to face Nikodemus and survive. Markmor's skills were attuned towards seeing and compelling. Markmor could "make" someone open a door. Nikodemus could "make" an artillery round destroy the door. Two different directions.

Lucia and her twin sister entered the room and started drawing him a bath. Markmor ignored them and went to his table. His table was made of ironwood and could have seated ten people. It was ancient. Over thousand years old. Likewise, the benches. The chair at the head of the table was almost, but not quite, a throne. A large crystal ball on a stand sat next to a dagger with a twelve-inch blade and hilt that looked like a snake coiled around a human skull.

Markmor gazed into the ball and saw Nikodemus, Rollins, and the other agents getting into three identical suburbans. Then he waved his hand, blanking the image. He went back to enjoy his bath and take out his frustrations on the two beautiful, naked, hapless women. The sounds of his slaps and their screams echoed off the mountains.

Chapter 12

Senator Rollins, Agents Bone and Smith and Nikodemus sat in the back two seats of the Senator's luxurious Suburban. Smith noticed that the doors were reinforced and very heavy as he closed his. He whistled and addressed one of the Secret Service agents in the front seats.

"Ballistics package, huh?"

The agent in the passenger seat nodded and turned around. Careful not to make eye contact with Nikodemus. He was still stunned. Nikodemus had taken bullets, then handed them back. The creases on the hood were hard to not notice.

"Doors, windows, floor panels, run on flats, a lot of extra weight. Custom engine pulls it, though."

He stopped talking abruptly as the connecting window rolled up. Senator Rollins took his finger off the window control and then poured four scotches without asking if anybody wanted any. His voice trembled more than his hands.

"That was the biggest bear I have ever seen. When its eyes locked with mine, I couldn't move. What happened?"

He turned to face Nikodemus as he handed him a tumbler of scotch.

"How did you know to come here?"

Nikodemus took a sip and slowly savoured the exquisite scotch.

"Senator, what do you want me to call you anyway?"

The Senator gulped his down and topped of Nikodemus.

"Call me Mike. You've goddamn sure earned it."

"Very well, Mike. This is the finest scotch I've ever tasted. What is it?"

"Glenfiddich, single malt, fifty years old."

Mike took another gulp, downing the rest of his. Smith and Bone both added their empty glasses to his in the rack.

"I'm more interested in how you knew I needed saving. Plus, what did you do to that bear? It looked like you used a howitzer on it."

39

Nikodemus chuckled a little and, after downing his drink, put his glass in the rack.

"Funny you should say that. It was a 105-mm sabot shell fired from a rack-mounted howitzer in a C-130."

Nikodemus paused as he took out his cell phone.

"I copied it three years ago."

Bone interrupted their exchange.

"Copied? Is that how you did the shots at the firing range?"

"Yes, it was. Mike, look at the text message on my phone."

He handed it over, and Mike looked at the screen. The text said unknown on the contact. The content said, "Rollins in imminent danger in twenty minutes. Near Divide Colorado. Believed to be glamoured animal of some sort. Intervene. I'll coordinate the location."

Mike handed the phone back.

"Who sent you that, and how did they know this?"

"The same guy that had me intervene in your daughter's kidnapping."

Rollins digested this and asked what everybody in the car was wondering.

"Does this person have a name?"

Nikodemus nodded but didn't speak. He looked at Bone and Smith.

"I've got to go. I'll be in touch. Sorry, but you have to get back to Fort Worth on your own."

Then the tearing sound started, and he popped out of existence.

Smith looked at his watch and cursed, "I'm supposed to pick up my kids from school in about thirty minutes. What do I tell my wife when I say I can't be on time?"

Rollins spoke with more authority with Nikodemus gone.

"Tell her the truth, Agent Smith. What calibre of the weapon were you using when you shot at the bear?"

Smith glanced at his MP4.

"5.56 Armour piercing rounds. They would go through a car. They were bouncing off that bear, though. What did that text say? 'Glamoured animal?' Whatever that means. I put five into his head except they didn't go into his head."

He shook his head. Then turned to Agent Bone. Bone was on the phone so he addressed the Senator.

"Markmor was here today, Senator."

The Senator narrowed his eyes.

"Who is Markmor?"

"Our adversary, sir. The person responsible for both attacks."

"Did you see him Agent Smith?"

Bone hung up and listened to Smith's answer.

"No, but when we arrived, Nikodemus said, 'Markmor is here. I'm going after him. Think you can handle the bear?'"

Bone joined the conversation.

"Nikodemus realised immediately that the bear wasn't ordinary. So he didn't pursue him. Instead, he protected you, us."

Smith looked at Bone.

"When did he tell you this?"

"He didn't. I just got off the phone with the Director of the Secret Service. They're apparently being updated from Nikodemus' office? For want of a better word. Oh, by the way. We're on the Senator's detail until further notice."

The speaker from the driver compartment came to life.

"Senator, is Nikodemus still back there?"

Rollins looked where Nikodemus had been sitting. The glitter wasn't real. It disappeared when he was gone.

"No."

The Suburban swerved a little and stopped.

"When did he get out?"

Bone rolled down the divider. The Secret Service agents both stared incredulously at the back seat.

"He bailed a few minutes ago. Why?"

"Because he's standing in the road up ahead. I thought I was seeing things."

Nikodemus was motioning for them to come up to him. He opened the rear door and got in. The Secret Service agents both gasped. One asked him.

"How did you open that door? It's triple-locked."

"I can open any door. One-way exit door. Padlocked door. Even a bank vault f I wanted to."

He grinned and opened a bag in his lap. It contained three small leather cases that looked like they contained badges. He passed them out to Mike, Bone, and Smith. They looked at what resembled a badge but had symbols on it that were changing. Shapes and colours.

"These are amulets. Magic amulets. They are…synced I guess is a good word. To each of you. If you need me, all you have to do is think it. I'll hear it and

41

respond. If you need to mark something or track something or even secure a door or hallway. Place this on the floor or a shelf and think what you want it to do."

Nikodemus took Smith's amulet and addressed the speechless group.

"Say somebody is following you. Throw this out the car window and think. 'Stop them.' If they're in, say, a car, it'll be like they hit a brick wall. Or you enter a building and need an entrance guarded. Place this there and think 'Nobody enters here.' Depending on the threat, they'll get bullets, fire, explosions, anything."

Nikodemus handed Smith's back to him.

"I've used one of these before in Syria. Fifty armed men with two technicals were chasing me, and I had two wards I was guarding. I dropped it on the road, and all fifty men were dead in less than two minutes."

Nikodemus opened the door and got out. Then he leaned back in.

"Those are for the real thing only. No demonstrations for shithead in Fort Worth. Tell him or don't tell him about them. I don't care. Don't use them unless you have to. Also, the one Mike has is going to shield his whereabouts from Markmor. I'll be in touch."

He closed the door, and then he wasn't there. Both Secret Service agents were freaking out. They looked at Bone with wild eyes.

"What the fuck is going on? Am I losing my mind?"

The window rolled back up before Bone could answer.

Chapter 13

Nikodemus stepped from between to Myron's castle in Ireland. It was empty, dark. Not what was supposed to be the case. Markmor was smiling from a scrying crystal. His voice sounded artificial and distant.

"Nikodemus, how are you?"

Nikodemus whirled at the sound and almost released a .00 buckshot round on the crystal. Then his eyes narrowed as he approached it. Markmor's image had a greenish tint and was slightly distorted by the edges of the crystal. The same tinny voice addressed Nikodemus.

"I see you've shielded the Senator. Won't stop me, you know."

He was trying to place a compulsion on Nikodemus as he talked. It wasn't working. Nikodemus grinned as he easily closed his mind to Markmor.

"I'll stop you, Markmor. If you're Lydia's brother, then that makes you Myron's son, right?"

Markmor's smile never faltered. He started trying another way to get into Nikodemus' head. Unsuccessfully.

"Really, Markmor? That might work on an unsuspecting woman. If your father wants you bad enough, he's going to find you. You know that."

The werelight torches flared to life as Myron and then Morgaine stepped into the room. Markmor scowled and the crystal went dark.

Myron looked at the crystal and then at Morgaine. Then he looked at Nikodemus and walked up to him. Standing with his face inches away from Nikodemus. He searched Nikodemus' mind. Nikodemus didn't try to stop him. Frankly, not sure if he would have been able to. He had nothing to hide.

Satisfied, Myron clapped him on the shoulder and addressed Morgaine.

"Morgaine, here stands a man of honour. Your sister is lying to me. Is she working with Markmor?"

Morgaine started stammering, and then she was lifted up, floating towards Myron. Myron's outstretched hand was trembling with rage. Morgaine started to choke, and he released her. She dropped to the floor and started weeping. Between sobs, she pleaded.

"Please, father! I didn't know anything! I came to you as soon as I suspected!"

Myron's voice shook the ground.

"When was that?"

"I could smell him, father. I didn't know where it came from or when it happened. I looked at her, and she knew I suspected. Then she went between, and I couldn't tell where."

Morgaine was on her feet now. Her voice gaining strength with every word. She walked over and stood next to Nikodemus.

"Niko and I can get him, father. I can find them, and he can kill them. If you just say, you want it."

Myron looked at Nikodemus and then returned his attention to Morgaine. Her words faltered under his baleful glare.

"Killing my only son isn't what I had in mind, woman!"

Myron stepped between, and the torches flickered out. Leaving Morgaine and Nikodemus standing in a darkened feasting hall in a suddenly abandoned seeming castle. Morgaine's breaths came in shudders. Nikodemus could copy and reproduce many things besides bullets and howitzer rounds. He reached into his "cabinet" and produced a crystal bottle of amber-coloured liquor and two glasses.

He went to the long table and set the bottle and glasses down. Then he dusted off two chairs and gestured to one as he sat in the other. Wordlessly, Morgaine shuffled over and sat down. She seemed suddenly old to Nikodemus. Like the light within her was getting dim.

"Hey! Did I tell you I'm practically an FBI agent now?"

Morgaine laughed at this, and her inner light burned bright again. She took the offered glass and sipped the contents. Its smoothness was indescribable. She drank the rest and pushed her glass towards Nikodemus.

"What is this? That's the best scotch I've ever tasted."

Nikodemus smiled as he poured them both another round.

"Senator Rollins had it. It's my new favourite."

"You aren't going to tell me what it is?"

"Nope."

Chapter 14

Markmor was torn. His father was getting annoyed. God help them all if he got really mad. What started as a simple act of defiance had turned into a revolution of sorts. Well, a revolt anyway. He didn't have any grand plans. Markmor had always enjoyed stirring the pot and watching others react to it.

Watching the great Senator Rollins. The new hope. Had been his main pastime until that idiot Nikodemus had shielded him. He thought about going after Nikodemus' pet FBI agents, but now they were protected too. Markmor decided to mingle. He knew a club in Dallas that he liked. In Deep Ellum. All the neon lights and black lights in the clubs made it easy to glamour women. Incredibly beautiful women. The classier they were, the dirtier the things he made them do.

He changed into something dark. A black suit jacket and pants. A powder-blue shirt that would glow in the black lights. The diamonds on his rings and his watch would glow brightly with a little werelight. These always lured the women in. Thieves too. It was almost as much fun to watch the fear grow in a big man's eyes as it was to watch a woman get down on her knees. Grinning, Markmor stepped between and exited in an alley behind a club called "Trees" in Deep Ellum.

Travelling between required enormous energy. When a person exited from between the "pop" was the physical reaction of the molecules of air being bombarded by molecules from another place. Depending on the size of the person, and the number of people travelling, it can be loud enough to break glass or quiet enough to go unnoticed. It was, however, detectable if a seeker was looking for it.

Nikodemus was, amongst other things, a skilled seeker. Since Senator Rollins lived in Fort Worth, Texas, Nikodemus had stationed his four apprentices in the area. Two in Fort Worth, one in Arlington, and one in Dallas. Deep Ellum specifically. Morgaine had given him what details she knew of Markmor's habits, and it had paid off. Yvonne was sitting outside Club Clearview. She was wearing sunglasses and headphones so no one would notice that her eyes were closed. She was waiting, like a fisherman watching his cork in the water. When Markmor stepped out of between and into the alley behind Trees she felt it. It was two streets over but still detectable. She was only a Level 2 so she had to use a cell phone to call Nikodemus.

"Somebody popped in near me."

Then she got up and went to the Dart train station. Her instructions were to report and then bolt immediately. Yvonne had seen what happens when you don't follow instructions like that to the letter. She shuddered at the memory. Within three minutes, she was on a train bound for Fort Worth. She felt Markmor probing the area. Looking for any seeker. Yvonne closed her mind and thought about shoes. Nothing but shoes. Markmor's probe touched her briefly and then was gone. She breathed a sigh of relief as the train got too far for his mental grasp to reach.

Satisfied, Markmor walked up to the entrance to Trees. There was a line of about thirty people waiting. They were behind a velvet rope. The two doormen had a combined weight of over six hundred pounds. He had been here before so it didn't take much of a push for them to raise the rope and let him enter. Much to the chagrin of people waiting. Markmor barely registered their protests. He was already hunting. Tonight, he wanted a Mexican girl. Long hair and long legs.

Chapter 15

Nikodemus hung up with Yvonne. He was sitting in Senator Rollins backyard with Agents Bone and Smith. He stood up.

"Let's go. Markmor is in Deep Ellum."

Smith was on his feet immediately. Bone stayed seated.

"Smith, you go with Nikodemus. I'll stay here with the Senator. Keep me posted."

Smith and Nikodemus exited the front door and walked up to a new Dodge Challenger with a Hellcat emblem on the side.

"Nice wheels, Smith. This yours?"

Smith grinned as he started the engine and gunned it a little to let Nikodemus hear the roar.

"Nope, this is a new Federal Pursuit car. It's the fastest production car on the market."

Smith turned on the strobe and siren as he got onto I-30. Nikodemus settled back and closed his eyes.

"FYI. I'm going to blank out until we get there."

Smith looked over at Nikodemus. He looked like he was asleep.

"What do you mean?"

Nikodemus didn't open his eyes. His reply was slow and barely audible.

"Markmor is a Level 12 Mage. I know you don't understand what that means."

Nikodemus breathed in deeply.

"I am a Level 7 Seeker. If he senses me near him, he'll step between, and I won't be able to track him. I'm clearing my mind and not looking for him. Punch me in the arm hard when you stop at the club. Double-park right in front of the door."

Then Nikodemus dropped off. Smith was going over hundred miles an hour and changing lanes quickly. Once, Nikodemus' head hit the side window on an abrupt left turn. Didn't even break the rhythm of his snores. Smith went up Main near Kennedy's X. The spot where John F. Kennedy was shot in 1963. Approaching Deep Ellum, Smith encountered barricades. He'd forgotten. On the weekends, parts of the club district were barricaded off to allow pedestrians full access to the streets.

As a patrolman walked up to the car, Agent Smith noticed the blue lights flashing off him and realised he still had the strobes on. He turned them off and opened his window. The patrolman looked at Smith, then at the sleeping Nikodemus.

"Problem, sir?"

Smith showed his credentials and addressed the officer. "We need to get to Trees, by the front door."

The patrolman whose uniform said "Diaz" was joined by his partner. Another Hispanic officer. His uniform identified him as Guiterrez who had heard the request.

Diaz looked at his partner. Then back at Smith.

"It's Saturday night. Pedestrian traffic only, sir. What's with him?"

He was indicating Nikodemus and was caught off guard by the vehemence of Smith's response.

"I don't goddamn care if it's Easter Sunday. I need to get to Trees, and I need to get there now! I want that barricade out of the way, and I want a goddamn escort!"

The officers jumped back and looked at each other. Smith got out of the car and breathed deeply.

"Look. Sorry, guys. I didn't mean to yell at you. We are after a very dangerous guy who is in Trees. He could kill all three of us without breaking a sweat."

This statement brought unease to the two officers. They looked at each other.

"That sleeping guy."

Indicating Nikodemus.

"Is the only chance we got. Don't ask me anything else right now. Get us in front of Trees, and I'm going to wake up Nikodemus. Then we'll sit back and watch."

Without another word, Diaz moved the barricade, and Guiterrez went to the back door of the Dodge. He got in, and after the barricade was back in place, Diaz got in the other back seat.

"This is the fastest way, sir. Our car is two blocks away. I'll direct you. Go straight, until you see green neon on the left. That's Trees."

Smith nodded and moved ahead.

"Turn on your strobes without the siren. People will move out of the way quicker."

Nikodemus startled them all when he spoke.

"No. Don't. Creep up on it."

Nikodemus sat up and looked in the back seat.

"Evening Officers. How unusual is it for a uniformed officer to go into trees!"

Guiterrez answered, "Not unusual at all. It's part of foot patrol."

Nikodemus considered this. Then to Smith.

"You have the amulet?"

Smith patted his jacket pocket.

"Right here."

"Okay, he can't turn you on me. Them."

Indicated the officers.

"He could."

Diaz sat forward and looked at Nikodemus.

"What the fuck you talkin' about? Amulet? Turning us?"

Nikodemus wasn't listening as Smith pulled up by the front door of Trees. There were throngs of people all along the sidewalk and the street.

"Okay, Smith. You show your credentials to get us in the door. I go in first. Then you. He's seated at a table in the back right corner. He has three glamoured women with him."

The officers prepared to get out. Nikodemus stopped them.

"You guys go across the street and watch the entrance. Our target is five feet seven inches, one hundred twenty pounds, pale skin, long wispy red hair."

Nikodemus stopped and looked at the officers.

"If he comes out, then it probably means that both of us are dead. He doesn't look like much, but he's the most dangerous person you will ever encounter. If he comes out, 'do not try to apprehend him.' In fact, I'd be more comfortable if you both walked back to where you were but I know you won't."

Agent Smith drew his weapon and checked the chamber.

"Leave that here, Bill. Bring the amulet. When I engage him, he will glamour probably the bouncer or bouncers against me. Drop the amulet on the floor and think about it defending me."

Diaz couldn't contain himself anymore.

"What the fuck are you guys smokin'? You're FBI? Listening to this shit?"

Then he stopped speaking because he felt like he was being choked. His partner was also. Nikodemus was looking at them and had his thumb and index finger pressed together. He held up his hand and opened his fingers. Both officers gasped and breathed again. Diaz crossed himself.

"Sorry, guys, but we don't have time for this now. Trust me when I say there is shit going on here that is absolutely next level. Stay clear."

Chapter 16

The interior of "Trees" was black lights on neon. Neon paint of every colour glowed from walls, booths, table edges, and even people. Any white shirt or skirt glowed. Waitresses had neon-painted shoes, jewellery, and even the edges of the trays they carried glowed.

Nikodemus and Bill moved over near the bar where they could see the tables against the back wall. For the first time, Nikodemus and Bill saw Markmor. He was sitting between two women. One of the women had her head in his lap. The up and down motion was synced to the beat of the techno music playing. Markmor was leaning back, smiling.

Nikodemus surveyed the bar and turned to Bill.

"I'm going to approach him. I don't see any bouncers except the two by the door. Don't do anything unless I look at you. Even if I get in a fight."

Nikodemus turned and looked Bill in the eyes.

"I've changed my mind about the amulet. Don't throw it down. As long as it's on you, he can't touch you."

Nikodemus was turning when Bill caught his arm.

"Where did you get the amulets?"

"His father."

With that Nikodemus broke away and started walking directly towards Markmor's table. He was about ten feet from it when a large black man rose from a table and stood in his way. The guy was six feet seven if he was an inch. Maybe three hundred pounds. He was in fact a line-backer for the Dallas Cowboys. Markmor's glamour was shining in his eyes.

"Private party asshole."

There was no emotion as he said the words. But he focused on Nikodemus. Then reached for him.

"Ssshhhh."

Nikodemus put one finger to his lips and touched the line-backer with his other hand. The linebacker faltered and fell like a ton of bricks. He was asleep. Markmor had by then zipped his pants up and was smiling as Nikodemus came up and sat at his table.

"Nikodemus! Good to see you."

He looked around Nikodemus at the sleeping line-backer.

"Too much to drink, I guess. Huh?"

Nikodemus smiled and reached into his "cabinet" and extracted another bottle of the Senator's scotch.

"You have to try this."

He produced two crystal tumblers and poured them each a drink.

"I copied this from Senator Rollins' Suburban. It's the finest scotch I've ever tasted."

He pushed one towards Markmor and took a drink from his own. Markmor smiled and took a drink also. He closed his eyes as he savoured it.

"You're not kidding. That is exquisite."

His demeanour changed. No longer friendly.

"What do you think you are going to do now? Seeker."

Nikodemus took another drink and sat back.

"I don't have any illusions of being able to do anything to you, Markmor. I'm delivering a message. I don't give a shit about any of this. I just want your dad off my back."

Nikodemus poured himself another and offered more to Markmor. Markmor nodded and placed his glass within reach. Nikodemus poured them both another.

"I know you're aware he wants to talk to you. He sent me because he doesn't like being in public like you and I."

Nikodemus turned and watched two stunning women leave the women's bathroom and head to the dance floor. Then he turned his attention back to Markmor.

"As far as I'm concerned I've fulfilled my assignment. I'm face to face with you, and I've told you to contact him. Are we cool?"

This last sentence was met by Markmor with a grin.

"Sure, Nikodemus. We're cool. Wanna party with these sluts?" Markmor gestured to two Latinas that were wearing matching miniskirts. They came over and sat on both sides of Nikodemus who stood and finished his drink in a gulp.

"Another time perhaps, Markmor. I have to go report to Myron."

He was walking away when he felt the hair on the back of his neck prickle. Then the lights and music turned off. It would have been pitch black except for the lights from all the phones in the crowd. Markmor was right next to him.

"Am I supposed to believe that's all you're here for?"

Nikodemus stopped and faced Markmor. Everyone was quiet. All eyes were on Nikodemus and Markmor. Several phones were video recording the exchange.

"I'm supposed to stop you. I can't figure out a way to do anything here. There would be too much collateral damage. Look, I got next to you. Isn't that enough? Straighten this out with your dad yourself. He's the one pulling the strings. You know that."

Nikodemus turned away, and then Markmor screamed. Nikodemus turned back, and Morgaine had Markmor by the hair. Then they both went between with a pop that knocked Nikodemus and several bystanders to the ground. Nikodemus stood up and looked at Bill.

"Let's get the fuck out of here."

People were screaming as Nikodemus and Bill ran out the front door along with a throng of people. Nikodemus slid across the hood and opened the door as Bill got in on the other side. They both jumped when officers Diaz and Guiterrez banged on the window. Bill gestured to the back and unlocked the doors.

"Sounded like a bomb went off in there."

This from Guiterrez. Diaz was on his radio.

"We're outside "Trees" now. No visible flames."

The dispatcher's voice asked.

"Was there an explosive device detonated?"

Guiterrez looked at Agent Smith who shook his head in the negative.

"No explosive device dispatch. Something loud but no smoke, fire, or injuries. Cause unknown."

Smith looked at Nikodemus. He was staring out the window at people running and gesturing at the club entrance.

"Who was that? The woman who took him?"

"Morgaine, one of his sisters."

"Is it over?"

"I seriously doubt it. His dad doesn't want to kill him. I don't know why he does what he does but… Shit, I don't know. Let's file reports or whatever. I'm ready to get some sleep."

The officers made no move to get out of the car. Bill looked back at them.

"Well, what's up?"

Diaz answered, "Our captain said to stick by you. This car checks out, but we don't know if you're who you say you are."

Bill started the car and moved slowly through the pedestrians.

"Well, we'll go to the office then."

Chapter 17

Neither Nikodemus, Bill, nor either officer noticed the two men watching them as they drove away. They were both dressed in black suits, sitting in a silver Mercedes in the parking lot across the street. They were employees of Draft and Associates, one of the most expensive and effective private investigation firms in the Metroplex, if not Texas.

They were waiting on results from the license plate. Greg Connor, the senior of the pair, was an ex-Marine. Twenty years in Delta Force. Mid-fifties. At six feet one inch and two hundred pounds, he was still deadly. Weapons or not. His companion Charlie Wilkins was also an ex-Marine but barely in his thirties. His strong suit was electronic surveillance and computers. He was only five feet nine inches and one hundred forty pounds. Champion Jujitsu fighter. The two of them could take most attackers apart.

Charlie's tablet beeped. Alerting them to email. Greg Connor leaned over as the results displayed.

"Well, Charlie, we got us a badass FBI pursuit car."

Charlie shrugged.

"You gonna call him, or should I?"

Greg sighed and took out his cell phone.

"Me. He hates you anyway."

Charlie chuckled as he powered the laptop off and looked at the entrance of "Trees." The crowd in front wasn't getting smaller. A Channel 4 News van had just pulled up. Greg was dialling his phone as he looked down at his handwritten notes. The number he called rang only twice before Curtis Vieth picked up.

"Hey, it looks like he was here tonight."

Greg paused as he listened to the reply.

"We didn't actually see him but something weird happened. We were cruising over by Club Clearview when it sounded like a bomb went off. It was in 'Trees.' It gets interesting, though."

Greg looked at his notes again then looked at Charlie. Charlie nodded at the windshield so Greg would look ahead. The Channel 4 News crew was setting up. People were crowding around hoping to get in the camera shot.

"We got here, and there was a new Dodge Challenger Hellcat parked right in front of the door. They had driven up even though the barricades were up. We started running the plate when two guys came out and got in. One looked like a federal agent; one was casual. Both white. An agent looked thirtyish. The casual looked fiftyish. Two Dallas police officers got in with them. They drove away, and the plate came back as the property of the FBI Fort Worth Office. It seemed like they were involved somehow."

Greg paused and started the car. Then he hung up.

Curtis said, "Go to the Fort Worth FBI building, and he'd call to get us a sit down with somebody."

Charlie looked at his watch.

"On Saturday night, or rather Sunday morning at 1:00 a.m. no less."

The Mercedes backed into the alley and started the winding course to get back to I-30. They didn't have the privilege of driving on the barricaded streets.

Chapter 18

Susan Simpson with Channel 4 News—'Your news right now'—wasn't happy. Every "witness" who wanted to talk to her was inebriated to greater or lesser degrees. She was about to leave when she noticed a group of women by the entrance to "Trees" all watching a phone screen intently. She walked up the steps to them.

"You guys have video?"

One of the women. A beautiful Latina in a skin-tight, red-sequined dress looked at Susan. Her eyes took in the microphone and the cameraman.

"Yes, but I don't want to be on camera. You can watch it. I'll even send it to you. But, no images of me. Got it?"

Susan looked at her cameraman quizzically. This was a first. Didn't want on TV?

"Sure, ok. I have to tell you, most people want to be on camera."

The Latina spoke to her three friends, and they walked away. She came over to Susan and started the video again on her phone.

"You'll get why when you see this. We noticed that Wayne Elliot, the Cowboys' line-backer, was sitting at this table."

The video was a little dark but still clearly showed the Cowboys' linebacker sitting at a table alone.

"It was weird that he was alone. I'd seen him before, and he had women crawling all over him. Anyway I had just started filming him when this guy showed up."

The video showed a fiftyish-looking man walking near Elliot's table. Elliot rose and flexed a little showing his muscles and said something unintelligible to the other guy. Then the guy put one finger to his lips like he was saying "Ssshhh." He touched Elliot with the other hand. Lightly. Then Elliot faltered and dropped to the ground.

Susan gasped as she saw this.

"So I figure! Wow! I'll keep filming this guy that…that did whatever to Wayne Elliot."

The video showed the guy sit down at a table with a skinny red-haired man. They talked a little, and the guy pulled a big crystal-looking bottle and two glasses out of his shirt.

Susan squinted a little and asked, "I didn't notice a big bulge in his shirt as he walked up. How did he hide a bottle that size and get in with it?"

The woman shrugged.

"That's nothing. Watch the next part."

After talking and taking a drink, the guy got up from the table and started walking away. The red-haired guy got up and walked after him. Right before he reached him, he made a curious movement with his left hand. Then the lights went off.

The camera adjusted to the light, and you saw the two men talk a little more. Again the guy who came in turned and started walking away. There was a flash of bluish light, and then a woman with long red hair was standing directly behind the skinny guy. She grabbed his hair. He screamed. The other guy turned around and then 'boom!' The screen went white, and when it came back, the skinny guy and the red-haired woman were gone. The other guy was knocked off his feet. He got up, and a younger guy who looked like a federal agent joined him, and they exited the frame.

"That's when I went to help my friend. Give me your cell number, and I'll send this to you."

Susan had never ever given her cell phone number to anyone, but she did this time without question. The woman sent her the video and walked away saying.

"Delete my number. I mean it. I don't know what I just saw, but I don't want any of those guys after me."

Chapter 19

Bill smiled as he pulled the Challenger into the FBI building prisoner entrance. While Guiterrez and Diaz were talking to their dispatcher, he was texting. Armed and armoured breach team. Hostage rescue was waiting for them. Diaz looked at Bill. "What gives?"

Bill looked at both of them and unlocked the doors.

"Well, your uniform checks out. But, we don't know if you're who you say you are."

Diaz's reply was cut short as he was yanked out of the back of the car and handcuffed. Nikodemus chuckled as he followed Bill. He and Agent Smith went through a pass key door and into the elevators.

The elevator doors opened two floors early with Deputy Director Glenn standing there. With a scowl on his face, he entered the elevator without saying anything.

Nikodemus broke the silence.

"You're looking well, sir. How are you doing this evening?"

Glenn said nothing for a moment. Then turned to Nikodemus and started to speak. Then he paused let out a breath and calmly addressed him.

"How did you do it?"

"What are you referring to, sir?"

Glenn dropped his composure.

"The goddamn fingerprints! The fucking pictures! Your DNA sample doesn't even test! What are you?"

Nikodemus smiled and offered his hand. Glenn looked at him strangely and then took the offered handshake.

"Hello. My name's Nikodemus. I'm a Level 7 Seeker. Mostly, I slay dragons, but today."

He paused for effect.

"I am the instrument of your will."

Nikodemus grinned at Bill and clapped him on the shoulder.

"I consider Agent Smith here, to be my unofficial partner. Tonight, we got close to the evil Level 12 Mage named Markmor. He was partying in Deep Ellum."

The doors opened, and as they walked down the hall, Nikodemus continued.

"I didn't realise it, but apparently, I was just supposed to get next to him so his sister Morgaine. Another Mage. Could snatch him. I don't know what the situation is now exactly, but as soon as I do, I'll report it to you immediately."

Glenn looked at Agent Smith.

"Is that your report?"

Smith nodded.

"Yes, sir. I'll add details of our targeting and arrival method and the aftermath, but that is a good summary of the important facts."

Glenn motioned to one of the conference rooms.

"Your night isn't over. Curtis Vieth has two investigators from Draft and Associates that will be here soon. They would like your input on an investigation they are involved in. Apparently, some red-haired skinny guy talked his daughter Julia into performing oral sex on him in front of her fiancée two months ago. The wedding is off, and Vieth wants to find the guy. Thinks he's a hypnotist or something."

Glenn looked at Nikodemus.

"Any thoughts?"

Nikodemus grimaced and looked at the floor.

"I bet she's a looker. Markmor glamoured her. So she did what he told her to do. He doesn't give a shit about anyone but himself. What exactly do you want us to tell them?"

Glenn looked thoughtfully at Nikodemus.

"You mean you'll do what I tell you?"

"Of course, I work on your behalf. Remember? Instrument of your will. I'll tell them everything or nothing."

"Well, you have to tell them something. Curtis Vieth is nobody to fuck with."

Glenn opened the door to the empty conference room. He didn't follow them in.

"I'll be watching from the observation booth. Bill, identify yourself."

He looked at Nikodemus.

"Call him Nick. Nick Demus."

Nikodemus chuckled at this.

"That's an alias I've used more than once."

The door closed behind them as Nick and Bill went to the conference table and sat down. It was nearly 2:00 a.m. It wasn't long before they were both sleeping with their heads on the table.

In the observation room, Deputy Director Glenn and Mike Walker, an NSA analyst, watched the two sleeping men.

"That's him huh? Nikodemus. The guy who took Agent Smith between. Rescued Senator Rollins' daughter and then the Senator himself. What is he exactly?"

Glenn didn't look at him as he answered, "Well, tonight, he told me he was a Level 7 Seeker, and he was the instrument of my will. What do you make of that?"

"Well, I'd use my instrument."

Chapter 20

Markmor seemed awful smug for someone who had incurred the wrath of the Great Myron. He glared at Morgaine, pointedly ignoring his father as he raged at him. Myron was screaming in his face. Markmor turned to Myron and interrupted him.

"I'm sorry, what were you saying?"

Myron got quiet. A cool appraising look came to his eye. Morgaine shuddered at the calm quiet of his voice.

"You're amused, aren't you, son? You think I won't do anything to you?"

Myron raised his hand, and the air crackled as he prepared to unleash something Morgaine could only imagine when Ethan popped in from between.

"Myron, stop! Markmor! What is Lydia doing?"

Markmor smirked and crossed his arms.

"Wouldn't you like to know?"

Ethan was a Level 22 Mage, like his brother Myron. However, he had no love for Markmor. So he didn't hesitate at all as he turned Markmor to stone.

Myron gasped and turned to his brother.

"How could you?"

"Myron! It's only temporary. Serve that ingrate right if I never lifted it. Lydia is interfering with somebody's dreams. I can't tell who. But it's bad. It's somebody with an amulet."

Myron's eyes widened.

"The Senator! Quickly, guard him. I'll look for Lydia. You, too, Morgaine."

As Ethan and Morgaine tranced out to be sleep-state guardians of Senator Rollins, Myron searched for Lydia. There was just one problem. Lydia wasn't interfering with the Senator. She was interfering with Agent Smith.

When a normal person sleeps, their subconscious and conscious reality are open for a mage of any level to view or even dabble with. A seeker can't guard a sleeping person. They can help them in a dream. They can join them. Since it was the first time Nikodemus had been sleeping near Agent Smith, he entered Smith's dream as an observer.

It was kind of dark for a guy like Bill. He was watching Bill as a boy being chased through woods that faded into hallways. Bill was screaming. When the monster pursuing him noticed Nikodemus, he recognised Lydia. She was cornering Smith. Nikodemus couldn't get to him but he could make himself heard.

"Bill! Drop the amulet and think of it protecting you!"

Nikodemus' voice echoed down the hallways. Then the small boy reached into his pocket and produced the amulet Nikodemus had given him. It was large in his small boy hands. He dropped it and closed his eyes. The monster was inches from the amulet when it produced lightning that burned it to a crisp.

As this happened Bill turned into a man. An agent. He looked at Nikodemus far above him and then at the ashes that had been a monster that was an amalgam of all his childhood and adult fears. His voice sounded in Nikodemus head.

"That was Lydia? Did I kill her?"

Nikodemus appeared next to Bill.

"No, you didn't kill her. That was a creation of hers not the bitch herself. The purple sky above them darkened as the silhouette of a giant woman materialised and glared down at them. Bill startled Nikodemus with the vehemence of his challenge."

"You want some more of that, you bitch! Come and get it!" Nikodemus chuckled as she glared one more time and then turned into mist.

"How are you here? In my dream. How did she get in my dream?" Fear entered Bill's voice as he implored Nikodemus.

"What was she going to do to me? How do I protect myself in a dream?"

Nikodemus patted the dream agent on the back as he picked up Bill's amulet and handed it to him.

"I can enter your dream if I'm asleep near you and you're asleep. A mage like Lydia, Myron, Markmor, or Morgaine can enter anyone's dream anywhere. It's the nature of the discipline."

Nikodemus changed his appearance before Bill's eyes. He was now wearing a tuxedo and holding a machine gun.

"My discipline is more physical. Therefore, I have to be near you. Markmor can control a person. I can knock them out. I can't make them do something. I can do something to them."

Nikodemus was about to speak again when they both were awakened by the door to the conference room opening. They sat up and looked at each other. Bill shook his head a little.

"Holy shit."

Chapter 21

Two men in almost matching black suits entered the conference room. They approached the table as Nikodemus and Bill stood. The older of the two addressed them.

"My name is Greg Connor. My associate is Charlie Wilkins. We are with Draft and Associates and have been retained by Curtis Vieth of Azle, Texas."

Bill stepped forward taking the offered hand.

"Hello, I'm Agent Bill Smith. This is my associate Nick Demus."

As they shook hands the younger man addressed Nikodemus, "I notice he didn't say Agent Nick Demus. Are you an FBI agent?"

Nikodemus smiled as he took the offered handshake.

"I am not. I am a consultant. Bill, you need to report that incident now while the details are still fresh in your mind."

Bill snorted and started to the table.

"I'm serious. The details will fade. Do it now. I'll entertain these gentlemen in the meantime."

Connor looked at Nikodemus quizzically.

"What incident? The one at 'Trees'?"

Nikodemus and Bill both looked at Greg Connor then.

"No. Bill, seriously with each minute you'll remember less. Go. Now."

Bill got up and without another word went to the door and exited. Nikodemus smiled and gestured to the conference room table.

"Gentlemen."

Both men sat down. Then Nikodemus said something that didn't register as a word in anyone's ears. The two men were motionless. Looking at nothing. Nikodemus went to the door and chased after Bill.

In the observation booth, Deputy Director Glenn and NSA Analyst Mike Walker were watching the frozen men sitting at the table. Glenn dialled a number on his cell.

"Get a medical team to Conference Room 2 now. No emergency, just need vitals."

Then he got up and went into the hall followed by the NSA analyst. They both caught up with Bill and Nikodemus by the bathrooms. Nikodemus was about to talk to Bill but as Glenn and Walker showed up, he turned to them.

"Look, I'm sorry about glamouring those guys. But Bill and I just had an incident that needs to be documented now. Did you notice how those two immediately knew I wasn't an agent?"

Glenn addressed Bill.

"Smith, what happened?"

"I was attacked."

"When?"

"Just now."

"Just now? By whom?"

"Nikodemus says it was Lydia. Markmor's sister."

Glenn was getting annoyed.

"He says? Just now? What, in the conference room?"

"Yes."

"What the fuck do you mean by yes? Nobody was in there but you two!"

Nikodemus joined in speaking calmly and slowly. As he did, Bill started breathing easier. He had been getting upset. "Sir. This is going to sound weird. Lydia attacked him in his dream."

The NSA analyst snorted his derision. Nikodemus looked at him.

"You're dealing with next-level shit here, guys. The attack was real. I was able to help him because I was asleep, too. The details of dreams fade quickly. That's why I'm insisting him to give a deposition or report or whatever you want to call it now. This minute. The details he remembers will help me nail that bitch."

Glenn was taken aback. Nikodemus was obviously very serious.

"Why are those two guys in a trance?"

"Because we need to do this now. They don't need to know about this. It's easier. When we're done, I'll sit down, and when Bill opens the door, I'll wake them. They'll never notice what happened."

Glenn was obviously trying to help, but he wasn't.

"We need to get a tech. We'll set up in an interview room."

Nikodemus interrupted him.

"Fuck it. Bill, your phone will record video right?"

Bill fumbled out his phone.

"Sure."

Glenn interjected.

"Come on. It won't take twenty minutes to get set up and do this right."

"Deputy Director, in twenty minutes, he won't remember shit. You don't understand. She'll be trying to erase his memory as we speak. Tomorrow, he won't remember it happened at all."

Nikodemus pushed record button on Bill's phone and handed it to Glenn.

"Hold this. Bill, the date is 21 June 2018, the time is 3:14 a.m. Start with your first memory. Describe the event."

Bill started slowly then the words started flowing. Glenn and Walker got wide-eyed as he progressed.

"Well, the first thing I remember is it was dark. It was my grandfather Willy's barn. It's outside of Arp, Texas. I was a kid. I stayed there one summer when I was nine. It felt like then. I was always scared of that barn. During the day, I'd always hear rustling in the corner and high above me. I'd seen a huge spider there once. I've always been scared of spiders."

Bill stopped looking into space and focused on Nikodemus.

"I'm rambling, aren't I?"

"Doesn't matter."

Nikodemus assured Bill.

"Keep going. Stream of consciousness. It's the only way you'll remember what I need to know."

"What do you need to know?"

"Don't worry about that. So, big spiders."

At Nikodemus' coaxing, Bill continued.

"I would never have gone into that barn at night alone, but there I was. I heard a sound from the corner and thought it looked like a spider the size of a small dog. I didn't really see it clearly because I ran out the door. Only the house wasn't there. Across a wide street, there was a building. It was one storey, white. Lots of windows. Going down the block to my right. It was dark except for a dim light above the door. I ran towards it. I could hear whatever it was right behind me as I ran."

Nikodemus interrupted.

"Did you hear any words from your pursuer? Man or woman? Creature? Whatever?"

"No. When I got in. It wasn't any brighter than the barn. I could hear kids chanting. No words. Just sounds in unison. I was scared shitless. I reached the end of the hall. It was a dead end. As I turned around, I heard you over the PA. 'Bill, drop the amulet and think about it protecting you!'"

Then I remembered I had an amulet. I remembered who you were and that I wasn't a kid. I dropped the amulet and when it got near it lightning smoked the thing. I went from scared little kid to feeling invincible. I never knew or thought about it being a person. Man or woman. Then you were beside me, and we were talking. Then the conference room door opened, and we woke up.

"Bill, this is important. The chanting. No words, right?"

"No, just 'Ya Ya Ya' or something like that."

"Was it Ya Ra Ya Ra Ya Ra?"

Bill jumped a little.

"Yes! That's what they were saying. What does that mean? How did you know?"

Nikodemus turned to Glenn.

"You can stop the recording. You should copy that and archive it. I knew what they were saying because I know that bitch. I know her and her sister well. I'm going to her father with this. He'll take care of her."

Glenn started to hand Bill his phone, but Bill gestured to him to keep it.

"The unlock code is 1621. Sixteen to drive, twenty-one to drink. Easy to remember, eh? I'll get it back after you copy the video."

Nikodemus asked the NSA guy.

"Who are you? I don't believe we've met?"

The other man shook hands with Nikodemus.

"NSA Analyst Mike Walker. I've been involved with this since the kidnapping. I interviewed Smith here regarding the dead mechanic from the bunker."

Nikodemus smiled.

"His name was Spencer. He'd been glamoured so many times he didn't ever remember his own last name. Why were you interested in him?"

"He'd escaped custody once a couple of years ago. Went between. We didn't know what that was at the time. The similarities. The glitter. The pop. Smith confirmed his identity from a mugshot. Didn't know his name, though. Spencer you say? No last name?"

They stopped outside the conference room door.

"Those guys I glamoured in there. I just paused them. I didn't insert anything in their mind. I couldn't if I wanted to. Others can. A Mage for instance. You do that enough, shit gets crowded out and lost. This can happen deliberately from my understanding. Like I said I can't do it. Spencer had it happen so much that part of his brain was like bad sectors on a hard drive."

He opened the door. Inside two men and one woman were observing the glamoured men. Nikodemus entered the room.

"Okay, guys get out."

He sat down where he had been earlier.

"Bill, get them out and close the door. As soon as you close it, open it. I'll wake them and say 'Maybe later.' That will be referring to your deposition. Act like you decided to wait and sit down. We'll start like nothing happened. Maybe they won't notice that they sat for thirty minutes."

Chapter 22

"Maybe later."

Greg and Charlie looked confused for a moment; then Charlie took out a small device.

"We'll be recording this. Ok?"

Bill sat down and smiled.

"Of course. What can we do for you?"

Even though Greg was obviously the senior of the team, it was Charlie that was doing all the talking. Greg was observing reactions, facial expressions, everything. He'd been a skilled interrogator. Human lie detector by more than one account.

"You saw the Channel 4 van at "Trees" right? Well, they were there. A woman gave Susan Simpson a video. Several videos are already on social media. You know that guy was Wayne Elliot, right?"

"You mean the big black guy, I guess. I thought he was a bouncer."

Greg entered the conversation.

"No, he's Wayne Elliot. Star multimillionaire linebacker for the Dallas Cowboys. Videos show him getting up on you, and you knocked him out by touching him. How did you do that?"

Bill gestured to Nikodemus to let him answer.

"Let's get to that later. That isn't why you're here, is it? Does Curtis Vieth have an interest in what happens to Wayne Elliot?"

Charlie took back over.

"Ok, fine. We'll come back to that. I take it you are familiar with Mr Vieth?"

"Yes, I am. I know his family has been involved in oil, dairy farming, and real estate for over a century. He has friends in high places. It's why this meeting is taking place at 3:30 a.m. on a Sunday morning."

Wilkins wrinkled his brow and looked at his watch.

"3:30? I thought it was barely 3:00."

He shook his head and looked at Greg. Then continued.

"Anyway who is the skinny red-haired guy in the video? We need his name and where we can find him."

Nikodemus answered him.

"Why? What are you going to do to him?"

"Can you just answer the question? You get us a line on him, and we're done here."

Nikodemus leaned forward.

"His name is Mark Moore. He's from Scotland, but he's in Dallas a lot. I think he may be in custody, though."

"Where? Dallas Police Department?"

"I doubt it. We'll find out and get back to you, though."

"Mr Demus. Who are you exactly? What is your involvement?"

This from Greg. He'd been watching Nikodemus the entire time.

"I told you. I'm a consultant."

"What is the name of your firm?"

"I'm not at liberty to say."

Charlie punched a key on his laptop and started a video. He turned the screen towards Bill and Nikodemus.

"Here's one of the videos. Get ready. I'm sure you'll be hearing more about this. Wayne Elliot is really, I mean really, really pissed. He wants your blood. He didn't even remember the event, but when he saw the videos, buddy, he wants a piece of you."

"Well, he should be careful what he wishes for. I was being gentle. He doesn't want to meet me when I'm in a bad mood. You tell him, if you talk to him, that I can do things that'll make that seem like a kiss."

Greg took out his phone and took a photograph of Nikodemus. Then he stood up.

"Let's go, Charlie."

Charlie looked at Nikodemus and Bill for a second and then closed the laptop and put it and the recorder in the small case he had brought with him. Bill handed them a business card as he followed them to the door.

"Here's my card if you need to reach either one of us."

Greg took the card but never stopped looking at Nikodemus. When the door closed Nikodemus looked towards the mirror.

"Watch them. They aren't leaving. Not until they see me leave to follow me."

Bill sat back down.

"Really? Why?"

"Ole Greg there didn't like it when I wouldn't give him the name of my firm. When he checks the picture he took of me, he's gonna be even more pissed."

In the booth, Glenn said to no one.

"Tell me about it."

Greg and Charlie were almost to their car when Greg took his phone back out to pull up the picture of Nikodemus. He stopped in the middle of the street.

"Son of a bitch!"

Charlie had continued to the car and looked back as he tossed his case in the backseat.

"What?"

"The picture of Mr Demus. It's corrupted or something."

He started walking again and got in the passenger seat. He handed his phone to Charlie.

"Look."

Charlie glanced at it and handed the phone back. The picture looked like a shadow with electronic interference. He had been about to start the car but didn't turn the key.

"So... I guess we're not leaving now?"

Greg was dialling a number. He didn't answer Charlie.

"It's me. Get a tail team to the FBI building in Fort Worth. We'll wait for them."

As he hung up his phone rang. Shaking his head he answered.

"Curtis. We just left. FBI says the guy's name is Mark Moore. From Scotland, the country not the little town in north Texas. Yeah. He's Scottish."

Greg held the phone away from his ear a little as Curtis Vieth's voice went up in volume.

"We're going to start looking for him now. Hey, at least we have a name. They said he's in Dallas a lot. Okay."

Greg hung up the phone.

"Rock paper scissors to see who has to walk to that McDonalds down there and get us something to eat."

The McDonalds sign was three blocks away. Luckily open twenty-four hours. Charlie just looked at him.

"Relax, old man. I'll go fetch you a grease biscuit. You know that shit's gonna kill you, right?"

"Make that two grease biscuits and a large coffee."

"Yeah, I know. The coffee hot and black, like your women."

Charlie got out and closed the door on Greg's reply. He started walking towards the McDonalds. On a monitor in Agent Smith's office, Bill, Nikodemus, Glenn and Walker watched the man walk down the street.

"So, what did you say about your picture?"

This was from Walker. He was watching the car. It was parked across the street near the corner. The passenger window rolled down a little and smoke started coming out.

"Got us a smoker, guys."

Nikodemus chuckled before he continued. He looked at Deputy Director Glenn and then at Walker.

"Sometimes my pictures don't come out very flattering. Or at all."

Bill studiously avoided Glenn's eyes as he got up and stomped out of his office. Walker looked puzzled.

"What's with him?"

"Well, he took pictures, prints, and DNA from me. None of it came out right. I think he's still mad about it."

Bill zoomed in on the car. As he watched, he wadded up a piece of paper and threw it at Nikodemus.

"You think?"

Chapter 23

Curtis Vieth lived on a five-thousand-five-hundred-acre parcel of land east of Azle, Texas. When his father Charles had died, Curtis had demolished the traditional ranch-type house and erected what is commonly being called a 'barndominium.' The house starts out as a metal building with a concrete slab and four-inch pipe frame. His was two stories and seven-thousand square feet of luxury behind the unassuming exterior.

Inside the building was a six-bedroom, two-storey house with wrap-around porches on both floors and a hot tub and sauna. The main living area had a cathedral ceiling and the longest bar anyone had seen in a private residence. That's what everybody said at the party when he finished the house anyway. When he divorced his wife Sheila, his daughter had chosen not to move to Florida with her. Between inherited land not being community property and his daughter not wanting to go with "the bitch." He had made out nicely. His daughter was everything to him, and she started school at the University of Texas at Arlington a year before. Before the incident. Before Curtis Vieth had started his mission.

To say Curtis Vieth was angry was like saying Hitler was vaguely anti-Semitic. His rage was visible on several walls, broken cabinet doors, and a large pile of broken glass that was being swept into a shovel by Julie who was older than Curtis by almost twenty years. At almost sixty, she had worked for Curtis' father Charles for most of her adult life.

Being a black woman working in a rich white man's house had its benefits. She made more than her younger sister who was an accountant. Charles had taught Curtis that if you can afford to pay someone well, they will work without complaint and be loyal. Loyalty can be priceless. Like when Charles got into an argument and ended up shooting a friend of his in the backyard, Julie had helped bury the man behind the fence. She wondered how long it was going to be before Curtis got a hold of the man he had so far paid $200,000 to find. There was a lot of land behind the barndominium Curtis had built for himself.

"Curtis, you need anything, hon?"

Curtis was staring without seeing the news on his seventy-inch LED TV. The sound was off.

"No, thanks, Julie. Sorry about this mess."

"Don't you worry yourself about that at all, Curtis. When you catch that mothafuck, hit him once for me. Will you?"

This caused Curtis to grin. He looked over at Julie. "You always know how to cheer me up."

His phone beeped indicating an email. Curtis opened the email. It was from Draft and Associates.

Curtis,

The attachment contains a freeze-frame photograph of Mark Moore. We're looking for him. There have been some developments that would be better explained in person. I can send Greg and Charlie to your residence or office. Or, if you prefer, you can come to our office.

Please let me know what you want to do. In the meantime, I will keep you apprised of anything new regarding this matter.

Nelson Draft

Curtis opened the attachment and looked at a fuzzy, low-quality picture in the dim light that showed a skinny wispy-haired man who looked about thirty a weighing maybe one hundred twenty pounds.

"I'm coming for you, my friend. Get ready."

Chapter 24

Lydia was standing in Myron's darkened castle staring at her brother Markmor. Well, a statue of Markmor anyway. She knew the basics of the spell to turn someone to stone. Not enough to reverse the one her Uncle Ethan had cast, though. Ethan was a Level 22. She wasn't quite a 12 yet. Still, she thought she could feel his mind trying to contact her. Fleeting wisps of it only. Then the torches flared with werelight as Myron prepared to step between back to his castle. Lydia cursed silently and stepped between at the exact moment that Myron, Ethan and Morgaine entered.

Myron and Morgaine immediately went to the table for some wine. Ethan was standing where he had entered. Staring at the spot in front of the frozen Markmor.

"Lydia was here."

Morgaine gasped and whirled on Ethan.

"She was? When? Why?"

Ethan looked at Myron. They shared a knowing look. Myron hadn't reacted to the statement from Ethan. He obviously knew already.

"It's why we couldn't find her in the Senator's dreams, child. She…"

Myron hesitated. Then looked towards the dais that the three of them had recently vacated.

"Nikodemus is coming. Apparently, he knows something we need to know."

Glitter started falling around the dais, and with a "pop," Nikodemus was standing on the dais. He looked at the three smiling. Then his gaze fell on Markmor. He chuckled a little and took out his phone. After taking a picture of Markmor, he pocketed the phone.

"I didn't know Markmor got stoned. I thought he just drank and coerced women to have sex."

Morgaine giggled, but Myron and Ethan looked puzzled. Finally, Ethan got the joke and laughed.

"Myron, he means 'stoned' as in 'on drugs' not executed."

Myron's demeanour wasn't pleasant.

"You make jokes about my son, Nikodemus?"

Nikodemus bowed his head in submission.

"I meant no offence, Myron. I thought you didn't want to kill him?"

Myron looked at Ethan as he spoke.

"He isn't dead, Seeker. My brother's spell is temporary."

Myron looked at his frozen son for a moment, then turned his attention to Nikodemus.

"You are here for a reason."

This was a spoken statement. No hint of it being a question. Nikodemus always marvelled at the abilities of a soothsayer. Myron was a Level 22 Mage with Prescient leaning. No telling how old he was.

"Yes, I did. Lydia attacked Agent Smith in a dream. Strictly by chance, we both fell asleep in chairs early this morning at the FBI building. I helped him. Your amulet zapped her."

"Ethan knew Lydia was attacking someone. How could you tell it was her?"

"Agent Smith heard children doing the chant from the Zil Academy."

"Also, there is a powerful man looking for Markmor. His name is Curtis Vieth. Markmor glamoured his daughter and made her do things that ruined her impending marriage to another powerful family. There is a private investigation firm called Draft and Associates looking for Markmor everywhere."

Myron nodded.

"We'll deal with all of this soon enough. Ethan, wake Markmor. It's time to get this thing under control."

Ethan grimaced.

"It's barely holding him. He'll go between as soon as he's conscious."

"Our seeker here will hold him."

Nikodemus winced a little as Myron said this.

"Of course, Myron. I'll bind him while Ethan loosens his grip. He won't like it. But, I guess you know that."

Myron said nothing to this. He opened his robe and pulled out a wand. Morgaine gasped when she saw it.

"That's the wand Merlin gave you. Isn't it?"

"Yes, it is, child. I forgot you've never seen it."

It was an unassuming-looking stick. But, the reverence shown to a stick by three Mages was almost palpable. Nikodemus had heard of the wand, though he never knew it was in Myron's possession. It was the fabled wand of King Arthur's wizard. Over a thousand years old. Worth a thousand times its weight in gold.

"How did you get that, Myron? How old are you?"

Nikodemus' question went unanswered as Myron held the wand like it was a powerful weapon. Which it was.

"Bind him, Seeker. Ethan, wake up this ingrate so he can take his medicine."

None of the group noticed Lydia behind a column. She was only ten feet from Myron. Directly behind Markmor. At the mention of Merlin's wand, her eyes gleamed with greed. She held a large black revolver in her hands. She closed her eyes as Nikodemus placed a binding spell on the statue. Ethan started his chant. Lydia waited until the last syllable released Markmor. Then she struck.

Lydia jumped from behind the column and fired three times. The first struck Myron in the chest. Then Ethan. The third was for Nikodemus. He wasn't there, though. He had flickered out. Lydia ran towards Myron and snatched the wand from his hand.

"Markmor! Now!"

At her screamed command, Lydia and Markmor both stepped between and out of the room. Not before Nikodemus flickered back in and took back the wand. He was left holding the wand as Myron and Ethan slowly sank to their knees.

"Give the wand to Myron! Quickly!"

Nikodemus stared at the wand in his hand for a moment and then handed it to Myron. Morgaine raced to her father's side and held his hand. The tip of the wand glowed bright yellow. Myron started breathing deeply. Then there was a thud as something hit the floor. Nikodemus looked around Myron and Morgaine and saw it was a bullet. The slug from Myron's chest.

Over to the side, Ethan fell over and a breath wheezed out of him. He didn't draw another breath in. Nikodemus went over to him.

"Morgaine! He's dying,"

Morgaine looked at Nikodemus and shook her head. Then Myron raised his head and spoke words that didn't register in Nikodemus' ears. There was a crackling sound, and as Nikodemus stared incredulously, Ethan turned into a statue lying on the ground.

"That will hold him, Seeker. You and Morgaine will go after my son. Bring him to me. Kill that bitch sister of his. Take this."

Myron handed the wand to Morgaine. She got wide-eyed and trembled as she held it. Then her demeanour changed. She looked at Nikodemus with eyes that held no fear at all.

"First, it's time I met the Senator."

Chapter 25

The Dallas, Texas Division of Draft and Associates was the flagship office. By definition, a "private" investigation firm needed to be unobtrusive. The Dallas office was unobtrusive to the point of being invisible. They occupied the top two floors of a building that was over hundred years old. It was situated near Kennedy's X off Main St. There were four parking garages close enough that employees and clients were never in the same parking garage.

Shuttle service from one, skywalk from another, closed-circuit hidden cameras on all approaches. Curtis Vieth was impressed. He had never actually been to their office and had agreed to meet there just to have something to do. Also to visit the Men's Club in Dallas. He entered a code that had been texted to him in the parking garage and entered a nondescript-looking steel door with the number 101 on the top corner.

He entered a short hallway with dim lighting. Until the door behind him closed. Then recessed lights came on above him. There was a camera above the door at the end of the hallway. Just as he reached it, the door opened, and Greg Connor was smiling at him.

"Good afternoon, Curtis. You're looking good. Welcome to the Dallas Office."

Curtis shook the offered hand, and the two men entered Draft and Associates' Dallas office. Curtis looked up at the twenty-foot ceilings. The lights were suspended and looked like they were floating crystals. He was just noticing the leather furniture and granite coffee tables when the best-looking female he had ever seen in the flesh walked in.

"Hello, Curtis, I'm Lori Foltom. Won't you please come this way?"

As she turned away, Curtis looked wide-eyed at Greg. He whispered, "Holy shit."

Lori Foltom was thirtyish, maybe one hundred ten pounds, long legs, well-defined curves. Everybody's type. Her long brown hair and green eyes made her look better than good. Eighteen to eighty men turned their heads and watched her wherever she walked.

Greg grinned and pushed Curtis along. Curtis was enjoying the view on a walk that was sadly only about fifteen steps. Curtis could have walked behind the woman all day. Lori opened the door and gestured inside.

"Nelson Draft will be along any moment. Would you like some coffee or anything while you wait?"

Curtis tried to speak but couldn't. Greg stepped in front of Lori as he entered the conference room.

"Love those shoes, Lori. What are they? Jimmy Choo?"

Lori got close enough to Greg to kiss him. But didn't. She giggled and didn't answer as she walked on down the hall. Curtis came in and after the door closed. He let out a breath.

"Women like that get men like me in trouble. Shit, she looks good enough to eat. You two? You know?"

Greg grinned and sat next to Charlie.

"Sometimes. She likes it rough, though."

Curtis just looked at him.

"She can be as rough as she wants with me, pal."

"Be careful what you wish for. She's gonna help us take down Mr Moore."

Nelson Draft entered the conference room while he was on his cell phone. He was fifty-five- or fifty-six-foot tall and looked like a pro football player. He had been at the University of Texas. It might have been twenty odd years ago, but he was still a formidable man. His navy-blue suit and gold cuff links, watch, bracelet and a couple of rings projected success. He was. He smiled at Curtis as he hung up.

"Good to see you, Curtis. Has Greg told you about our plan?"

"Only said that the goddess that I followed to that door was going to be involved."

Nelson chuckled.

"Yeah, we're going with the honeypot. Seeing as we can't find Mr Mark Moore on any database anywhere. We've got facial recognition software hacked into half the traffic and security cams in the downtown area. We've had a couple of hits."

Charlie was punching buttons on a keyboard in front of him as Nelson talked. On one wall of the conference room was a large monitor. It came to life with a succession of grainy traffic cam and security cam footage.

"Granted, our source pic of Mr Moore isn't very high quality. But, with enhancement, we did get these four hits. All in Deep Ellum. All on a Friday or Saturday night. At either the club 'Trees' or at 'Club Clearview.' Well, outside these clubs."

Nelson signalled Charlie, and the monitor went dark.

"We're trying this Friday at 'Trees'."

Chapter 26

Deputy Directors Perkins and Glenn, NSA Analyst Mike Walker, Dallas Police Chief Keith Hill, and DHS Officer Mark Dudley were seated at a conference room table in the Fort Worth FBI office. Glenn signalled to Agent Charles Bone to begin his presentation. The lights in the room dimmed a little as the main monitor powered up, and Bone started his narrative.

The screen showed the holding tank of the Fort Worth sheriff's department.

"This is the first footage regarding the events at hand. I assume you have all read the reports in front of you. This was after a man known only as Nikodemus appeared out of thin air at the home of Senator Mike Rollins. Disappeared again. Reappeared with the missing daughter. Elizabeth is her name."

Bone zoomed in on the paused video.

"Gentlemen, I saw this with my own eyes. He had informed us he was taking an agent with him to arrest the individuals responsible. He then took Agent Bill Smith and disappeared again. We knew he was coming back to the holding tank. The video camera was rolling. Only..."

Bone started the video rolling. It showed static and five blurry figures appear. Then the static cleared, and there were only four.

"The camera did not function when Nikodemus was in the frame."

The screen changed to show several photographs in a row that were blurry and distorted.

"Here are attempts to photograph Nikodemus in the booking area. His prints and DNA wouldn't process either. We have no idea as to his real identity."

Bone turned off the monitor.

"At this time, I will bring in Range Warden Bill Jantzen to tell you about his experiences with Nikodemus at the firing range."

Jantzen entered the room. Nodded to all present and placed several plastic bags on the table.

"Good afternoon, gentlemen. These are slugs removed from the practice area of the firing range. At his request, I patted this man down. He was unarmed. He then gestured at the wall, and there was a tearing sound. I then removed this .44 calibre hollow point slug from the wall."

Jantzen picked up a baggie and slid it down the table to the DHS agent.

"Then he gestured several times. He 'fired' a .44 slug, a .50 Teflon-coated sniper round, and a .00 buckshot shotgun round into the same wall."

"Thank you, Jantzen, that will be all."

Jantzen nodded at Bone's statement and left the room. Bone picked up the remainder of the baggies and slid them to the other side of the table. Mike Walker picked up the baggie with .00 buckshot slugs in it.

"After the demonstration at the range, Nikodemus took me and Agent Smith to Divide, Colorado. I went between. It was instantaneous. Texas to Colorado in one breath."

There were murmurs around the table as all present digested this.

"In Colorado, he vaporised a bear with what he said was a 105-mm sabot round. It was deafening. I was knocked to the ground. The huge bear was spread out over fifty yards. I have never heard anything like it."

Bone paused, remembering how it had sounded like the sky ripped open.

"He made a statement in the Senator's car after that event regarding the 105 round. He said, he "copied" it three years ago."

The DHS officer put down the plastic bag of .00 buckshot he was holding.

"Copied, you say? This implies someone fired a 105-mm sabot round at him."

"It does indeed."

"To my knowledge, only US Military has these rounds. They're depleted uranium and would go through this entire building."

The DHS officer was writing as he talked. "I'll start finding out when we fired the round at him."

Agent Smith was waiting outside Agent Bone's office when he left the meeting.

"Nikodemus called and said Morgaine wants to meet the Senator."

Bone paused, then put the folder in his hand on the desk before taking his seat. Smith seated himself in front of the desk.

"Did he say when?"

"No, what do you think?"

"We do it here. I'll clear it with Glenn. He wants to meet her, too. The Senator leaves for Washington in two days. So, tomorrow, I think. Two o'clock."

Chapter 27

"How could you lose Merlin's wand?"

Markmor was pacing in front of his table. The twins were hiding in the bathroom. Sensing their fear made Markmor smile. Lydia wasn't smiling. She was pouring a drink.

"This is the thanks I get? I shot our father and Ethan. For you! The wand wasn't even part of it until I saw it. I tried. I had it in my hand. Then, when we stepped here, it wasn't."

Lydia downed the liquor and closed her eyes. Feeling its fire slowly burn down her throat.

"Do you realise what that wand can do? Do you, Lydia? I never knew father had it. How could he have it this long and not use it?"

"How do you know he didn't use it, Marky?"

Markmor scowled at her.

"Don't call me that."

"Okay, brother. I'm tired. I'm going to sleep. What are you going to do?"

Markmor said nothing as Lydia left. Then he called out.

"I'm going out."

Chapter 28

Susan Simpson was waiting for Wayne Elliot when he arrived. He entered "Bally's Sports Bar" without his usual entourage of assistants and scantily clad women. He had returned her voicemail almost immediately the day before. The man wanted answers. He wanted to get his hands on the guy who dropped him at "Trees." Susan did too. Answers anyway.

"You got a name yet?"

Wayne sat down and started with no preamble. He looked at Susan, and she felt like a zebra looking at a lion.

"No. Not yet. I think the FBI is involved. I saw what turned out to be an FBI vehicle pull away from the front door of 'Trees'."

Elliot snorted his derision.

"You think? You sounded like you knew more than that in your message."

Susan reached over and put her hand on his arm.

"I called Draft and Associates. I was going to get them on this. They said they're already on it for another client."

The doors to Bally's opened as Greg and Charlie walked in. Charlie was carrying a tablet under his arm.

"Here they are now."

Wayne turned around and stood. He smiled and shook Greg's hand.

"What's up, Greg?"

"Oh, the usual, Wayne. You're looking good."

The two men sat opposite Susan as Charlie slipped in next to her.

"You know him, Wayne?"

"Hell, yeah. This is one detail-oriented, tenacious motherfucker."

At Susan's quizzical look, Greg smiled and said, "Don't ask. Charlie, show Wayne what we know."

Charlie turned on the tablet and turned it so Wayne and Susan could see it.

"I'm gonna spare you viewing the videos we've gleaned from social media. You've seen them. Here are two still frames of the persons of interest."

The tablet showed stills of Markmor, Nikodemus, and Morgaine.

"We are after the skinny guy. Mark Moore. We met Nick Demus at the FBI office. We don't know who the woman is."

"He's a Fed?"

"No, he's a consultant. Didn't tell us the firm. Seemed tight with them, though."

"You got an address for Mr Demus?"

Charlie said nothing. He turned off the tablet. Wayne looked at Greg.

"Come on, Greg. I just want to talk to him."

"Right, Wayne. Just talk. No, we don't have an address. He's not in any database. That grainy, crappy picture is the only one of him we have. I tried to take his picture when we were at the FBI building, and it came out fuzzy."

Charlie started to speak but stopped at a severe look from Greg. Wayne noticed it. "What? Come on, Greg, you owe me."

"Ok, tell him, Charlie. Tell him what Mr Demus said."

Wayne and Susan were staring at Charlie. He started playing with the silverware in front of him. Without looking up he spoke.

"I told him you wanted a piece of him. He said, and I quote 'He should be careful what he wishes for. I was being gentle.' No shit. Those were his exact words."

Wayne started breathing hard. Greg leaned in.

"Easy, Wayne."

They were interrupted by Greg and Charlie's phones' text alert tones. Greg's sounded like a bullet ricochet. Charlie's was a woman's voice saying, "Text alert, sugar."

Neither moved for a second. Charlie looked at his phone. Then at Greg.

"Mr Demus and an unknown female just got out of a taxi in front of the FBI building."

Chapter 29

Deputy Director Glenn, Agent Bone, Agent Smith, and NSA Analyst Walker watched the taxi pull up in front of the FBI building on the monitor in Agent Bone's office. It was two o'clock. Nikodemus and a red-haired woman got out.

"Well, so much for running plates. I'll meet them downstairs."

Smith was out the door before he finished the sentence.

Nikodemus offered Morgaine his hand as she exited the taxi. She was dressed in a purplish business suit that was slightly iridescent in the afternoon sun. The skirt was short enough to make men look twice. Her hair was down. Long and flowing. The sun made it look like fire. She looked like a model.

"Morgaine, you look good enough to eat."

"Maybe later, Nick old chum."

Nikodemus was dressed up to match her in a black suit, white shirt, but no tie. Dark wayfarer glasses hid his eyes. Nikodemus opened the door to the building just as Agent Smith exited the elevator.

"Can I help you?"

This from the same black guy that Nikodemus seemed to see every time he entered the building.

"Thank you, no. Smith here is expecting us."

As Agent Smith came up to them, he was trying not to stare at Morgaine.

"Uh, hey, Nikodemus. Uh. Uh. Y-Y-Y-You must be Morgaine!"

Morgaine extended her hand as her glamour exuded into the lobby. Nikodemus shook his head. Great, now everybody will be in love with her.

"Delighted, I'm sure. Agent Smith."

Smith stood there staring saying nothing. Nikodemus stepped up and punched him in the arm. Hard. Smith jumped a little and rubbed his arm.

"Crap! What did you do that for?"

"Do what for? Come on, lover boy, take us upstairs."

Still rubbing his arm Smith led the way to the elevator. When the doors closed, Nikodemus turned to Morgaine.

"Turn it off."

"Whatever do you mean?"

"The glamour will make this weird and confusing. You're gonna freak out when you meet Rollins. I'm serious. He's the only righteous man I've ever seen in the flesh. It's why your father is protecting him."

Morgaine looked at Nikodemus innocently but the glamour faded. Smith was still looking at her like candy in a window.

"Who's in there, Bill?"

"In where?"

"Jesus! Bill, the goddamn conference room! Remember? The reason we're here?"

The elevator stopped, and the doors opened. There were four Secret Service agents standing outside the conference room door. Plus, Agent Bone. Even with the glamour turned off, they were all practically drooling. Nikodemus turned to Morgaine. She was looking hot.

"Okay, diva. Let's get this dog and pony show started."

Morgaine giggled as she walked up to the closest Secret Service agent. She reached up and caressed his cheek.

"My, my. Aren't you big and handsome? What's your name?"

"His name is agent, Morgaine. Come on."

Nikodemus opened the door, and Morgaine entered the conference room. Seated at the table where both Deputy Directors Allen Perkins and John Glenn were sitting. The NSA guy, Mike Walker; the DHS representative, Mark Dudley; and at the head of the table was Senator Mike Rollins.

Morgaine was smiling at each until she saw the Senator. She did a double take and blinked. Walker and Dudley looked at each other curiously. Then Morgaine turned to Nikodemus.

"Holy shit."

She looked at the Senator again and then, with little warning, popped between and was gone. Nikodemus shook his head.

"Perfect. Well, what did you think of her?"

Bone didn't look happy.

"I thought you said she wanted to meet him."

Nikodemus walked over to the table against the wall with coffee and water bottles. He opened a bottle of water and, after drinking most of it in one long draft, went and sat down in a vacant chair at the table.

"Well, I guess she just needed to see what all the fuss was about. You remember my first reaction to him, don't you?"

Senator Rollins voice was quiet but got everyone's attention.

"I remember Nikodemus. You looked at me like I was a man with three heads or something. Just like she did. What exactly is this righteous without being self-righteous thing you said? You also said my soul 'shines like a beacon'."

Everyone turned towards Nikodemus who looked at the Senator for a moment before he answered.

"Well, Mike, it's like this. I have known many people who held political positions of power. Usually, they walked over people to get there. More than one killed an opponent to get there. They did it to gain power. Not to help people or make the world a better place."

Nikodemus looked around the room.

"Some of these guys have done it to a greater or lesser degree."

Nikodemus returned his attention to the Senator.

"I am a Level 7 Seeker with Protector leaning. This means I am a trained guard amongst other things. I can look at someone and see a little bit into their character. If one of you in this room was a spy or, for whatever reason, working against us, I could tell by looking at you."

Nikodemus had stopped addressing the group directly. He was facing the mirrored wall.

"It's why I can see all six people in the observation room. And…"

Nikodemus turned his attention back to the Senator and went to sit directly across from him.

"I can tell you never cheated anybody in your life. You never threw anybody under a bus to get here. You genuinely want to make the world a better place. I've never seen anybody like you. Morgaine hasn't either."

Nikodemus stood up and started pushing his palms towards the water table that was fifteen feet away. The table moved against the wall and then started making a creaking sound before it snapped and folded up its entire length against the wall. The coffee maker and all the water bottles crashed to the floor.

"It's why I will die to protect you."

He looked back at the Senator. Everyone was speechless.

"Now that she's seen what this is about. It's why Morgaine will kill her own brother and sister."

Nikodemus sat back down.

"To protect you."

Nikodemus grinned and let his sunglasses slide down to cover his eyes.

"Did that answer your question?"

Chapter 30

They made a weird-looking procession. Greg and Charlie in a black four-door Mercedes, followed by Wayne in his metallic blue Viper, then Susan in her Toyota Corolla. They were conspicuous because there weren't three parking places near the spotter car across the street from the FBI building.

Charlie was driving; Greg was looking at the front door.

"No way, not to see that goddamn big blue Viper. You know they have cameras watching everything."

Charlie killed the engine. They were double-parked, three cars in a row.

"Something's gonna happen, Greg. You know it. If Wayne sees Demus. It's gonna be on. FBI building or not. What the fuck do we do?"

Greg was on the phone. He disconnected and looked at Charlie.

"Curtis is about two blocks away. Wait till his big yellow H2 parks behind Susan."

They weren't wrong.

Agent Torrez opened the conference room door without knocking. Normally an infraction. Bone's scowl softened as Torrez said something in his ear. Torrez looked at the destroyed table then over at Smith.

"Apparently, we have a car convention of sorts in front of the building. One of the cars is Wayne Elliot's Viper. They double-parked across the street. Smith, come with me. You"

Bone was looking at Nikodemus and then the destroyed table.

"Stay here."

Once the conference room door closed, Bone held Smith's arm and stopped near the elevator.

"Torrez, I want a forensics team ready to examine the table in the conference room. I want ballistics, physics, everything. Have them hold in the lab until I call them."

Bone pushed the call button on the elevator. Torrez received a text.

"Sir, a yellow H2 just pulled up and parked behind the Toyota Corolla. We've run all the plates. We have a Draft and Associates' car, Wayne Elliot, Susan Simpson, -she's press in case you didn't know -and Curtis Vieth of Azle, Texas."

Smith shook his head at the mention of Curtis Vieth.

"That's the guy, sir. You know, the one looking for Markmor. That Greg Connor and Charlie Wilkins were hired to find. This should be interesting."

As the elevator door opened, Agent Bone turned to Smith.

"On second thought stick close to Nikodemus. Don't let him get where Wayne Elliot can see him. Get him out of the building."

"And go where exactly?"

"You're his 'unofficial' partner, right? Go somewhere, I don't care. Just get him out of here without Wayne Elliot seeing him."

The door to the elevator closed before Smith could reply. The door opened to the lobby. Wayne Elliot was smiling and signing autographs. The information desk attendant had left his booth and was part of the group of about ten people trying to get next to Wayne to take a selfie.

"Richards!"

At Bone's parade ground volume, Michael Richards, the information booth attendant, nearly jumped out of his skin.

"What are you doing?"

Richards gulped and ran around back to his booth. He offered no explanation. Just sat down and stared at his entry logbook. Then started writing in it. Bone ignored him. His bellowed enquiry had taken the enthusiasm level of the autograph session down several notches.

Greg was grinning at Bone. Behind him were Susan Simpson, Charlie Wilkins and Curtis Vieth. He walked over to the information booth.

"That's Greg Connor, Charlie Wilkins, Susan Simpson, Curtis Vieth and of course Wayne Elliot here to see Mr Nick Demus. He's a consultant. For what company I have no idea."

Greg glanced up and acted like he hadn't noticed Agent Bone until then.

"Agent Bone here might know his firm."

Bone walked up and was looking through the doors at the four double-parked cars across the street.

"Those vehicles are parked illegally."

Greg glanced at the cars and then returned his attention to Agent Bone.

"Indeed they are. I'll have Charlie move them. Would it be possible to speak with Mr Demus?"

"Mr Demus is a private citizen. You would have to ask him. Why are the four of you here now exactly?"

Greg looked over at Charlie and indicated the door. Without a word, Charlie got Susan's keys, then Curtis', then Wayne Elliot's and went out the door.

"Well, Special Agent Charles Bone. Seventeen-year veteran, agent in charge on the Rollins kidnapping that never made the news. Divorced once. Remarried. Three children. Youngest about to graduate from the University of Texas, Austin. I'm here because we spotted Mr Demus and an unknown female get out of a taxi and enter here."

Susan was listening intently and had put her phone on record as they entered the building. Greg leaned against the counter of the information desk before he continued.

"I got all that information on you without much effort. Not so with Mr Demus. Can't find him in any database. Just like we can't find Mr Mark Moore. Now, why is that?"

"Your data mining capabilities are not my concern. Mr Connor. What is your interest in Mr Demus anyway?"

Elliot entered the conversation like a wrecking ball.

"I would like to have words with Mr Demus. That's why I'm here. Where is he?"

Elliot was close, leaning over, looking down on Agent Bone. The intimidation was lost on the agent, though. Agent Smith looked at Elliot like he was about as intimidating as a baby seal.

"My concern, Mr Elliot, is that you are starting to invade my personal space. I find your demeanour threatening and will act accordingly if you so much as get a piece of lint on my jacket."

Agent Bone had subtly signalled the two lobby security agents, and they had sauntered over to stand behind Agent Bone. Their MP4's slung low were hard to ignore.

"And, Mr Connor, the last time we met you called ahead of time. Or rather, Mr Vieth called ahead of time. It is a pleasure to meet you, Mr Vieth. I'm sure the Deputy Director can make time for the son of one of his oldest friends. If you would care to follow me, I can take you to his office."

Agent Bone's tone when he addressed Curtis Vieth was friendly and deferential. A drastic change from the emotionless tone when addressing Elliot. Greg Connor was impressed. No wonder he was the agent in charge of whatever. Their little visit seemed dead in the water until Curtis saved them.

"Thank you very much, Agent Bone. I was hoping to introduce my friends to Allen."

Agent Bone smiled at Greg.

"Of course, Mr Vieth. I'll get a conference room."

He motioned towards the elevator, and the procession started past him. As Connor started to pass, Bone caught his arm.

"Touché', Mr Connor."

Chapter 31

Morgaine stepped from between onto the dais in her father's castle. Myron was standing by the statue of his brother Ethan. Ethan was frozen in repose on the floor. He didn't look up. Morgaine went to Myron and took his hand in hers.

"I saw him, father. I've never seen a soul like his. He's pure. It was scary. I didn't know what to say. Imagine that, me not knowing what to say."

"How long were you in his presence?"

Morgaine let go of his hand and went over to the liquor cabinet.

"Maybe ten seconds. Long enough. Now, I understand. What I don't understand is why Markmor is doing what he is doing. How could Lydia shoot you? Shoot Ethan? What is happening?"

Myron walked over to the council table and sat down in his chair at its head.

"This isn't Markmor. Someone is pulling his strings. Lydia's too. He just doesn't realise it. It's someone dark. Now, Lydia, and Markmor, too, I suppose, know about the wand. Things are going to get worse before they get better."

Myron sighed and then looked at Morgaine. The weariness in his eyes seemed inconsolable.

"We need a Necromancer."

Morgaine came to the table with two tumblers of amber-coloured liquor.

"We also need Nikodemus to advance to Level 8."

"I don't understand why he didn't a long time ago, father. He's already doing things that are supposed to be beyond his capabilities. He can 'make.' Why hasn't he advanced?"

Myron drank half his tumbler before he answered.

"Because he would have to be beholden to a mentor. A mentor can make you do things. He never liked being told what to do."

"He's been doing what you tell him to do."

"Yes, but only because it involved protecting someone. He has Protector leaning. His brother had a bad experience with a mentor. It cost him his life."

"Well, besides that, do you know of any Necromancer that is still alive?"

"Yes. Only one. Leviathan. The same one who killed Nikodemus' brother."

Chapter 32

Bill and Nikodemus were sitting in Bill's Challenger in the parking garage. Charlie was still a little unsettled by the incident with the table in the conference room.

"I know you well enough to start asking questions, right?"

Nikodemus looked over at Bill and then settled back in his seat.

"Sure. I'll try to answer some questions."

"What do you mean, some?"

"Well, if I asked you questions about FBI procedures or training that wasn't public knowledge, you wouldn't be able to tell me, would you?"

Bill nodded.

"No, I suppose not. Okay. Uh…"

"You want to know how I broke the table?"

"No, I want to know how you got into…this. Magic or Seeker or whatever in the first place."

"Well, Bill, it wasn't by choice. In fact, it was kind of an accident."

Nikodemus paused and looked out the windshield. He wasn't seeing the concrete wall. He was remembering a dark night long ago. He had a faraway look in his eyes.

"My brother Roger and I were supposed to be asleep. It was late. I was twelve, and he was fourteen. Summertime, though. Didn't have to get up or anything. We had snuck out and were going down the alley behind our grandparents' house. They lived in Rockdale, Texas. It's kind of out in the sticks."

Bill interrupted him.

"Do you mind if I record this? Information on your background is something Glenn is asking me about every day. I'm not going to lie. Anything you tell me I'm going to tell him anyway. This way there won't be any…you know, screw-ups on my part."

Nikodemus shook his head.

"Sure. Why not."

Bill took out his phone and pushed "record."

"This is Agent Bill Smith and Nikodemus. This recording is being made with Nikodemus' permission on 8 June."

"Okay, my brother Roger and I were fourteen and twelve, respectively, and we're wandering around unsupervised in Rockdale, Texas, at 3:00 a.m. on a summer night. It's 1977. We aren't doing much but looking at stuff. We were just bored. Then we saw it."

Bill leaned closer.

"The graveyard was on the edge of town, and we were maybe half a mile from it. We saw this weird bluish light, like lightning, except it was on the ground, and there weren't any clouds in the sky."

"Roger said, 'What the hell is that?' I said nothing. I was scared, but Roger was curious. He was the leader, so towards the graveyard we went. We got near the gate. There hadn't been any more "lightning." There were voices. They sounded weird. Talking in some language I didn't understand."

Nikodemus shivered a little. He looked at Bill.

"I was scared shitless. The voices. I can't describe them. We didn't make a sound as we stepped in the gate. It was ajar a little. But, as soon as Roger's foot touched the ground inside the gate, all of them whirled around and looked right at us."

"There were six of them. They were wearing dark robes. One of them was holding this big walking-stick-looking thing. Only, it looked like it was alive. I was staring at it when I realised Roger wasn't beside me anymore. He was floating towards the guy with the stick. The guy reached out and touched Roger about the same time that the sheriff turned on his spotlight at the gate."

Bill let out a breath. He didn't say anything, though. He just looked at Nikodemus waiting for him to continue.

"Then there was this pop as they all went between. They took Roger with them."

"I pissed my pants and screamed as I ran to the gate. The sheriff couldn't understand anything I was saying. He had seen the others but now they weren't there. He walked through the graveyard with his flashlight while I sobbed at the gate."

Nikodemus was looking at his hands as he continued.

"Rockdale isn't a big town. Sheriff Mark Shaw knew who I was. He took me to my grandparents' house and rang the bell. My grandfather Lanar came to the door, looked at me, then asked Mark. 'What the hell is my grandson doing in a police car at 4:00 a.m.?'"

We went into the house, and my grandmother came in. Both of them were looking at me like I was some kind of criminal.

"Mark, would you like some coffee?"

She was always nice.

"Yes, thank you, Mary. Before you get worked up, James here didn't do anything."

Bill interrupted.

"Your name is James? James what?"

"Will you shut up and let me finish my story, please?"

"Okay, sorry, James."

"If you ever call me that again, I'll let you have a taste of the fire I gave that lawyer. I mean it."

Nikodemus was glaring at Bill, and it was scarier than he thought possible.

"Maybe this recording thing isn't a good idea."

Bill pleaded.

"Look, I'm sorry. I won't let them hear this. I'll keep it and do a transcript without the names, city, or year. Please, what happened next?"

"Well, I could finally talk. I said, 'They took Roger.' My grandfather jumped up and was going to go upstairs except Roger came walking down them. Yawning, like we woke him up. I couldn't believe it. I was relieved until he met my eyes. It wasn't him in there. It was someone else. He smiled and went back upstairs."

"My grandfather told me to go upstairs while they talked to the sheriff. I didn't want to, but I had no choice. I got to the foot of the stairs, and he was at the top, looking down, smiling. It wasn't a pleasant smile. He walked towards our room before I got to the top. I went into the bathroom and locked the door. I looked in the mirror, and he was behind me. Then he wasn't."

Nikodemus looked at Bill with a profound sense of loss.

"Roger ran away the next night, and I never saw him again. It wasn't him that night anyway. I went to the graveyard during the day. Somebody had dug up a grave, and the body was gone. Some old gypsy according to my grandfather's interpretation of the article in the newspaper. His name was Levi Athan."

Nikodemus and Bill sat in silence for a minute. The sounds of the city outside the parking garage are the only sounds.

"I knew that Roger's disappearance was connected to that corpse. Back then we didn't have the internet. My research abilities at twelve years old were limited. I couldn't go to the county clerk's office in Rockdale because they would tell my grandparents."

Nikodemus paused a minute. Then reached into his cabinet and pulled out a bottle of scotch and two glasses. Bill's eyes got wide.

"Holy shit."

"It's the Senator's scotch, you know, from Colorado."

Nikodemus poured two glasses. Gave one to Bill and then drained his in one gulp. Bill did the same. Both of them closed their eyes, savouring the smoothness. Nikodemus took the glass back and put both glasses and the bottle back in his cabinet. It was like they appeared out of thin air and then disappeared. Bill was stunned.

"Here, hold this, Bill."

Nikodemus had a Colt Peacemaker .44 in his hand. Bill took it and was in awe. It was blue steel, ivory grips, long barrel.

"This thing is worth $20,000 to a collector, Nick."

"Here, take two, then."

Nikodemus handed him another identical to the first.

"Check the serial numbers."

Bill looked, and they were identical. 400405.

"Show those to Bone later. Right now, I'm bored. Let's go do something."

Bill started the car, and they left the garage. It was on the north side of the building. The convention of cars they were avoiding was on the east side. So Bill turned left to avoid that side. Neither of them noticed Markmor and Lydia standing inside an out-of-business dry cleaner's. They passed within fifty feet of them as they headed over to Commerce and into the Fort Worth Stockyards.

Markmor opened the door and followed Lydia out onto the street. Without a word, they started walking after the car.

Chapter 33

"Well, if it isn't Wayne Elliot here in my office. Bone, will you take a picture of us, please?"

Deputy Director Glenn posed behind his desk with Elliot as Bone took a picture with his phone.

"One more, Bone. I think I blinked on that one."

Bone took another picture and then introduced everyone.

"I would like to introduce Greg Connor and Charlie Wilkins with Draft and Associates, Susan Simpson with Channel 4 News, and of course, you know Curtis."

Deputy Director Glenn smiled at Curtis and then rested his gaze on Susan Simpson.

"If you're press, then you are probably recording this, right?"

"Actually, I am. Do you care to comment on the whereabouts of Mr Nick Demus? I understand he's a consultant for the FBI. Could you give me the name of the firm he works for?"

Deputy Director Glenn smiled as he sat down.

"I can't comment on personnel involved in active investigations."

"Are you confirming that Mr Nick Demus works as a consultant for the FBI?"

"I can neither confirm nor deny any knowledge of Nick Demus."

Deputy Director Glenn glared at Curtis.

"Your father and I served in the Army together, Curtis. His influence helped me get to where I am today. I've covered his back, and he's covered mine."

Deputy Director Glenn stood up and his voice started rising in volume until he was almost shouting.

"But he never! Ever! Brought the goddamn press into my office to record what I said!"

Glenn went to the door of his office and opened it.

"Curtis, you called me at 3:00 a.m. At home, and I got you a meeting. But bringing the press into my office, recording me no less. That about does it. You have exhausted your favours that would have lasted your entire life by bringing this woman in here. All of you, get the hell out!"

He went behind his desk and punched the intercom.

"I'll need an escort for five out of the building immediately."

He sat down without another word and avoided Curtis' eyes. Curtis was dumbfounded, as were they all. Then the door opened, and four armed, armoured men entered.

"If you will all please come with us, this can be as painless as possible."

Wayne Elliot stood up bristling. He was head tall and outweighed the biggest agent by at least fifty pounds. One agent moved to the left closer to Elliot. She had a taser in her hand. Only when she spoke were you aware that it was a woman.

"Easy big boy. Fifty thousand volts. Feels like a freight train hitting you. This ain't the fifty-yard line. This is the office of a deputy director of the FBI. Be smart."

Wayne looked at her and let out a breath. Then he joined the line going to the elevators. Two elevators were being held. Three agents got in one elevator with Wayne Elliot. One plus Agent Bone got in the other.

When the elevator with Wayne Elliot closed its doors, one agent hit the hold button. Then he took off his mask.

"Sheila, put the taser down."

He looked up at Elliot.

"This is about that thing at Trees, huh?"

Elliot was looking straight ahead.

"Yeah."

"Look, I'm a big fan, man. I've seen the dude. Nikodemus."

"I thought he was Nick Demus."

"Well, all our stuff says Nikodemus, one word. Look, here's my number. Call me tonight after 6:00, and we'll talk. Maybe have a drink?"

Wayne was used to people trying to get next to him. But this guy actually had something he wanted. He smiled his biggest PR smile as he put the card in his pocket.

"Hell, yeah, we'll have a drink. All you guys are invited. How about "Clubhouse" at 8:00. Drinks are on me."

The agent pushed the go button.

"Cool, man. I'm Ricky Kirby. I'll see you then."

The elevator opened on Bone standing there.

"What took so long?"

Elliot smiled as he exited.

"Selfies."

Elliot stopped and addressed Bone.

"Look, I'm sorry. I was worked up, and I shouldn't have come here. Not like this. I didn't mean any disrespect to you or anybody."

Agent Bone shrugged and then smiled at Elliott.

"Think nothing of it, Wayne. If I may call you Wayne. Would you mind doing one last selfie with me?"

Elliot smiled and posed with Bone as he took the picture using his own phone.

"Thanks, Wayne. Have a good day."

Wayne exited the building to find his four companions waiting on the sidewalk. Curtis wasn't happy at all. None of them was. Wayne grabbed Greg's arm, and they walked down the sidewalk.

"Hey, what do you say we all get in Curtis' H2 for a minute?"

Greg looked at Wayne quizzically. Wayne smiled.

"Trust me. You want to hear this."

They all got into the H2. Wayne sat in the passenger seat in front. Greg and Charlie had Susan Simpson sandwiched between them. Susan was warming up to being pressed against Greg. She was giving him that look. Much to Charlie's disgust. He never understood why women went for the old geezer.

"His name isn't Nick Demus. It's Nikodemus, one word. And…"

Wayne paused until Curtis finally asked, "And what?"

"Turns out the agents with me are big fans. Ricky Kirby is going to meet us for drinks at "Clubhouse" at 8:00."

Greg smiled and punched Wayne in the shoulder.

"Ha! Here I thought it was a bust. But Wayne delivers when it counts. Okay, Charlie and I will be there at 7:00."

Susan leaned forward and spoke up.

"What about me?"

Greg leaned over and gave her his best bedroom eyes.

"I'll come by and get you at say 4:30 if you'll give me an address."

Susan handed him a card after writing on the back of it. Then she let Greg open his door and helped her get out to the ground. She smiled demurely and went and got in her car. Greg got back in and closed the door. Curtis was grinning like a Cheshire cat.

"Damn, man. You're smooth. Why 4:30?"

"I like to take at least two or two and a half hours the first time. Then, buddy, they're mine."

Chapter 34

Sitting in Myron's castle, Morgaine watched Leviathan as he looked around. Leviathan was a large man. Over six feet tall with long dark hair, flowing beard and even darker eyes. He was dressed in a modern-looking black suit with a red collared shirt. His shoes were black as well. Again, modern looking in appearance. Except for the hair, he would have been at home in any urban setting. His appearance was in discord with the Scottish Castle Hall and Myron in flowing purple robes.

Necromancers had always creeped Morgaine out. The discipline itself was dark. But, sometimes, like now, they were the only solution. Leviathan was looking at Ethan's statue form.

"He's at the doorway, you know, Myron. Seconds from it. I can hold him, but you have to heal him. It must be done fairly quickly."

Leviathan looked over at Morgaine. She felt his gaze travel up and down her body. She acted like she didn't notice. He knew she did, though. He smiled and wandered towards her.

"So you're Morgaine. The favourite daughter of Myron. Level 12, eh?"

"Yes, nice to make your acquaintance, Leviathan."

He took her offered hand and kissed it.

"The pleasure is all mine, kitten."

Myron's voice snapped Leviathan back to the matter at hand.

"Enough! What will the cost be for this service?"

"Nothing for you, Myron. Who knows? I might need your help sometime. It is my honour to be able to help as distinguished a Mage as yourself and Ethan. My mentor had held the two of you in the highest esteem."

Myron softened a little.

"It was a shame about Aspekt. I knew him a long time. Did you ever find out exactly how it happened?"

Leviathan was gazing at Morgaine again. She didn't react, though. She wanted to hear this. Aspekt was the most powerful Necromancer anyone had ever heard of. His recent death was unexplained. Death to a Necromancer being a relative thing. Supposedly.

"Does he speak to you?"

Leviathan avoided Myron's gaze. Myron locked eyes with Morgaine. She could tell something was off.

"No, he doesn't. I don't know why. I still don't know what happened exactly? He helped you with the kidnapping thing, didn't he? The last I heard from him was when he left to assist you."

Leviathan stepped back from Ethan's form.

"Do you want to do this now?"

"No, I haven't fully recovered from my injuries. I should be ready in a couple of days. I just wanted to get your assessment. I thank you for coming. Would you care to stay for dinner?"

Morgaine cringed at the invitation. She hoped it didn't show. Leviathan smiled at her as he replied.

"I appreciate the invitation, Myron, but I have a matter that needs attending to. Perhaps when we wake Ethan, we can have a banquet."

Without another word, Leviathan went to the dais and went between. Myron was looking at Ethan's form.

"Something isn't right, Morgaine. Aspekt would have made me do somersaults for what Leviathan offers for free. Plus, I don't believe he hasn't talked to him. Two Necromancers. One of them dead. That's what they do."

Myron went to the liquor cabinet and pulled out a dusty decanter from the back. Morgaine had never noticed it. He poured himself about three fingers. Then he picked up the tumbler and looked at the liquid. It was golden and sparkled as he swirled it around.

"What is that, father? I never noticed that decanter before."

She walked up closer and watched the sparkles dance around in it.

"This is called Elixir. The bottle isn't always there."

"What do you mean the bottle isn't always there?"

Myron drank all of it. He closed his eyes. Then answered.

"Exactly what I said, child. Sometimes it isn't there."

Morgaine looked at the cabinet, and the bottle wasn't there.

Chapter 35

Agent Bone and Agent Ricky Kirby were in Bone's office.

"So, you're meeting him tonight at 8:00?"

"Yes, sir. You saw the video. He thinks it's on the low."

"What exactly is that supposed to mean?"

Agent Kirby suppressed a chuckle.

"It means, like, he thinks you won't know about it. He thinks he's going to get the information you wouldn't give him."

"Good. You haven't been privy to much of it anyway so you can't give anything away."

"What is my primary objective here, sir? If I may ask."

"Find out what they know. Convince him that going after Nikodemus is a bad idea."

"Yes, sir."

"The Senator will fly out in a couple of hours. Once he's gone, I'll be by my phone. Keep me updated."

"I will, sir. Thank you, sir. I won't let you down."

Chapter 36

Nikodemus and Bill were at a cowboy bar in the Stockyards called the White Elephant. Neither of them had drunk very much. Women kept eyeing Nikodemus. Finally, Bill couldn't take it anymore.

"How come they all look at you, and none of them looks at me?"

Nikodemus took a drink of his beer and grimaced.

"The ones looking at you are doing it so you don't notice it. Besides, you look like a cop."

Bill signalled the bartender. She came over and smiled at Nikodemus. Then looked at Bill.

"What can I get you, fellas?"

"Two shots of Patron Silver and two more beers."

Nikodemus shook his head.

"Switching to tequila is never a good idea, Bill. You start with tequila and work down to beer. Not the other way around."

"You've got your way. I've got mine."

Bill raised his shot, and Nikodemus did the same.

"To...what? Nick?"

"To the statute of limitations."

This got a couple of chuckles from lawyers in earshot. He had thought he felt him earlier, but just then, Nikodemus caught a glimpse of Markmor in the reflection of the mirror behind the bar. He was standing with Lydia across the street in the shadows. Still smiling he leaned over to Bill.

"Don't react, but Markmor and Lydia are across the street watching us."

Bill nodded and smiled back. Still grinning, looking away from Nikodemus he asked, "What do we do?"

"Nothing yet. I'm going to text Morgaine. Who knows if she's even on this continent, though? If she doesn't answer, we're gonna have to play it by ear. You have your amulet?"

"Yep."

"Good. Let's see if she answers."

Markmor was looking at the hundreds of birds in the trees and lined up along the buildings. He grinned as an idea began to form.

"Sister, I'm going to send all these birds into that bar. When Nikodemus comes out, bind him."

Markmor began a low chant. The birds all took flight and started circling in a big tornado of avian mass. The White Elephant was open on two sides. Markmor grinned as he anticipated the carnage that was getting ready to ensue.

"They're all going to try to hit Nikodemus. Get ready."

In the bar, Nikodemus could feel something. Then he heard the birds. A guy walked in and commented.

"What's with the birds? They look like a tornado or something."

Nikodemus stood up.

"Bill, when I say 'now' fire your gun in the air."

The bartender's eyes got wide at this statement. Nikodemus addressed both of them. Several people near him could hear also.

"When he fires his weapon, hit the floor and stay there. Bill, take your amulet in your hand and think about protecting the people behind you."

"What are you going to do?"

"A few rounds of .00 buckshot. Then I'm going to face him in the street. No matter what happens don't come outside."

Just then a woman screamed outside.

"Now!"

Bill fired his weapon, and everybody got down, just as a black mass entered the bar from one side. The birds seemed to be screaming in one voice. Everyone who saw it was screaming too. Bill along with several bar patrons watched in fascination as Nikodemus turned to face the mass.

When the mass was almost upon him he started gesturing. The ripping sounds were so close together they sounded like a giant zipper.

Pffft. Pffft. Pffft. Pffft. Pffft. Pffft. Each shot shredded scores of birds. The mass wasn't visible as birds. It looked like a shiny cloud expanding and shredding as Nikodemus systematically decimated the swarm.

It went on for fifteen or twenty seconds as Nikodemus advanced out the door of the bar. Dead birds and blood covered every surface, including Nikodemus.

Covered in blood, he stepped in the street and shouted in a voice that literally rattled windows and set off car alarms nearby.

"MARKMOR! Enough! Face me, you chickenshit!"

His voice shattered birds near him. Then the rest flew away. Silence fell over the street as all the street lights went out and Markmor stepped out of the shadows. Nikodemus paused before he unleashed anything on him. Markmor couldn't make, but he could deflect something. He would deflect it into bystanders naturally. They were starting to line the street. Battles to the death by magic didn't happen twice in a lifetime.

Markmor was a Mage but his leaning was technically more Enchanter. As a seeker with protector leaning, Nikodemus could make. Markmor could enchant a mind. But not Nikodemus. His Protector leaning shielded him. Lydia was still in the shadows. Under a scaffolding. She was looking down the street to her left. Wondering why she wasn't helping Markmor; Nikodemus looked down the street and saw that she was. Six glamoured, tattooed Latinos were shuffling towards Nikodemus. Two of them were armed. They had probably accosted Lydia and got glamoured for their trouble.

Nikodemus looked back at Markmor, and he was grinning.

"Go ahead, Seeker. Show me your best shot."

Markmor prepared to deflect whatever Nikodemus sent his way. He was between Nikodemus and Lydia. The scaffolding however was stretching up three stories. Nikodemus unleashed five .00 buckshots and then two carefully placed .50 Teflon-coated rounds into the scaffolding. Boards started falling before the two precise rounds severed two main braces. The entire thing came crashing down on an unsuspecting Lydia. She didn't even have time to cry out.

The Latinos were twenty feet from Nikodemus when they stopped and started blinking. Markmor started to turn his attention to them but was interrupted by Agent Bill Smith's piercing voice.

"FBI! Clear the street! We have an active shooter!"

The Latinos scattered before Markmor could get their attention and glamour them. He wasn't grinning anymore. He looked over at the pile of boards and steel supports that covered Lydia. Then he glared at Nikodemus. The pop when he went between was purposefully hard. It broke the windshield on the car nearest him. The bystanders on both sides of the street screamed and covered their ears. Nikodemus tried but couldn't tell where Markmor had gone. He turned to Bill.

"I need a shot."

Then he walked over to where Lydia was. There were four oilfield workers looking at the pile. You could tell they were oilfield by the company shirts and the fact that they were out drinking in jeans covered with grease and oil.

"Hey, guys help me uncover her, will you?"

All four plus Nikodemus started pulling boards and scaffolding parts off Lydia. Bill and a couple of guys from the White Elephant joined in. Once some of the 2 x 6's were off, several men together lifted a large scaffolding support off the pile. Lydia cried out. She was still invisible beneath the pile.

"We should call an ambulance, maybe."

This was from a worker with a shirt that said, "Colton" on the breast pocket. Underneath "Paragon Oil Services."

Bill stepped back and called for EMTs. Then he called Agent Bone.

"I'm in the Stockyards at the White Elephant with Nikodemus. We were attacked by Markmor and Lydia."

Bill paused as he listened to Bone's response.

"No, we're ok. Lydia was injured by a scaffolding that collapsed on her."

He paused again.

"Well, Nikodemus kind of made it collapse on her."

Another pause.

"Because Markmor had attacked us with a million birds."

All the work had stopped as they listened to Bill.

"Yeah, I know. Then Lydia had glamoured these cholos."

Bill paused. It was obvious Bone had interrupted.

"Well, I don't know, sir. It is what it is. I'm just making sure you knew what was going on."

Bill paused as Bone talked for some length of time.

"Sir, this happened in front of maybe a hundred people. Markmor went between so hard it broke a couple of windshields."

Bill paused again, and Bone's shouting was audible to everyone near him.

"Sir, Nikodemus responded to an attack."

"Sir, bystanders are assisting us to uncover Lydia. I've called EMTs. I have to go. Just keeping you informed. Would you like to speak to Nikodemus?"

Bill hung up on Bone shouting into his phone. He grinned and looked at the guys.

"You'd think an FBI agent in charge would be more understanding. It's not like I shot somebody."

Nikodemus laughed.

"Did you have to tell him I made the scaffolding fall? It could have been an accident."

The same worker, Colton laughed and shook his head.

"Buddy, this is by far the most interesting night of my life."

Chapter 37

Susan Simpson watched Greg adjust his ankle holster. He then checked the little silver automatic that went in it.

"What kind of gun is that?"

Greg smiled as he took it back out of the holster and handed it to her.

"It's a Llama .32 calibre."

Susan held the gun and pointed it at the TV.

"Seems kind of little."

"It's my backup gun. This."

Greg pulled out a large blue steel revolver.

"Is a Colt .357 magnum with hollow points? Big enough for you?"

Susan grinned and lowered her eyes until she was looking below his waist.

"You know it, big boy."

Greg holstered both guns and put on his sports jacket. He was looking good. Susan didn't know how old he was, but he was something to look at.

"Hey, I'm not going with you tonight."

Greg's eyes widened, and he looked at her.

"Why not? Did I do something wrong?"

Susan laughed a little and got up off her sofa and went to kiss him goodbye.

"No, I checked my email, and I have a ton of stuff that has to be in by midnight. Besides, you're just getting information anyway. Kirby and whoever will probably be more relaxed without a reporter around anyway."

"You're probably right about that."

Greg left, and Susan sat down at her computer. She pulled up some notes on her tablet, plus some handwritten notes and hunkered down to write. She worked for two straight hours before a text on her phone distracted her.

It was from Carl, one of the cameramen she used. The text said, "Call me now."

Susan hit the dial button. When Carl answered the noise in the background almost drowned out his voice.

"Susan! Can you hear me? I can't hear you. You need to get to the Stockyards right now. There is some crazy shit going on. I'm looking at a fucking tornado of birds. HOLY CRAP! They're like, attacking the White Elephant. I think that guy from the video in "Trees" is in this. I gotta go. Get out here now!"

Susan jumped up, and, after putting on her shoes, raced out her door. A few seconds later, she came back and picked up her car keys and her phone. Then ran back out. She got in her Toyota and dialled the station as she was backing out.

"Tommy? Sorry, Phil, you sound like Tommy. Is Bill in? I need to talk to him."

Susan honked at a car in the parking lot that was in her way. Then she sped around them. She was almost onto 635 when her manager Bill Thornton got on the phone.

"Bill, Carl just called me from the Stockyards did... Okay, well, I'm headed out there. It'll take me maybe twenty minutes. Send a camera crew, and I'll meet them in that Wells Fargo Bank parking lot on Main. It's near the White Elephant. Okay, thanks."

Susan accelerated as she got onto 121 South towards Fort Worth. She thought a minute and then called Greg's cell phone. It went to voicemail. She hung up and turned-on voice to text.

"Something is happening in the Stockyards. I think it involves your guy. I'm headed to the White Elephant, sugar."

Greg, Charlie and Wayne Elliot were sitting in a booth at "Clubhouse." It was a strip club in Dallas owned by the band Pantera. Heavy metal music, women in leather and chains. No FBI guy. They were an hour late. Not promising. Greg ignored the call. Couldn't hear it in here anyway. He did look at the text. His eyes widened. He showed the text to Charlie and then Wayne. Without a word, all three got up and practically ran out.

As soon as they were outside, Charlie couldn't help himself.

"Can I call you 'sugar' too?"

Susan came across her camera crew on Main St. FBI barricades were covering the road. Susan got out and went to the van. Billy Thompson opened the window; he didn't look happy.

"Billy, let's go down side streets."

"That guy there."

Billy pointed to a large black man wearing an FBI flak jacket and holding an AR-15 assault rifle.

"He said I can wait or turn around. He said if I start down a side street trying to bypass this barricade, he would take my biggest camera and shove it up my ass. I believe him."

Susan walked towards the barricade. The agent who had talked to Billy looked at her, shook his head in the negative and pointed back the way she had come. She went back to her car, pulled out of the line and turned around. She went back up Main until she knew she was out of the field of vision of the barricades. She pulled into a 7-11 parking lot and took out her phone. She opened Maps and looked at an aerial view of where she was.

She zoomed out and then in looking for another way deeper into the Stockyards.

Chapter 38

The front of the White Elephant looked like Armageddon. Well, bird Armageddon anyway. Agents in FBI windbreakers and some civilians were scooping up dead birds with shovels and putting the remains in dumpsters. A fire truck was hosing the area off. Lydia had been dead by the time she was uncovered. Nikodemus and Bill were standing there looking at her body when Bone walked up.

"Nikodemus, are you responsible for this clusterfuck?"

Bill answered for him.

"She is, sir. And Markmor, of course. He's the one who glamoured the birds. She."

Bill indicated Lydia's lifeless body.

"Glamoured six members of the Texas Syndicate. They were armed."

Bill looked at Bone, and they locked gazes.

"She was controlling them, sir. Like remote control robots. She was shielded by Markmor. She was going to have them start shooting."

Nikodemus interrupted, joining the conversation.

"If she hadn't been standing under that scaffolding, I'm not sure what I would have done. Anything I threw directly at Markmor would get deflected into innocent bystanders. All those Syndicate members were looking at me. They were going to start shooting. If I had taken them out in front of people, there would have been pandemonium. Well, worse pandemonium than there was."

Just then an agent came up to Bone and said something into his ear. Bone shook his head in the negative.

"Keep the barricades up. This isn't even close to contained. So, where is Markmor now, Nikodemus?"

Nikodemus was still looking at Lydia's corpse.

"You know, a Necromancer could interrogate her corpse."

There were shocked gasps from all around. Nikodemus hadn't been paying attention. Several agents and bystanders had heard him make the statement. They all stopped and stared at him. Bone had an incredulous look on his face.

"Interrogate her corpse?"

Nikodemus smiled calmly and looked at Bone.

"The way I found out who was behind Elizabeth Roth's abduction was interrogating Spencer's corpse. You really interrogate their spirit. Or their soul, I guess. Depending on how you look at it. Morgaine can arrange it probably."

Nikodemus stopped talking and looked at Bone quizzically. As if to say. Well, do you want me to? Bone was just staring straight ahead when his cell phone rang. Nikodemus and Bill went into the White Elephant and sat at the bar with the four guys from Paragon Oil Services. They all grew silent as the two men joined them. Nikodemus suddenly burst out laughing for a second and then gestured to the bartender.

"Shots of Patron all around, darlin!"

Nikodemus turned to the four guys.

"Gentlemen, you have seen things you aren't supposed to see. I don't know what agent Bone is going to do about it. Probably lock you up, or well, I guess killing you would be easier."

Bill burst out laughing at this. He reassured the guys.

"No, he won't. Well, probably won't. You wouldn't believe how much paperwork that would generate."

They all downed their shots and raised them to the bartender.

"What are you anyway?"

The question from Colton caused everybody to fall silent. They all looked at Nikodemus. They weren't hostile about it. They were curious. Nikodemus downed his shot and then leaned back against the bar.

"Well, I'm a Level 7 Seeker with Protector leaning. Lydia, that's the dead chick, was a Level 12 Mage with Enchanter leaning. Satisfied?"

They all look at him blankly. Nikodemus took a beer bottle out of Bill's hand and stood up. He walked over to an empty table and sat down. He could see everybody at the bar from there. Bone and several senior agents had walked in. He got back up and took a barstool from the bar and pulled it out where he could see everybody.

"Okay, Magic User 101. There are five major disciplines in magic. Mage, Sentinel, Seeker, Enchanter, and Necromancer. Mage and Sentinel are light. Enchanter and Necromancer are dark. Seeker is split between light and dark. Within the major discipline's you can minor, if you will, in a speciality or more than one specialities. This is called leaning."

There was a crowd of about fifty or more people listening. No one was saying anything. They were hanging on his every word. He finished his beer and was handed another without asking. He drank most of it and continued.

"How you advance in levels is another lecture. But, I'll give you a rough idea of how the leanings work. Morgaine's father is Myron. He is a Level 22 Mage with Prescient leaning. He is the most powerful magic user alive that I'm aware of. Prescient means he can tell the future. He is sometimes referred to as a soothsayer. Lydia and Markmor, that's who attacked us tonight, are both Level 12 Mages with Enchanter leaning. Enchanter is technically another major discipline. It is the dark version of Mage. It's like they have a double major. It's how they can control people and animals they 'enchant' them."

Nikodemus took off his jacket and drank some more beer. Somebody set a hamburger on the table by him. He took two quick bites and continued.

"I'm Level 7. Protector leaning is something like Sentinel. If I were to advance past Level 10, my leaning would be Sentinel instead of Protector. I am a guard. I can make. That means I can reproduce things I have encountered. Like bullets."

Nikodemus punctuated this statement by gesturing at the corner of the ceiling. A .44 round shattered the mirrored tile covering a security camera. He gestured again and a .00 buckshot round vaporised the camera.

"Those were .44 magnum and .00 buckshot, respectively. I can't control people. I can't get in their heads. I don't want to. A Mage can read your mind if you aren't shielded. My Protector leaning shields me."

Nikodemus stopped and ate the rest of the burger. Then he drank the beer he had in his hand. He was offered another. He declined.

"Okay, one more thing I'll tell you. 'Going between.' I know several of you heard that loud pop that broke a couple of windshields. If you were looking in the right place, you saw the skinny red-haired guy disappear. This is called 'going between.' It is teleportation, I guess. Any discipline past Level 5 can go between. If you can afford it. You don't pay in money. I'm not going to go into the currency The pop is the sound of either the vacuum created by molecules leaving a space or being bombarded by molecules coming from another place reacting to the molecules you displace."

"This concludes part one of the Magic User Basics for Dummies Lecture Series. Bill, I'm going to have to see Myron. I don't know if I'll see you tomorrow. If you don't hear from me tomorrow, I'll contact you soon after that. Now, if you'll excuse me. I'm beat. I'm going to sleep for a while."

Glitter started falling, and Nikodemus went between and was gone. Nobody said anything for a minute. Then Colton and his buddies started clapping. Then yelling. Soon everybody, except Bone, was yelling. Above the din, Colton could be heard yelling.

"Now that was a fucking magic show!"

Chapter 39

Markmor stepped between into his castle in the Alps. He had company. Leviathan and two of his familiars were there. His girls were screaming as Leviathan's ghoulish companions were abusing them in Markmor's bedroom. Leviathan sat in Markmor's chair at his table and was drinking some of his best liquor and smiling at the sound of the girl's screams.

"Markmor, finally. Where's Lydia?"

Markmor's anger was abruptly replaced by sadness. Lydia, his partner in crime was gone. He sighed and sat down wearily at the table with Leviathan.

"She's down. I think she's dead. A scaffolding fell on her."

"I told you to follow him, not make a move against him, you ingrate!"

Leviathan's gaze wasn't pleasant. He threw the crystal tumbler he was drinking from against the wall. In the bedroom, the girls' screams had abruptly ceased. Leviathan's minions came in covered in blood. They smiled at Markmor and then went and sat on the dais with their gazes averted.

"Everything was going exactly according to plan. Hell, Myron asked me to assess Ethan. I was in. Now this. What did you do anyway?"

"What does it matter now? It didn't work. Nikodemus doesn't seem like a Level 7. I've beat Level 9's that couldn't make as fast as he can. He dropped something on a bear I glamoured that...well, it was, I don't know what it was. It sounded like thunder."

Leviathan went over and got another tumbler. He looked around and found another of Markmor's best. This time scotch, and came back to the table. He toyed with Markmor's dagger that was lying next to the previous bottle.

"Nikodemus could already be a Level 11 if he wanted to. He figured something out about the Seeker Discipline at Level 7 that doesn't exist in any other discipline. Seekers can be light or dark. In Nikodemus' case, he is light and dark At Level 7, you can take any leaning almost to the point of interface. He has done it with five different leanings."

Markmor squinted at Leviathan.

"Five leanings?"

"He is a seeker with protector as his declared leaning. He can make. You've seen that. He can shield. It's how he absorbs bullets and copies them. He can project. By projecting 180 degrees out of phase with this plane. He becomes invisible. It's quicker than going between, and you can still see and hear what's going on. Because he can project to negative planes, he can shake the ground by speaking a kind of half-ass demon."

Leviathan drank the scotch and stood up. His minions stood also. Leviathan walked to the dais and then turned around and faced Markmor.

"By staying Level 7, he doesn't have a mentor. He is a free agent. With his extended leaning and years of experience using them, he is like a… Well, he's kind of like a Supercharged 1968 Camaro. It isn't a new car, but it can do some impressive stuff. It's only a matter of time before Myron and Morgaine find this place. You should pick another. If your sister's dead, I'll find out what she knows."

Then Leviathan and his minions went between and were gone. The pop was loud, and it broke glass on every table and a mirror in the bathroom fell. Markmor looked towards the bedroom and could see one of his girls' arms around the edge of the bed. There was blood on the floor. Markmor put his head in his hands and wept. Then he took his dagger and went to the dais and stepped between.

Chapter 40

Susan's cell phone rang. She was going through a neighbourhood in east Fort Worth trying to find a way into the Stockyards. She looked at it. It was Greg. She put it on speaker.

"Hey."

"Where are you?"

"I'm trying to get to FM 180 by going through a neighbourhood. It's taking forever. Where are you?"

"We're stuck on an exit ramp of 820. Traffic is at a standstill."

"Yeah, there are FBI barricades on Main. I'm sure whatever happened is over anyway. I was getting ready to give up and go home."

"If we can ever get off this ramp, we'll head back to the Dallas office. Keep me posted."

Susan hung up, and her phone rang again. It was Carl.

"Carl, they have barricades up. I can't get to you."

"Forget that. You aren't going to believe what I've got."

"What?"

"Look, I'm almost to the I-20. I'm going to the office. Meet me there."

Susan looked at her watch.

"It's almost ten o'clock."

"Trust me, Susan. You want to see this."

Susan hung up and realised she had finally found FM 180. Instead of heading into Fort Worth, she headed towards Dallas. Thirty minutes later, she arrived at the station. Carl's car was parked in the red zone right in front of the door. He must really have something.

There was a crowd in the editing room. Susan walked up to Gene Terrell, a large, overweight man with glasses and an engrossed look on his face as he was watching the screen.

"Gene, what's going on?"

Gene turned to her. "Is this your story? Carl said it was for a story you're working on."

Susan looked in and saw what looked like a horror movie shot of a swarm of something attacking a building. Then she recognised the front of the White Elephant. Her eyes widened as Nikodemus walked out gesturing at the swarm. Something he was doing was blasting them apart. Then she saw from the dead ones on the ground that they were birds.

"That's the guy from the video in 'Trees.' The guy who KO'd Wayne Elliot. No question."

Susan couldn't tell who had said it, but she had to agree with them. It was definitely him. Then the camera panned over to a bunch of Latin-gang-member-looking guys that were shuffling like zombies. Then they stopped and looked at each other.

"That's when he blasted the scaffolding off the building. It fell on the woman who was controlling the Mexicans."

Susan recognised Carl's voice.

"Watch this."

Then there was a pop, and the camera was dropped. It was still recording. It showed Carl's face close up as he inspected it, and then it panned over to show a cracked windshield. The video ended.

"Is Susan here yet?"

Susan looked over until Carl noticed her.

"Susan, the next video is the one I'm talking about."

Carl stood up and disconnected his phone from the monitor. There was whining from everyone.

"Don't worry, you'll get to see it. I just want to go over it with Susan for her story."

Susan, Carl, Gene and Charles Bills, the station manager, looked at each other after the final words on the video.

"Now, that was a fucking magic show!"

Susan and Carl were squirming in their seats. Gene and Charles just looked at each other and shook their heads. Susan was writing notes and talking excitedly.

"Okay, we'll start with a teaser tomorrow and lead up to a full-week series for next week. What do you think, Charles?"

Charles pursed his lips and looked at her.

"I think none of that is going to happen."

Susan stopped writing.

"What do you mean? This is gold!"

"Sure, right next to the aliens in Hanger 18."

Carl joined in.

"Look, I saw that with my own eyes."

Charles was unmoved. Gene took up the narrative for him.

"Which is why you believe it, Carl. Anyone else won't. You know what we can do with CGI."

"There were FBI agents in the crowd."

Charles tone was dismissive.

"You really think the FBI is going to back your story? Do you?"

Charles turned his attention to Susan. She was obviously furious.

"Dammit, this started with the incident at Trees. I'll get some more images of the scaffolding and the dead birds, and we'll have physical confirmation."

"You really think that those barricades will go up before that is all cleaned up?"

"What about the oilfield guys? Paragon Oil Services. I could call them."

"No, you won't. This story is dead. Finished. Good evening."

Charles made a shooing gesture. Carl and Susan got up and left his office. Gene closed the door and sat in one of the recently vacated seats. Neither of them said anything for a minute. Then the phone on Charles' desk rang. He punched the speaker button.

"Mr Bills, there is an Agent Bone with the FBI on line one for you."

Charles pushed the button for line one.

"Agent Bone, before you say anything, I should inform you that I saw a video of a Magic User Lecture that was very interesting. However, I have decided not, I repeat not to give it any serious consideration as newsworthy material. You might see it on Conspiracy Theory Shows sometime in the future. But not on this station. Not on my watch."

There was a pause on the phone. Then Agent Bone answered.

"I appreciate your candour. Mr Bills. And your discretion. I'm glad we see eye to eye. If possible, I would like a copy of that video."

"Of course, I'll transfer you back up front, and you can give delivery details to my staff. Please feel free to call me again if I can be of further assistance."

"Thank you, I will."

Then Charles Bills transferred the call and the problem to his staff.

Chapter 41

Agent Smith, Nikodemus, and NSA Analyst Mike Walker watched Bone hang up the phone.

"Told you so, sir. I was a little off that night. Plus, there is a cost when I make. I wasn't near depleted, but I was weary. Those guys had really pitched in to help. They were ordinary guys that asked me a reasonable question. This isn't the first time Magic Users have come to the attention of the media. No one ever believes them."

Nikodemus grinned at Bill. He didn't grin back.

"Bill, you can go ahead and let them hear the recording of our conversation in the parking garage. Start running the names. You'll identify me. Then, well, I guess we'll see what happens."

Nikodemus stood up.

"Agent Bone, what are the chances of your loaning me one of those fancy new Challenger pursuit cars?"

Bone shook his head.

"Those cars are government property, sir. I don't think…"

Bill interrupted by tossing his keys to Nikodemus.

"Don't wreck it."

Nikodemus smiled and left the room. He came back a few seconds later.

"I don't know how to get to the parking garage. Codes and whatever."

Smith got up and went with him. When the elevator doors closed, neither of them said anything. Nikodemus got out and gave the keys back to Smith.

"Never mind, I really just wanted to see what Bone would say. I knew you had my back."

"Where are you going?"

"Myron is calling a conference. Morgaine and I are going to be at his castle tomorrow."

"Where is that?"

"Scotland."

Nikodemus walked down the ramp and out of the parking garage. Bill's text alert went off. He looked at his phone.

"Recording?"

It was Bone. Bill sighed, and then went back to the elevator. While Bill hadn't forgotten about it, he had decided not to share it. But now, he headed up to Bone's office.

Chapter 42

For the first time ever, Nikodemus stepped out of between a mile from Myron's castle. It didn't look as grand from the outside. It looked kind of abandoned. It was built into a cliff overlooking the ocean, almost looking like it was falling into it. More square edges than English castles, with grass growing on the roof and on most of the towers. It had two towers flanking the road that curved around the mountain to the front portcullis. Nikodemus walked up to the entrance and realised that it hadn't been opened in centuries. The only way in or out of Myron's castle was between. He was standing there looking at it when he heard Morgaine's voice down the dark hallway leading to the grate.

"What are you doing out there?"

"I've never seen the outside of it. Only the feasting hall."

Morgaine popped out of between and was beside him.

"Neither have I. God, it looks rundown. No wonder he doesn't stay here."

"I thought he lived here. You too."

Morgaine's laugh was like the tinkling of ice hitting glass.

"God no. I have a house in Prague. Father has one in Rome. This is for meetings. Mostly."

Morgaine took his hand and pulled them both between and onto the dais in the feasting hall. Ethan was still a statue. Myron was sitting at the table. There were three places set. Nikodemus had never actually sat at the table. He had stood before it many times. Myron smiled at him and indicated the seat immediately to his left.

"Nikodemus, it's good to see you. Please, won't both of you sit down?"

Nikodemus and Morgaine sat and removed the covers from their plates. They were empty at first then entrees appeared on them. Nikodemus had a large steak and baked potato. Morgaine had a salad with curious-looking breadsticks.

"How did you know what I liked, Myron?"

Myron was eating his fish and pasta. Between bites, he answered.

"I looked in your mind for a moment, Seeker. I hope you don't mind."

Nikodemus dug in without another word. For a few minutes, all three ate without talking. Myron finished first and leaned back. Looking at Ethan's statue. Nikodemus noticed.

"Why haven't you healed him or whatever."

"He's too close to death. I'd need the services of a Necromancer. The one I've contacted is giving me a bad feeling. He's lying to me. I don't know why."

"I thought you could foretell the future."

"To a certain extent, I can. Regarding certain things. Necromancy is a dark art. I can't always grasp the ramifications of their actions. With the Senator, I could tell we needed to intervene. Markmor is being influenced by someone dark. Either a Necromancer or a high-level Enchanter."

Myron stopped talking and looked at Morgaine.

"Your sister is dead, child."

Morgaine stopped in mid-bite. She looked at Nikodemus. He looked at the ground. Morgaine looked like she was going to cry, but then she just let out a breath.

"She shot my brother. She helped your brother attack Nikodemus and a crowd of people in a public place."

Morgaine turned to Nikodemus and started to speak. Then instead addressed Myron.

"How could a Level 7 Seeker kill a Level 12 Mage? She would have deflected anything he could throw at her. Or Markmor."

She turned back to Nikodemus.

"How did you do it?"

Nikodemus looked from Myron to Morgaine and back. Myron nodded to him.

"She had glamoured a group of armed thugs against me. She was concentrating on them. Markmor was between her and me. He was ready to deflect anything I sent at him into the crowd. She was standing under a scaffolding. I had a split second before the thugs started shooting. I brought the scaffolding down on her."

Morgaine looked at him, then smiled. She reached out and put her hand on his. Nikodemus looked relieved. Myron had walked over to his brother's statue. He was looking at it as he spoke.

"Nikodemus, what do you know about your brother's death?"

Nikodemus stiffened at the mention of his brother. His voice was barely audible when he replied.

"Why?"

"I just wanted to know the extent of your knowledge on the subject."

"He was taken by a Necromancer. Someone else was inhabiting his body. It was ten years before I was able to make any real enquiries into the subject. It's why I'm a seeker. Because I wanted to find him. All I know is a gypsy name, Levi Athan."

"So your enquiries were under the last name Athan? Correct?"

Nikodemus nodded.

"You were involved in the death of the Necromancer Aspekt."

This wasn't a question it was a statement. Nikodemus pursed his lips and took a drink before answering.

"Yes."

"Searching for your brother, correct?"

"Yes."

"Because you thought Aspekt was his mentor?"

Nikodemus voice was getting colder every syllable he spoke.

"Mentor? He wasn't a mentor. He was a captor. They took him when he was twelve years old. We didn't know anything about Necromancers or Mages. We just saw something weird in a cemetery at night and went to investigate. We were kids. They took my big brother from me."

Nikodemus was close to shouting. He breathed deeply and got himself under control. Morgaine touched his arm. He didn't even notice. He got up and started pacing.

"Two years ago, the Necromancer Maal died in Mexico. Were you involved in that?"

"I bear a grudge against every one of their kind. Why are you asking me this, Myron? Why now?"

"Because just as you are Nick Demus, so is Levi Athan actually Leviathan. He is the Necromancer I contacted. He says Aspekt doesn't speak to him. I don't believe him. I think he is the one behind all this. He is the one responsible for Lydia's death. I fear Ethan will never be awakened."

Myron paused and looked Nikodemus squarely in the eyes.

"I think he is the one responsible for your brother's death also."

Nikodemus stopped pacing.

"I know why you haven't advanced past 7. You don't want a mentor. You've pushed several leanings almost to interface. Some of them are dark. You are light and dark. With the right catalyst, you could finish this."

Myron reached inside his cabinet and produced Merlin's wand.

"This is that catalyst, Seeker. It isn't much use to me anyway or any Mage. Merlin wasn't a Mage. He was a wizard. His discipline became what is now a Sentinel. His power was in the physical realm. His undoing was a woman. She tricked him. She asked him 'Speak the charm of making.' He told her, and she took his power from him. But not this."

Myron walked up to Nikodemus and held out the wand. He held it like a person would hand over a knife, pommel first. Nikodemus looked at it a moment and then reached out and took it from him. Immediately, the tip started glowing yellow, then orange, then red. Then the light died. Without a word, Nikodemus put it in his cabinet. He looked at Myron and grinned.

"Okay, so what's the plan?"

"Your Investigators are going to do most of the work for us. Markmor is going to fall for a trap they set. You will be there to make sure he doesn't escape it."

"And Leviathan?"

"Well, Seeker, we'll see."

Chapter 43

"So where is their office?"

Carl and Susan were sitting in her Toyota in a parking garage off Main. Susan's phone received a text.

"According to Greg. We take the skywalk across and go to a door with 101 on the corner. Here's the code."

She showed Carl her phone. They got out and after taking a skywalk across to another parking garage they found a door with 101 on the corner. Carl entered the four-digit code and the door opened onto a dimly lit hallway. Once the door closed behind them, the lights brightened, and Greg came out a door at the other end.

"Susan, you're looking lovely. And…you must be Carl."

Carl shook his hand, and Susan kissed him quickly on the lips.

"We've got something, Greg. My station says it's too unbelievable to air. It makes the Trees video look tame."

Greg took them straight to the conference room. Charlie, Nelson and Curtis Vieth were waiting. Charlie motioned Carl over. Carl handed Charlie a memory card, and Carl's video started playing on the main screen.

The first video ended, and Charlie rewound and started screenshotting stills of Nikodemus, Markmor, and couldn't isolate Lydia. He moved it backwards and forwards over one silhouette. Carl and Susan looked at each other. Susan touched Greg's arm.

"Guys, that isn't the interesting one."

Charlie, Greg, Nelson, and Curtis all stopped talking and looked at her. Susan smiled and turned to Charlie.

"Play the next video."

Charlie looked at his screen and exited the first video. He pulled up the second video and started it. On screen, Nikodemus' voice started.

"Okay, Magic User 101."

Chapter 44

Agent Bone walked into the conference room and took his seat. He looked around and noticed Deputy Director Glenn, NSA Analyst Mike Walker, DHS Mark Dudley, and several people he didn't know. He was the last to arrive. Deputy Director Glenn nodded to his second, an agent that Bone couldn't remember at the moment. The main screen came up with a driver's license.

"We have identified Nikodemus. After running dates and names from Agent Smith's conversation, we can confidently say that Nikodemus is Mr James Lanar Montrose III. He was born on 16 October 1964 in Tomball, Texas. His father, James Lanar Montrose Jr., died in 2002 of complications from emphysema. His mother died in 2004 in a car accident. He has or had a brother named Roger Lancer Montrose. Born 22 July 1962. He went missing in 1977. No records since that time."

The screen changed and showed a series of older driver's licenses and a couple of mugshots.

"A couple of arrests. One for possession of marijuana at age nineteen. Another when he hadn't paid an expired inspection sticker ticket and then was stopped for a minor traffic infraction and was taken in because of the unpaid ticket. He graduated from Sam Houston State University in 1991 with a business administration degree. Worked in advertising until his mother's death. Then dropped off the face of the earth. His most recent driver's license expired in 2004."

Nobody spoke for a moment. Bone looked at Deputy Director Glenn.

"So now what? We know who he is."

Glenn surprised everyone with his response.

"Give him a badge. Put him on Senator Rollins' detail."

Glenn got up and left without another word. Bone and Walker smiled at each other. Bone got up.

"Shortest meeting I've ever been to."

Walker got up with him.

"Last thing I was expecting, eh?"

Bone said nothing as he left. He texted Agent Smith.

"See me regarding Nikodemus. He's getting a shield. Both of you will report to Rollins' detail tomorrow."

Chapter 45

Markmor had been busy. He had toyed with the idea of setting up another lair deep in some wilderness. The only problem being he would have needed help. Which he couldn't ask for at the moment. So he did the next best thing. He rented a suite at the "W" Hotel in downtown Dallas. His suite came with a living room with couches and TV. Near the windows was a table that would seat fourteen. The entrance was sunk in an alcove with a curtain. Food or whatever could be brought in without anything in the room being visible. There was also another alcove behind a curtain on one wall. It was for luggage but would be perfect for hiding henchmen, or a body, for that matter.

There was a bathroom for the living room, and the bedroom had a large king-sized bed. Its bathroom had a full shower and jacuzzi hot tub. At $1,200 per night, it was extravagant. But, Markmor had a quantity of gold and a buyer he used on a regular basis. He had sold $40,000 worth of gold that day and with a $5,000 deposit and a little glamouring he had checked in and felt fairly anonymous. His suite was on the twenty-second floor, and there was an outdoor pool on the sixteenth. It was open twenty-four hours. There was a nightclub called "Ghost Bar" on the thirtieth floor of an adjoining building. New hunting grounds. Markmor devoured the rib-eye steak and baked potato while he watched the news. All in all, he felt happier than he had been in a while. He would glamour a couple of women and bring them to his room to enjoy at his leisure.

The voice of Senator Rollins on the TV changed all of that. The byline said, "Live from Washington, D.C." Markmor was scowling at the TV when his cell phone text alert chimed. He looked at it. It was Leviathan.

"Where are you?"

So the texting began.

"New digs. No blood or dead girls anywhere. Thanks by the way for killing two women I spent months breaking in."

"No matter. Where exactly are you?"

Markmor hesitated. A Necromancer couldn't find him. But this Necromancer was owed.

"Meet me at 'Ghost Bar' in Dallas. I'll be there at 11:00 p.m."

Leviathan didn't answer the text. He knocked on the door. Markmor jumped at the sound. He went and smiled as he opened the door. He drew the curtains first. Leviathan was standing there with two different minions. They were tattooed skinheads and didn't fit in. Markmor ushered them in, all the while smiling at Leviathan. He then pulled back the curtain on the luggage alcove.

"They can wait in there."

This wasn't a question. Markmor wasn't going to sit and take it anymore. He, after all, wasn't without power. When the goons hesitated, he put a compulsion on them so hard that it made their ears bleed. They groaned and hurried to the alcove.

"If I hear one god-damned sound out of you or if you shit or piss in there, I'll make you eat your own dicks."

Markmor closed the curtain and smiled at Leviathan as if there had been no interruption.

"You really should get help that is more in keeping with your standards of appearance. These are really beneath you."

Leviathan grinned and sat down.

"That's more like the Mage that I allied with."

He looked around.

"I like this. Especially the curtains on the door."

He indicated the luggage alcove.

"That too. I'm sorry about your girls. But, you really had to get out of there. Morgaine was close to locating it."

Markmor smiled as if it was of no consequence.

"I'm glad you're here now, though. Would you care for something to eat or drink? I can get you anything you want probably."

Leviathan noticed Senator Rollins on the TV. His eyes went cold. His voice was no longer jovial.

"He has to be stopped. What are you going to do about it?"

Markmor had no ideas at all, but he wasn't going to admit that to Leviathan.

"I've been thinking of nothing else. His amulet is a problem. What are the chances of you getting next to my father again?"

Leviathan was picking at Markmor's leftovers and watching the TV. The national news had ended. The local news had the same story on Rollins. The locals had people on the street answering the question. "Would you vote Rollins for President?"

"I don't know. I think he could tell I was lying about Aspekt. Nikodemus killed him. Apparently, he has killed several Necromancers."

Markmor looked sharply at Leviathan.

"He has? Why? How many?"

"He's looking for his brother. He's killed five that I know of."

"How?"

"He usually brings something down on top of them. Not unlike he did your sister. That way there's no trace of his work on them. He needs to be dealt with. Soon."

Markmor went to the windows and looked out on the Dallas skyline as the sun went down.

Chapter 46

Morgaine and Nikodemus were in a hotel room less than a mile away from Markmor. The difference is that they were enjoying themselves. Morgaine lay nude on the bed while Nikodemus was just coming back in from the hall with ice. They had gone around the world twice. But, seeing her lying there like that caused a stirring. She saw the look in his eyes and sat up putting on his white dress shirt. If anything it made her look sexier.

"Enough! Are you never sated?"

"You are irresistible, what can I say."

"I can say make me a drink."

Nikodemus poured them both some of the Senator's scotch. Added two handfuls of ice and passed her one. They silently toasted to one another and took a sip. Morgaine's text alert sounded. She looked at her phone.

"Father says that something is changing regarding Markmor. Draft and Associates are going to be looking in the wrong place."

"Does he know the right place?"

Morgaine shook her head.

"Apparently, not."

Her text alert sounded again.

"He now says we should follow them anyway."

"I guess next he'll say 'answer unclear try again later' might as well get a Magic 8-Ball."

Morgaine didn't answer him. Another text had come in. She looked up at Nikodemus.

"Have you tried to use the wand yet?"

Nikodemus was shaving, wearing a T-shirt but nothing else. Morgaine was gazing at his exposed butt. He stopped and looked at her.

"No reason to yet. Why?"

"Father says it might… Well not be the solution but… When you do use it anything you try will be enhanced."

Morgaine finished her drink and went to put on her clothes. She and Nikodemus had gone shopping earlier. Just for this occasion. She had chosen a dress that was form-fitting but comfortable. It was purple, like most things she wore. Short hem on the skirt showed off her legs. She had found some purple Ugg boots to wear with it. Much more comfortable than heels. Slightly more chic. Nikodemus was black and blue. Black slacks, black alligator belt, black lace-up dress shoes. They looked like wingtips but were actually golf shoes. They felt good and had good traction. A royal blue long-sleeved shirt finished his ensemble. Nikodemus preferred silver over gold so he had a silver chain around his neck, a silver link bracelet, and a silver watch with a black face and wristband. Morgaine's jewellery consisted only of a gold chain with a large purple amethyst pendant. She carried no purse which Nikodemus had commented would seem odd. So she had suggested he find one to carry instead.

Nikodemus put on some sunglasses that were barely tinted blue. They were almost clear. Morgaine smiled at him as he posed for her.

"Very nice. You look like a man on the prowl."

"I've already found you. This is for you, my dear."

"Father said you had pushed several leanings almost to interface. He said you are light and dark. What did he mean?"

Nikodemus paused and then went and poured another drink. He went to the mirror and looked at himself. Without looking at Morgaine he answered.

"A seeker can be light or dark. If you haven't decided, you can test different leanings until you find yours. I realised that if you push a leaning almost to interface you have capabilities of most of the leaning. A mentor helps you decide and prevents you from trying more than one at a time."

Nikodemus turned away from the mirror and looked at Morgaine.

"Protector leaning is light; Sorceror leaning, which is Enchanter when you reach 8, is dark; Maker leaning can be either or both. Diviner…"

Nikodemus paused in his narrative. He reached in his cabinet and drew out the wand.

"It's hard to believe that this was Merlin's. How did your father get it? How old is he?"

Morgaine looked from the wand to Nikodemus.

"He's not a thousand or anything. He is an advanced healer. I'm not much older than you. I remember him when I was a child. He didn't look much different than he does now to tell you the truth. I don't know."

Nikodemus' text alert sounded. He looked at it and dialled a number.

"What's up, Bill?"

There was a pause. Nikodemus smiled at Morgaine.

"No kidding. That's the last thing I would have expected. So… What now?"

Another pause.

"Ok. See you tomorrow."

Nikodemus hung up and looked at Morgaine.

"You'll never guess."

Morgaine just looked at him.

"I'm getting a badge. For real. I'm an FBI agent as of tomorrow. Bill and I are partners, and we're assigned to Senator Rollins as part of his Secret Service detail."

Morgaine looked at him impatiently.

"What?"

"You didn't exactly finish answering my question."

"Oh that. Well, where were we? Oh yeah Diviner. Dark. You know that. Like I said, without a mentor, you can try all of them."

"That's what I don't understand. I've always had a mentor. How have you not?"

"You always had one because Myron is a Level 22 Mage, and he's your father. If my father was a magic user of any discipline, I would have one. You trust him. I've never trusted any person that could be a mentor. They always had a hidden agenda that I was going to fulfil. Your father can draw energy from the ambient to go between. He transfers it to you. It's like it's free. I have to mine energy. From different sources. You wouldn't understand."

Nikodemus gestured to the door. "Speaking of which, we are going to take a taxi so we don't make a splash Markmor will detect. I have four apprentices stationed around Deep Ellum. If they feel him, they'll text me. Let's go get something to eat before we start this shindig."

With that, they both went out and closed the door.

Chapter 47

Charlie, Greg and Lori were in the conference room at Draft and Associates' Dallas office. Lori was modelling her dress for the night. It was tight, black, and short. Her heels were four inches long and made her rear end pooch out at just the right angle.

"Jesus, Lori. You look good enough to eat."

Lori smiled at Greg's compliment. She looked at Charlie for his input.

"Kill your brother or your best friend hot."

Charlie was always more reserved than Greg. He had never seen Lori in full hair and makeup.

"How do we keep every other guy off you long enough to hook our fish?"

Just then Nelson Draft entered with Malcolm Crews. He was a tech guy that developed and maintained some of the more sophisticated surveillance technology that Draft and Associates employed. He handed Lori and Charlie both a bracelet. Lori's was feminine, gold, and silver intertwined. Charlie's was larger. Kind of like an ID bracelet. Lori looked at hers.

"What's this?"

Nelson reached over and pushed a button on a controller in Malcolm's hand.

"Shit!"

Lori screeched and dropped the bracelet.

"What the fuck!"

The fury in her eyes aroused Greg like nothing else. Lori knew this and smiled at him before turning a baleful glare on Nelson.

"They're shock bracelets, Lori. We now realise that Wayne was hypnotised or glamoured or whatever. You saw those Texas Syndicate Vatos in the video. If you look like you're glamoured, that should snap you out of it."

"Who's going to be watching?"

Nelson nodded towards Malcolm.

"Malcolm is. Greg and I decided that we couldn't blend in like him. You and Charlie are young enough to look like regulars. Greg will be outside with two guys. He'll be monitoring."

Nelson reached over and pushed the other button. Charlie was still holding his bracelet. He dropped it but didn't make a sound.

"Just wanted you both to know what it felt like. You're starting at Club Clearview at 10:30. Give it an hour or two. Then Trees. If no bites, then knock off at 1:00 a.m. and come back here."

Over at Hotel W, Leviathan had just turned his minions to stone. He smiled at Markmor.

"Don't have to worry about them shitting the floor now, eh?"

Markmor laughed and handed Leviathan a small envelope.

"That's a spare key. It will get you into Ghost Bar without having to wait in line or pay a cover. It's a privilege for Hotel W guests."

"Ghost Bar?"

"It's on the top floor of the building next to us. If you want, I'll get you your own room."

"Thank you, Markmor. I might take you up on that. Right now, let's just try out this 'Ghost Bar.' I like the name."

"Sounds like someplace a Necromancer would feel at home, eh?"

Chapter 48

They didn't feel at home. There were so many Japanese tourists that made Markmor think he was in Tokyo. He had gone through an Asian phase, but none of these was hot enough. It was early, but it didn't look promising. Markmor leaned over to Leviathan.

"This rots. I know a much better area. I say we finish these drinks and blow. I'll get us a taxi."

"Taxi. Let's just between it."

"We can but it'll only take about ten minutes to get there. Seems like a waste."

Leviathan downed his drink and nodded.

"Perhaps you're right. We need to conserve our energy for the prey."

"Exactly."

Downstairs Markmor glamoured his way to the front of the taxi line. He and Leviathan got in.

"Deep Ellum."

The taxi driver started his metre and pulled away. Markmor was right. Ten minutes later he paid the cab and smiled at Leviathan. There were twenty or thirty absolute knockout twenty somethings wandering around the streets.

"Why is it barricaded?"

Markmor smiled and indicated the entrance to "Trees."

"On the weekends they close it to vehicle traffic so the drunk people don't get run over."

They walked towards the entrance that was crowded with miniskirts and long brown legs. Leviathan smiled at a woman that noticed him. He reached out with glamour, and she got out of line and stood next to him, holding his arm.

"I'll be in a minute. I want to enjoy Sara here first."

He smiled and walked towards the side of the building. Markmor went into the club. Leviathan led her around the corner and then towards the alley. The woman was smiling dreamily like they were in an amusement park. Leviathan put his hand on her throat and started pulling her soul out of her body. His eyes showed abject terror, which was like a drug to Leviathan. Then her eyes went blank, and he tossed her into the nearby culvert. He used a little telekinetic push to shove her body out of sight. Then he sighed like a man that had just enjoyed a sexual encounter. Which it was to him. Then he walked around the corner whistling, never realising that a security camera had recorded everything. He went to the entrance and glamoured his way in, avoiding the line, just as Markmor had. He found Markmor at the back. Sitting at a table with one woman beside him. Another woman's heels showed under the table. Markmor waved and gestured to a seat.

Their table in Club Clearview was near the dance floor. Charlie had gone to the bar and made a circuit if the place. Then he walked up to their table. There were two guys trying to get her to dance. He sat next to her. Charlie had once been in a firefight in Falusia that started with ten of his and twenty-five Falusians. He had been the sole survivor. He didn't have to fake the thousand-yard stare. He just thought about his dead friends and looked at them. They were gone in five seconds. Lori leaned over and kissed his cheek. She'd seen his look. Maybe Charlie was deeper than he looked.

"Thanks. I was getting ready to deck one of them. I'm sick of this place. Let's go to "Trees." On their earpieces Greg's voice answered, 'Fine by me. That music makes me want to kill somebody.'"

Malcolm got up and headed to the door.

"I'll go get set up. Say something in case I don't spot you when you come in."

Malcolm was gone. Lori and Charlie stood up together, and as another guy started to talk to Lori, she took Charlie's hand and leaned against him. The guy looked at Charlie wondering how a guy who looked like him could get prime stuff like her.

"You're out of my league, you know?"

"Nah. They probably think you have a giant dick."

Charlie burst out laughing. Lori joined in, and they went out the door. Looking like a happy if mismatched couple. Two blocks later, they saw the entrance to "Trees." There was a long line. Greg's voice in Charlie's ear informed him.

"Malcolm is in place."

"How did he get through the line?"

"A hundred bucks to the doorman. I bet Lori can get you both in."

Lori pulled Charlie to the left, and they walked up to the front of the line. The bouncer took one look at Lori and pulled the rope aside.

"You're a lucky man, my friend."

He smiled at Charlie. Charlie smiled back and shook the offered hand. Lori grinned at the bouncer. He was black, fortyish, six foot four pushing three hundred pounds. A beast by any other name.

"Luck has nothing to do with it. He's packin."

All three bouncers had heard this and burst out laughing. The first guy started leading the way.

"Holy shit! I'm Cyrus. Ya'll get the VIP section. Sugar and King Salami, follow me please."

Cyrus led them to a cordoned-off section of tables that were opposite where Markmor was sitting. They drew a lot of attention as Cyrus got them settled and had a bottle of champagne delivered.

"On the house, sir. Please don't hesitate to ask if I can be of further assistance."

Lori laughed and leaned against Charlie. The waitress came over and poured two glasses. Malcolm's voice was emotionless in their ears.

"Contact. Nine o'clock. Corner table. He is at a table with two women and another gentleman. Subject two. White male, forties, long dark hair, dark beard. He noticed you, Lori."

Greg took over.

"Sit there for a few minutes. Let's see what he does."

Charlie and Lori sipped champagne. They couldn't look at Markmor's table without being obvious. So they just drank their champagne. Lori took out her cell phone and pulled Charlie close like they were going to take a selfie. The phone was angled so they could see Markmor's table. He was looking towards Lori. He made a shooing gesture, and both the women left his table. The other man said something to him and got up. He went into the bathroom. Charlie watched the door. He never came out. After a little while, he went in to check. Empty. There were no windows. He pushed the transmit key on his watch.

"The other guy disappeared. Went between I guess."

Malcolm's voice in his ear was agitated.

"No, shit. Mark Moore is at your table. Lori has a funny look in her eye. Get out there."

"Ok. As soon as he looks at me, shock me. Then every fifteen seconds until I say so. Got me?"

"Yeah. Hurry. She's getting up and going to his table."

Nikodemus' apprentice Yvette was in line at "Trees" when she felt Leviathan go between. She texted Nikodemus.

"Somebody went between inside 'Trees'."

His answer was immediate.

"Confirmed. Bolt. Now."

She got out of line and went towards the DART stand. Nikodemus and Morgaine had just left Pappadeaux. Cajun food and beer. He considered and then turned to Morgaine.

"We're going between. In the alley behind Trees. I've mapped it. Ready?"

He didn't wait for her answer. Pop. They stepped out of the alley and went towards the entrance. Greg was in a surveillance van barely twenty feet from where they stepped out. He hesitated and then opened the door.

"Nikodemus."

Nikodemus and Morgaine stopped and turned around. Nikodemus squinted at him.

"Greg? With Draft and Associates, right?"

Greg got right to the point.

"Mr Moore is in there. Charlie and another agent named Lori are working him. They have shock bracelets on. Another agent is in the crowd. Here."

Greg handed Nikodemus an earpiece. He produced another and handed it to Morgaine.

"They have built-in microphones. Malcolm. Give me visual."

In their ears, Malcolm's voice spoke.

"It's up. Getting ready to shock Charlie. Then Lori."

On a tablet that Greg turned so Nikodemus and Morgaine could see, Markmor was at a table. With a woman next to him.

"Is that Lori?"

Greg nodded in answer to Nikodemus' question.

"By the way, his name is Markmor. One word. Brilliant idea the shock bracelets, really."

On the screen, Charlie had come up to the table, and Markmor was smiling at him. Nikodemus could see the glamour taking hold then BAM! Charlie jumped as the shock hit him. Markmor frowned at him. Then Lori jumped the same way. She lost her dreamy look and stood up. Markmor stood and pointed at Charlie. Charlie started backing away before he jumped as the bracelet shocked him again. He grabbed a hold of Markmor and could be heard above the din.

"Hit me again, Malcolm!"

This time, the shock hit Markmor too. He pulled away and cried out. Greg looked away from the screen just in time to see Nikodemus sprint for the door. He used his shushing trick like he did to Wayne Elliot on all three bouncers. A woman in line screamed as all three fell like bowling pins. Knocking over the velvet rope and two guys at the front of the line. Nikodemus was through the door. He had the wand out. Ready to push Markmor through the wall. Then Leviathan stepped from between right in front of him. His two tattooed skinheads had pepper spray in both hands and hit Nikodemus with a cloud. Nikodemus projected himself to Negative 1. He had inhaled a little of the spray. Nobody could see him at all except Leviathan. His dark art meant that he would see a faint outline. Leviathan ran to Markmor. He knocked Charlie aside and grabbed Markmor's arm and went between. His two minions were still spraying pepper. Even though it was choking them. Leviathan had placed a compulsion. Nikodemus was standing in the cloud. Unaffected because he was 180 degrees out of phase. He touched each of the skinheads on the arm and screamed into their ear killing them instantly. This was getting out of hand. Blue and red lights were flashing out front. Two Dallas police officers entered. It happened to be Guiterrez and Diaz. From the first incident. They were almost on him when Nikodemus flickered back in. Directly in front of them.

Guiterrez went wide-eyed but kept his weapon in his holster.

"Guiterrez, good to see you again."

Just then Bone and Smith walked in. Smith motioned Nikodemus over. He handed him a badge. Nikodemus opened it. The picture was from his most recent driver's license. Pretty old, but undoubtedly him.

"Having an older picture will make the whole thing look more authentic."

He looked around. Then back at Nikodemus.

"So, partner. What happened here?"

Bone had walked over and was listening also.

"Markmor was here. A Necromancer was here also. I think his name is Leviathan. He's the Levi Athan from the graveyard thing in Rockdale in 1977. Leviathan had two goons."

Nikodemus indicated the motionless, tattooed, shaven head corpses.

"They had pepper spray. Two cans each. It slowed me down long enough for Leviathan to pull Markmor out of the frying pan."

Greg Connor walked up.

"Agent Bone, I'm sure you remember Greg Connor with Draft and Associates. He had two operatives wearing shock bracelets inside. A man monitoring them would shock them if they looked glamoured. It was a brilliant idea. I think we should do something similar to agents likely to be in contact with a magic use event."

They were interrupted by Dallas police.

"Agent Bone, you need to come look at the security camera footage. There was a murder behind the building. By the bearded guy that did whatever and disappeared with the red-haired guy."

Nikodemus turned to him.

"Did he put his hand on her throat and just look at her until she fell down?"

Both police officers stared at him.

"How did you know that? How did you know it was a woman?"

"Because I know the type. His profile is that he enjoys it more than sex. When he was through, he looked like he had just won the lottery, didn't he?"

Agent Bone snorted in disgust. Nikodemus continued addressing the officers but was really talking to Bone, Smith and Greg.

"This guy will make Markmor look like a choirboy. Myron thinks he's the one behind the whole thing with Senator Rollins."

"What are you talking about? Senator Rollins?"

The two police officers could tell the subject was getting way above their pay grade. Two more officers walked in from outside. One of them addressed Guiterrez.

"Found the body in the culvert. Homicide is on the way."

"Let me see the video. Bill, you and Bone should too. We've got another face to find."

Chapter 49

Leviathan and Markmor stepped out of between into Markmor's room at Hotel W. Markmor was shaking. Leviathan was cool as a cucumber as he turned on the TV and went to the wet bar.

"Drink?"

"Hell yes."

Leviathan poured them both a couple of fingers of vodka and offered one to Markmor. Leviathan chuckled.

"I don't know how, but I knew something was getting ready to happen. That's why I went between and roused them. Pepper spray turned out to be fairly effective."

"Did Nikodemus do that thing you mentioned about projecting to Negative 1? It was fast."

"Yes. We were gone by the time he did it, but he also spoke in their ear in his kind of half-ass demon. It kills instantly."

Markmor shuddered as he downed the vodka. Leviathan was staring into space. Deep in thought. Markmor thought. Then his eyes rolled back in his head, and Markmor could tell he was communing with the dead. It was how he communicated with Aspekt. His mentor. It didn't take long. Then he blinked and looked at Markmor.

"Time is getting short on the Senator. We are going to hit him when he returns from Washington. That gives us tomorrow and part of Monday. I'm going to round up some helpers. We can't keep them here. I'll find a place. You need to rest up and stay here. They're looking for you, me too now. I'll be back sometime tonight."

Then Leviathan went between. Markmor looked at where he had been for a minute and then lay down on the couch.

Chapter 50

"Agent Demus, I find your analysis of the video…unusual, to say the least."

Bone, Smith, Nikodemus, and several Homicide Detectives for the Dallas Police Department were at the police station. The conference room not as nice as the FBI's didn't smell good either. Smith was sure that something was stuck to the seat of his pants.

"Well, what would you say the cause of death is then? Detective Harris, is it?"

Detective Bill Harris had been on Homicide for twenty-six years. He had seen many causes of death. But, he was stumped on this one. Coroner hadn't reported back in yet.

"We'll see what the coroner says."

"I predict 'natural causes' or 'undetermined.' I'll take any bets that you want to place against that."

There were no takers. Harris wasn't amused.

"This is no laughing matter, Agent Demus. That woman has a family. What would they think if we were taking bets on the cause of death?"

Nikodemus demeanour changed. It was scary to Smith, and he knew him. His eyes were cold. His voice was equally cold.

"You don't see me laughing, do you? Roll back and stop right before he left the alley."

Detective Harris nodded to the tech, and the video rewound and stopped with Leviathan smiling broadly, looking satisfied.

"You see that look? He just ate. Something he loves. Her soul. Back up to where he puts his hand on her throat and roll it forward at half speed."

Without asking the tech did as Nikodemus bade him. As the video advanced the woman's eyes were from dreamy, to abject terror, to dead and lifeless. Then Leviathan tossed her aside.

"That guy there. His name is Leviathan. Spelt like the creature from the deep. They have a lot in common in fact. He can kill you just by touching you and holding your gaze."

There were gasps around the conference room from the police personnel present there. These personnel noticed that there were no similar gasps from the FBI agents. Bone took up the narrative.

"We, unofficially, of course, have a standing kill order on this man. I don't know how you handle such an instruction within your guidelines, but you need something similar. Do not try to apprehend this man. Kill him on sight. I never will officially admit to such a statement, but if you want to protect the citizens of this city, you will do just that."

Bone handed Detective Harris a blown-up photo of Markmor.

"This is the other subject. His name is Markmor. His capabilities are different but just as deadly. We have been after him in regard to an attempt to abduct the daughter of Senator Rollins and a subsequent attempt on the Senator's life."

Bone paused a moment.

"Have any of you heard about the incident outside the White Elephant in Fort Worth last week?"

There was some indistinct murmuring. Harris narrowed his eyes at Bone.

"We've heard things. Apparently, the FBI confiscated or erased security cam and traffic cam footage for the entire thing. We heard about a tornado of birds attacking a bar. Texas Syndicate guns acting like zombies. Can you tell us anything?"

Smith and Nikodemus were looking at each other. Bone glanced at them.

"Nikodemus, tell these gentlemen what happened. Everything. At this point, law enforcement needs to know what we know."

Nikodemus got up.

"You want to let them record it?"

Bone was gathering his things.

"I'm not here."

He looked at Nikodemus and then walked up to him. The seriousness in his gaze was echoed in his tone.

"Nikodemus, I don't know what the hell has happened to my world. A month ago, I thought magic was bullshit. You've proven and shown me different. These men are our brothers in arms. Arm them with the information they need to get us through this."

Bone walked out. The policemen were speechless. They looked at Nikodemus with a mixture of awe and fear.

"Okay, guys. Stop looking at me like that. I'm going to give you some information that needs to stay within our ranks. By our, I am saying yours and mine. We're together on this. Fighting a common enemy. Protecting the same thing."

"Wilson, hurry up. Get the goddamn camera set-up."

Detective Harris' voice broke the reverie. The tech Lance Wilson was just staring at Nikodemus until he heard Harris. It only took him a minute to get set up. Nikodemus looked at Bill, then up at Harris.

"You got anything to drink around here? You're going to want it once you hear this."

Harris nodded to another detective.

"Sanger, get the bottle from my desk and some glasses."

A detective, presumably Detective Sanger, left the room and came back with a bottle of Wild Turkey American Honey and three glass tumblers. He also had a number of paper cups from the coffee area. Detective Harris poured himself, Nikodemus, and Smith drinks and then passed the bottle to Sanger. Most of the remaining men got drinks in paper cups. The bottle was returned to Harris still a third full. Nikodemus took a sip. Thought for a minute. Then began.

"Okay. I am Agent Nick Demus, and this is Agent Bill Smith. It hasn't been officially designated yet, but we are heading the FBI task force on magic. I'm sure it'll be called something different because if you say you believe in magic, you're nuts, right?"

There were a few chuckles around the room. Most were listening intently. The dead girl in the morgue didn't seem funny.

"The FBI first became involved with Markmor when he abducted Senator Mike Rollins' daughter Elizabeth. She was taken from outside John Phillips High School. She had an ex-Navy Seal for a driver who was at the spot when she was taken within ten seconds. Didn't see anything."

Nikodemus took a sip and addressed Detective Harris.

"Have any of you seen footage of a subject disappearing?"

Harris said nothing but shook his head in the negative.

"It happens. The subject Markmor and Leviathan can appear and disappear without warning."

Nikodemus and Bill expected snorts of disbelief, but there was only silence Then someone in the back spoke.

"Guiterrez said you appeared out of nowhere. His partner said the same. You can do this, right?"

Nikodemus couldn't tell who had spoken. He shook his head.

"Okay, turn off the recording for a minute. Okay. Back up to tape over those two questions."

Harris addressed his tech.

"Do none of that. Keep it rolling. Why would you want him to stop? Are you done?"

Nikodemus looked at Bill.

"Yes, I can do these things. Other things too. If that is on this tape that's all anybody listening to it will focus on. This is a briefing to save your officers and detectives' lives. Not to mention innocent civilians. Now, back up the fucking tape!"

Harris just looked at him.

"Okay, Bill. We're out of here. Let me know what the coroner says. Or don't. I thought we were going to finally have some interagency cooperation. But no. We're doing this as a courtesy, out of respect for your men and their abilities. You don't want that to happen I guess."

Bill got up, and they started to walk out. The detectives in the room all pleaded at once. Harris finally nodded. The tech pulled up the video and clipped it where Nikodemus requested.

"The rest will actually be a second video. I'll edit them together when you're done."

Nikodemus nodded.

"'What's your name?"

The tech blinked and smiled at Nikodemus. Usually, nobody cared.

"I'm Lance Wilson. I'm actually a civilian contractor for IT."

"Well, nice to meet you, Lance. You need to get with Malcolm. I don't know his last name. He's a tech for Draft and Associates. He has a video from inside Trees. I'll tell him to get you a copy."

Nikodemus went up to Detective Harris. He smiled and offered to shake his hand. Harris stood up and shook.

"Sorry, if I was getting a little pissy. Let's continue."

Nikodemus went back to his spot at the end of the table. Bill had refilled his glass. He took a sip.

"Where was I? Oh yeah appearing and disappearing. It's called going between. We were able to take Elizabeth back unharmed. Through interrogation of a subject, who unfortunately died, we learned of Markmor's involvement. One of you said something about Texas Syndicate zombies. They were glamoured. Kind of like hypnosis. You get glamoured; they can make you shoot your partner or yourself. Malcolm at Draft had fitted his operatives with shock bracelets. When he noticed them glamoured, he would shock them, and it brought them out of it."

Somebody interrupted.

"Would a stun gun work?"

"Without a doubt. Just remember they can glamour more than one person. All of this is somehow connected to Senator Rollins. He now has additional protection but is still in danger. The subjects Markmor and Leviathan are very dangerous. You saw the video. Leviathan can kill you without a weapon."

Nikodemus set his glass on the table. Considered for a minute and then went up to Bill.

"Let me see your amulet."

Bill took it out and handed it to Nikodemus who showed it to the room and then handed it back.

"This is a magic amulet. I know. We're not playing D&D. Senator Rollins has one that is similar. It can shield him. It can protect him. It was issued by a Mage named Myron. Okay incidentally. Markmor is a Mage. Leviathan is a Necromancer. I am a…"

Nikodemus paused.

"FBI agent. Anyway. If you hear about someone hearing a popping sound in an alley or somewhere. It might be somebody going or coming between. So to end this briefing. Be sure everyone has pictures of the two subjects. Also, anything about Senator Rollins that you hear. Pass it along, okay? Lance. Stop the recording."

Lance turned it off.

"Okay, now I'll tell you something. In Fort Worth, Markmor glamoured a shitload of birds and sent them after me in the White Elephant. I shredded them with a 12 gauge. Then the Texas Syndicate guys showed up. I brought a scaffolding down on the woman that had glamoured them. I can do things."

Nikodemus projected to Negative 1. Everybody but Bill freaked out a little. Nikodemus walked over and sat down on a table in the middle of four detectives.

Then he flickered back in. They all jumped when he appeared inches from them. He projected again and went to sit down next to Detective Harris. He flickered back, and Harris spilt his whiskey on himself.

"By the way, the 12 gauge is in my hand right now. If we were someplace I could demonstrate, I'd show you. When Lance gets the footage from Malcolm, study it. We'll be in touch. Remember, if someone is glamoured, they move a little slower and have a vacant look in their eyes. Detective Harris?"

Harris looked at Nikodemus.

"I thank you for your time."

Then Nikodemus projected and left the room. He was waiting by the car when Bill showed up. Bill grinned and got in.

"Well that was weird. By the way, Harris actually shit himself. He was telling me to go and wasn't getting up. It became obvious when I started to smell it."

Bill started the car and put on his seat belt.

"But, all in all, I think it was a good meeting. We're supposed to go to Senator Rollins house and get gate codes, and apparently, we'll have rooms to stay in. All that. He gets back Monday night."

Nikodemus was looking at his new FBI badge.

"I want to flash my badge at somebody. FBI! Take off your clothes and assume the position!"

Bill laughed as they left the parking lot.

"Kind of early to hit a strip club but…"

Chapter 51

The weather turned out to be perfect. The Senator picks a Saturday, three months in advance. Without even looking at the forecasts. Agent Smith marvelled yet again about how things seem to always work out for the man. His room at the Rollins Inn, the name Nikodemus had given the place, was nicer than any hotel room he could have found. His room connected with Nikodemus' through the bathroom they shared. Nikodemus was still apparently asleep. Or busy. Having women pop in between had advantages.

"Oh!"

The naked woman that walked into the bathroom from Nikodemus' side grabbed for a towel to cover herself. Her red hair had caused Bill to think it was Morgaine. But she was too young. It was Yvonne or Yvette. One of Nikodemus apprentices. They were twins. Bill went over and closed the door to the bathroom.

"Tell Nikodemus I'll be downstairs or in the backyard when he gets out."

He didn't wait for an answer. When he went into the hall, he found Nikodemus waiting for him.

"What would your wife think, Bill? Seeing a naked woman in your bathroom"

"Shut up."

Bill smiled, and the two-headed downstairs.

"Was that Yvonne or Yvette?"

"Yes."

"Whatever."

They had barely been there over a day, and Nikodemus already was friends with Senator Rollins entire staff. Family too for that matter. Mary Rollins and her friend Jeanette Ledbetter (Janet's mother) were in the kitchen talking to cook when Nikodemus and Bill walked in.

"Nick, you must try these cinnamon rolls. We saved you two."

Mary offered Nikodemus a plate, and he sat down in a chair between them. Mary and Janet were smiling at Nikodemus like he was Santa Claus or something

Bill wasn't jealous or anything but jeez. Everywhere they went, women fell all over themselves pleasing him.

"I'm not going to say no to that ladies. Mary, lovely as always. Janet, I didn't think you could top the thing you were wearing yesterday but…"

Nikodemus didn't finish his sentence. Instead, he took a cinnamon roll and stuffed most of it into his mouth. Bill, unnoticed, went over to the table that had three Secret Service agents from the Senator's detail. They were all watching the exchange and shaking their heads. Bill sat next to Walt Carmoney, the senior agent.

"They're eating out of his hand as usual. Didn't even say hi to you I noticed."

Bill took a coffee Walter poured for him. Took a sip. It was quality stuff.

"God, I love this coffee. Thanks. I wonder if they'd be so lovey-dovey with him if they knew he had two red-haired women in his room right now."

Bill looked at Walt.

"One of them walked into the bathroom naked right before I came down."

"Get a picture or anything?"

This from Steve Spencer. They didn't ask how they were there. These guys had been in Colorado. They'd seen people going and coming between.

"No, I didn't take a picture of the naked woman with skin like Carrera marble and long-flowing red hair that looked like fire in the light from the skylight. I can't get the image out of my head, but no, I didn't take a picture."

Janet and Mary were laughing and constantly touching Nikodemus on the arm or sometimes on his leg. Janet especially was getting very touchy. Nikodemus grinned over at Bill. Bill looked away in disgust. Then Elizabeth walked in. The Senator's daughter Elizabeth had just turned seventeen and was starting to look like something out of a magazine. Of course, she went up to Nikodemus as well. Bill couldn't take it anymore. He got up.

"Nick. Let's get to it. Shall we?"

All the women looked at Bill like he was taking their pony from them. Nikodemus got up amid pleas to stay.

"Ladies, we will continue this conversation later I hope. Elizabeth, try not to break any hearts today."

Ray Brooks was waiting by the door. He smiled at Nikodemus and preceded Elizabeth to the car. Three hundred yards away. On a hill behind a closed down laundromat. Leviathan watched Elizabeth and Ray through a telescope. They got in the car and headed out. He stayed on the back door and saw Nikodemus and

Bill step out onto the porch. He was watching Nikodemus. He turned, and Leviathan swore he was looking him right in the eye. He jerked away from the telescope. He looked over at the eight minions he had gathered. They were sitting on the ground against the wall in the few inches of shade that the wall provided. They were quiet and were watching him. Waiting for instructions.

Two were policemen. Still in uniform. A day and a night in the same uniform. They were a little rumpled but should pass once it got dark. They were both off duty for the next three days, so they weren't listed as missing by the department. Their families were dead in their respective houses. Leviathan smiled as he remembered killing their wives. Two respectable-looking Latina women. Maybe pass as staff, maybe not. Four black, armed, gangbangers. They had said their gang affiliation when Leviathan glamoured them, but he hadn't really been listening. Leviathan looked at his watch and took out his cell phone.

"Nikodemus and Agent Smith are definitely there. I'm ready on my end. It gets dark in eight hours. Check in with me before sundown."

Markmor's voice sounded tinny from the speaker.

"No problem. I'll be over there by four o'clock anyway. I'll come to the laundromat."

Leviathan put his phone in his pocket. He went into the shade of a large oak tree and leaned against it. He cleared his mind and prepared to commune with Aspekt. His group of minions watched his eyes roll back in his head. He looked on darkness. Swirls of smoke and then Aspekt's silhouette drew near him. Leviathan spoke the traditional greeting.

"Master."

"Are you not your own master now?"

Aspekt's voice was almost subsonic. They were conversing on a plane somewhere between Planes 1 and 0. Before the planes became dark, his voice reverberated through Leviathan's body. Well, his ethereal body anyway.

"You wish to tell me something?"

Leviathan tried to see Aspekt more clearly but to no avail. He never became quite whole during their communing.

"We will kill the Senator tonight. Hopefully Nikodemus also."

"You should take one task at a time. Remember, Myron is involved. The Senator and two agents carry amulets he sanctified. He gave Merlin's wand to the Seeker. Either kill the Senator or the Seeker. Trying to do both will mean you will accomplish neither. Possibly get taken. You know the Mage you have corrupted will die, don't you?"

"Yes, it was the plan all along. He whines more than any wife I ever had."

Aspekt's laugh seemed to echo throughout eternity. He faded, and Leviathan opened his eyes. The sun had risen so there wasn't any shade by the wall anymore. His minions were sweating. They stayed where they were told, though. Leviathan thought about making them sit there all day but realised they were barely going to pass as normal as they were.

"Get up. Move to the other side of the building in the shade. I'll bring you water soon. You…"

He indicated one of the policemen. The name on his uniform said "McDade."

"If anyone comes near here, you will kill them if they see any of you. Try to remain unseen. I will be back soon."

With that, Leviathan stepped between and was gone.

Chapter 52

Leviathan had never heard of a medical alert necklace. Never seen the "I've fallen, and I can't get up" commercials. If he had, he would have disabled the one on Officer John McDade's mother-in-law who happened to be visiting when Leviathan came calling. Hers had a feature that detected a fall.

It hadn't gone off during the thirty minutes of hell on earth that Leviathan subjected McDade's wife Ann, his daughter Amy, and Ann's mother Bea too. He had stuffed the bodies standing upright in a linen closet at the top of the stairs. The linen closet had a notoriously tricky latch that popped open when the vagaries of rigor mortis, settling body fluids, and the central air conditioner next to the closet kicking in happened to come together.

The door popped open, and the bodies of Ann and Amy fell into a heap. Bea's body was stiffer, and after leaning forward finally seesawed over the mound and went tumbling down the stairs. Setting off the medical alert necklace. The alarm went off. GPS located the necklace, and an operator's voice came out.

"Mrs Winston, are you all right? We detected a fall. Can you hear me?"

After a pause of ten seconds.

"Mrs Winston we have detected your location to be 1515, Elm St., Lancaster, Texas. We are dispatching units now."

Twenty minutes later, EMTs were knocking on the door. They looked in the window and saw Mrs Winston's body on the stairs. They stepped aside, and the firemen with them took the door down. The inside of the house was cold. The A/C was set on 60 degrees. When the three cold bodies were verified to be long dead, the EMTs went back out to wait for the police.

Chapter 53

Having a Prescient leaning didn't mean that you sat down and asked what was going to happen. It felt more like a premonition. Especially if the possible event was unpleasant. Myron had chosen Prescient as his leaning because it felt like he had always had it. This was how leanings were supposed to be chosen. Myron mused on Nikodemus. Five leanings almost to interface. Capabilities that needed discipline and practice to hone effectively. The wand would help but still wouldn't allow him to break the barrier to the next level. He could make, but he couldn't apply his influence to an amulet. He could glamour by making someone stop and not realise they've stopped. But he couldn't influence them to do his bidding. He could make them feel like they were on fire, though. Unheard of until Nikodemus did it. He didn't even try to be a Healer. Instead, he went straight to possibly dark leanings. He could project himself out of phase. In and of itself not considered anything. Nikodemus had discovered he could still see and hear in this plane without being in it. A new discovery. He had spent enough time on Negative 1 that he could speak a mumbled kind of demonic. With this, he could shake the ground in this plane. Caused by Plane 1 reacting to Negative 1 sound waves. If spoken directly into someone's ear, it was instantly fatal.

Myron shook his head. He was sitting in a chair he had put near his brother. He sat there a lot lately. It wasn't until he was gone that Myron realised how much he depended on Ethan's counsel. He wasn't gone exactly. Not yet. Myron's premonitions showed two possible outcomes. Meaning that something was in play that he was unaware of. He felt it had to do with Leviathan and possibly Aspekt. If Nikodemus killed Leviathan, then there was only one other Necromancer alive that Myron knew of. Not that he knew her. He had heard of her. Nefernefernefer, an Egyptian that was supposed to be older than seemed possible. Myron pushed thoughts of her out of his mind as he gazed at Ethan's form.

Morgaine walked in dressed in a modern businesswoman's suit. It was purple of course. The skirt seemed too short to Myron, but he had given up trying to influence his children on how to dress long ago. She came up behind his chair and put her hands on his shoulders.

"Well, I'm going to the Senator's party. Hans and Gunther will be on guard."

She stopped and looked at Ethan.

"Are you going to wake him?"

"If I did it now, he would finish dying."

Morgaine kissed her father's head and walked towards the dais. She stood a moment and then went between.

In Nikodemus' suite of rooms at the Rollins Inn, an area had been designated as between arrival area. Morgaine stepped through and encountered a woman with a schedule pad sitting at a table.

"Morgaine, you are logged in. Here are two items Nikodemus left for you."

She indicated an earpiece and a laminated ID badge. She looked at it and recognised the picture as having been taken from a security camera in the FBI building. There was also a bracelet-looking thing with a small battery on it.

"Nikodemus said you could rest here or go downstairs at any point of your choosing. The bracelet contains a microphone. Raise it to your mouth, and it will turn on."

The woman raised her wrist to demonstrate.

"Morgaine has arrived. Confirm."

In her earpiece that she had just put in Morgaine heard Nikodemus' voice.

"Welcome to the party, Morgaine. Let me guess, you're wearing purple."

The woman smiled at Morgaine. Then she stood up and went to a small refrigerator and took out a coke.

"Would you like one?"

Morgaine shook her head in the negative.

"My name is Melissa Barnett. Let me know if you need anything. Downstairs and to the left there is a room that the law enforcement agencies are using for briefings and whatever. I'm pretty sure Nikodemus is there."

"Thank you, Melissa. Tell Nikodemus I'm going to lie down for a little bit. I'll be in his room."

She walked into the bedroom and encountered Yvonne and Yvette. Sitting on the bed. Both were wearing thongs and nothing else. They saw her and smiled widely.

"Hell yes! Now we can have some fun. Morgaine, get your beautiful ass over here and take that skirt off."

Morgaine smiled and allowed Yvette to assist her in undressing. They placed her outfit carefully over a chair. Melissa barely heard the squeal as Yvonne jumped on the bed and wrestled Morgaine onto her back.

Downstairs the Dallas police, Fort Worth police, and the FBI were reading the same bulletin. Fort Worth Police Officer Mike McDade's family had been found dead in their Lancaster home. McDade's whereabouts were unknown. His partner Billy Gage was also unavailable. Upon visiting the Gage's residence, the body of his wife Susan had been discovered in their den. All the bodies had no markings whatsoever. Cause of death undetermined.

"What do you think? Leviathan's work?"

Nikodemus looked at Bill, then at the officers in the room.

"Probably. We need pictures of these two guys. Unit number on their cruiser."

"Cruiser is in impound."

This information from Detective Harris.

"Okay. If Leviathan did this, then he's going to use them. Try to mingle them in. The bodies are a couple of days old, right?"

Nods of assent from two detectives.

"That means they've been wearing their uniforms that long. Probably haven't shaved or showered. They'll look wrinkled and maybe unshaven. Hit them with a taser on sight. In fact, when in doubt, taser anybody."

Agent Bone was looking at papers and spoke without looking up.

"Not the Senator, though. Bill and myself are also protected. I'll have pictures distributed. It's nearly four. Three hours to go. Let's go over the grounds again."

The room emptied of everyone except Nikodemus, Bill, Bone, and the two lead detectives. Bill Harris with Dallas Police Department and Mike Hall with Fort Worth Police Department. Smith looked around.

"Where's Morgaine? I thought she was here?"

Nikodemus was looking out the window at the patio where tables were being set.

"She's probably playing with Yvonne and Yvette. We've still got some time. I'm going to go get some exercise."

Nikodemus walked out. The men left were speechless.

"We're getting ready to maybe fight off all kinds of weird shit tonight, and if I'm hearing right, he's going to go romp around with three women."

"Three, hot, red-haired women."

Detective Harris looked at Smith.

"Oh, well, then I guess it's ok."

"Greg Connor, Charles Wilkins, and Malcolm McDonald with Draft and Associates are here. I've directed them to the briefing room."

This from an agent at the front gate. His announcement over their earpieces received a reply the same way from Agent Bone.

"Confirmed."

After a moment Greg, Charlie, and Malcolm entered the briefing room, Greg spotted Bill and walked up to him.

"Hey, Agent Smith. Where's Nikodemus? I wanted to go over something with him."

Bill thought for a minute and then started up the stairs.

"Follow me. I'll show you to his room."

Detective Harris and Agent Bone kept their faces expressionless until Greg was gone. Then Lance, the tech from Dallas Police Department, came up to Malcolm.

"You're Malcolm, right?"

Malcolm shook his hand.

"Yeah, nice to meet you in person. Lance, right?"

Lance was grinning. So were Agent Bone and Detective Harris. Harris and Bone went outside. Charlie came up to them.

"What's so funny? Private joke?"

Lance was deadpan.

"Ask Greg when he comes back down."

Bill and Greg were outside Nikodemus' door. Nothing seemed out of the ordinary. Bill knocked.

"Nikodemus. Greg Connor is here to talk to you."

Then the door was opened by a nude, except for a thong, beautiful red-haired woman. Yvette looked Greg up and down. Greg was speechless.

"Come on in, Mr Greg Connor. Bill? Do you want to come in?"

She was playing with her hair and smiling at him innocently. Bill said nothing. She grabbed Greg by the arm and pulled him into the room before closing the door in Bill's face. Bill stood there for a minute. Then went downstairs.

"Shut up," was all he said to Charlie when he saw him.

Greg entered a bedroom with Nikodemus wearing only a towel standing at the entrance to the bathroom. What he realised was a twin to the double hot ginger that had opened the door sat on the foot of the bed. Like her sister, wearing only a thong. Then he saw Morgaine. She was nude; she walked out of the bathroom with no shame at all. She walked up to Greg and greeted him.

"Greg. I've heard a lot about you. Nikodemus left out the part that you were gorgeous."

For once in his life, Greg was speechless. For a moment. Then he tried to be nonchalant.

"Likewise, I'm sure. I didn't really get a good look at you the other night."

He gazed up and down her near-perfect form. All three women had creamy skin with no tan lines. Long flowing red hair. Greg felt himself getting aroused. Yvette and Yvonne's giggles made him realise he was visibly aroused. He looked over at Nikodemus.

"Hey, I had something I wanted to go over with you, but it's nothing that can't wait a few...hours."

He was looking from Morgaine to the twins.

"I'm Yvette."

"I'm Yvonne."

"Of course you are."

He spied a bottle of something on the table with glasses and an ice bucket.

"Say, I'm thirsty all of a sudden."

Yvette and Yvonne giggled, and both went over and made a point of bending over. Showing their shapely rear ends to Greg as they made him a drink. They pulled him to a chair at the vanity. Nikodemus was looking in the mirror, combing his hair.

"Easy girls. I don't know if he's married or anything."

"I'm single!"

Greg said this louder than he meant to. Greg tasted the scotch and couldn't believe how good it was.

"My God! This is the best Scotch I've ever tasted in my life! What is it?"

Morgaine had put on a purple robe and swatted Yvette on the rear end so she would move over and let Morgaine sit on Greg's right leg.

"It's Senator Rollins' private stock. Exquisite, isn't it?"

Greg started kicking into womaniser mode.

"No, you're exquisite. This is good."

Morgaine's laugh tinkled like icicles. To Greg sounded almost musical.

"Aren't you the silver-tongued devil? Nikodemus, let us play with him, please?"

"Please."

"Please."

Greg joined in as his heart started beating faster.

"Please Nikodemus. Please."

Nikodemus turned around and grinned at Greg.

"Sorry, Greg. We've got work to do. Plus, you probably wouldn't be able to walk when they got through with you."

Greg's face was crestfallen. Morgaine kissed him lightly on the lips.

"Don't worry, Greg. We'll be here after the party."

Her musical laughter again mesmerised Greg. Then all three women went into the bathroom. The shower turned on, and you could hear Yvette and Yvonne giggling as they started washing Morgaine. Nikodemus closed the door to the bathroom. Much to Greg's chagrin. Greg looked at Nikodemus and shook his head. Nikodemus quickly pulled on a pair of jeans, a button-down shirt, and a pair of loafers without socks.

"This shindig doesn't start for two and a half hours."

Greg's statement was almost a plea.

"They were messing with you, buddy. They're mine. Come on. Now, when you get downstairs, act like you just got some to Bill. He's been going nuts."

"I don't know what to say. I have no words."

"Just limp a little."

They walked into the briefing room where all the agents on site had gathered to view Malcolm's video from Trees. They all looked up at them, and Greg limped a little over to the table. Charlie noticed it immediately.

"Greg? I pulled something a little. A minute ago. I'll be fine. Continue."

But they didn't continue. They just stared at Greg. Nikodemus smiled and left the room headed for the kitchen. When it became obvious they weren't going to continue. Greg sat down.

"What?"

"What do you mean what? You know what. You were in the room with them?"

The Secret Service agent was deadly serious with his question. Greg looked up innocently.

"Yeah, so?"

"Bill says that Yvette answered the door naked."

"Bill is mistaken. She was wearing a thong."

The agents and police officers present all groaned. They rolled their eyes at Greg. Several left the room with disgusted looks on their faces. Bill was just looking at him. Greg looked back.

"Hey, she asked you if you wanted to come in."

Bill got up and left in a huff. Greg chuckled, leaned over, and got himself a coke from the bucket of ice on the table. Nikodemus came back in.

"Malcolm, is everybody up to speed?"

"Yep."

"Greg, shock bracelets?"

"We have them with us but going to see what you thought about them."

Nikodemus got a coke before he answered.

"No, not yet. Lance, show him the stuff on McDade and Gage. I'm going to look around and pick spots for the girls."

He went out just as Mary Rollins walked by.

"Nikodemus!"

She smiled broadly and took his arm.

"I have some more of my friends for you to meet."

They walked off down the hall. Lance looked after them and then started pulling up the requested information.

Chapter 54

Markmor drove a car he had glamoured away from a parking attendant at the Hotel W. It was going to be on the security cameras, but he didn't plan on going back there. He was carrying over $50,000 in cash in his cabinet. Plus several gold bars and coins were stashed. Following Leviathan's instructions, he hadn't gone between so close to where Nikodemus was. Leviathan was there waiting for him. Markmor could see his minions sitting against the wall of the closed-down laundromat.

"I'm ready. When do you want me to do it?"

Leviathan was smiling at Markmor. This always kind of creeped him out. The Necromancer's smile always seemed kind of unnerving. Like a tiger showing his teeth.

"Oh, the plan is kind of fluid at this point. I'm not sure if those two."

He indicated the men in policemen's uniforms.

"Will pass. They're kind of rumpled looking."

Markmor had been thinking the same thing.

"Yeah, but if they don't, they'll be a distraction, right?"

Leviathan was looking at the two Latino women he had glamoured. He was starting to think he didn't need them. Not for the party anyway.

"Exactly. If they pass, we wait for the sound of mayhem. Then these four will go in with guns blazing."

Leviathan was looking at the four gangbangers. They grinned at the prospect.

"If they don't pass. The mayhem will be immediate. Then these four will go in with guns blazing."

Markmor smiled at Leviathan.

"Sounds like at some point. Those four will go in with guns blazing, and in the confusion, I go for who? The Senator or Nikodemus?"

"Either or both. I will be distracting, Myron. I'm going between to his castle as soon as you engage. I plan on temporarily disabling the amulets. That should give you your window."

Markmor said nothing. If he didn't disable the amulets, then it wasn't going to go very well. The Senator would be basically untouchable. Nikodemus, formidable already, had Merlin's wand. He missed Lydia. For the thousandth time, he considered asking Leviathan if he had spoken with her spirit. He was afraid of the answer.

Leviathan got up and addressed the glamoured minions.

"You four find a place of concealment near the property. Not on it. The vacant lot across the street two houses to the north looks good. Stay in the trees all the way. You don't belong in this neighbourhood and would stick out like sore thumbs. Hide. Now, get going."

The four gangbangers got up and started walking without a word spoken by them. Markmor looked where they were going. It would be a hot hour-long trek through the woods. Maybe longer. He didn't envy them. Leviathan then addressed the two policemen.

"I have a stolen sheriff's car from Granbury, Texas, for you. Don't drive in the driveway or anything, but you can use it to get near there. It won't stick out with uniformed men in it. When it is time for you to go into the party, I will alert you like this."

Leviathan looked at them, and they both heard what sounded like a bell tone. But it vibrated through their body.

"That's the signal. When you hear the clarion, go to the gates. If you get in, find the Senator and shoot him. If you are challenged, draw your weapons and start shooting anybody you see. Go on; the keys are in it."

He indicated the bay door on the laundromat. They opened it, and inside was a blue and white sheriff's car. Palo Pinto County sheriff was emblazoned on the side. They started the car and drove off. Markmor looked at the remaining two Latino women. They were in their twenties and not half bad looking. Leviathan noticed and smiled as he walked up next to Markmor.

"Which one do you want?"

Markmor looked at him and then back at the women.

"I'll take the tall one. With the long hair."

Leviathan released his glamour on her, and Markmor placed one seamlessly. The woman was wearing workout clothes that were black with pink flowers and form-fitting. She walked up to Markmor and followed him to the car.

"I'll head in as soon as I hear shooting. How will I know if you were successful on the amulets?"

Leviathan had already taken the other woman into the vacated garage. He pulled the door down without answering. Markmor had considered enjoying a little action here until he heard the woman scream from the garage. He just got in and drove away.

"I'm going to call you Bonita. Now, get to work."

Her head dropped below the line of the dashboard as he drove away.

Chapter 55

Senator Rollins annual fundraiser was always organised as a joint effort from the Secret Service, local FBI, and local law enforcement. Communication was maintained through radio, telephone, and in recent years with real-time video link. Deputy Director Glenn had invited the Dallas and Fort Worth Police Departments to monitor from the FBI offices. With the recent developments regarding Officers McDade and Gage, the stress level was higher than usual. Director Glenn was reviewing Agent Bone's assessments of the party and in particular the physics and ballistics analysis of the table that had been destroyed in a conference room last week.

Results of analysis regarding an unknown event in Conference Room 2 on 12 June 2018 in Fort Worth, Texas.

Stress analysis showed that two-thousand-three-hundred-eighty-foot pounds of pressure was applied evenly along outward-facing edge of the table. Duration of application unknown. The table was against the east wall of Conference Room 2. Pressure then changed angle slightly causing the table to fold along the centre axis. Table flattened against the wall with no visible reduction of pressure. Pressure released. The table falls to the floor.

Additional note.

How pressure was applied resembles the action of the table in a mechanical press. The actual source or cause of this event is unknown.

Director Glenn turned his attention to one of the monitors. Nikodemus had Mary Rollins, that is to say, Mrs Mike Rollins, hanging on his arm, and she was introducing him to two women. Their attire and accessories were what Glenn referred to as muted hyper/expensive. They were affluent but not flashy. Old money women from money families married to money. Nikodemus seemed to fit right in. He had them all smiling and laughing and touching him in seconds. Glenn looked at his watch. A little less than two hours to go. Nikodemus looked like he hadn't a care in the world.

Mary was smiling at Nikodemus when he felt it. He stopped talking in mid-sentence and looked around. Mary was concerned. He didn't look happy.

"Nick, what's wrong?"

Nikodemus was still looking around almost frantically. He looked at her, and his expression scared her.

"Something's wrong, Nick. What is it?"

"Mary, Susan, Judith, please forgive me. Something just occurred to me that I haven't taken care of. It really is lovely to meet you both. Mary's friends have all turned out to be so interesting."

He looked at the two newcomers with laughter in his eyes.

"And attractive. But I must attend to something. Please excuse me."

Without waiting for their replies, he rushed off and grabbed Bill and Greg by the arm. He pulled them into the house towards the briefing room. He let go of Bill and activated his wrist mic.

"Agent Bone, Detective Harris, please meet us in the briefing room. Will you?"

Charlie and several others noticed Nikodemus walking quickly to the briefing room and followed them. After waiting until Bone and Harris were there, he motioned for the doors to be closed.

"Markmor is near. I felt it."

The murmuring amongst them silenced. He looked around before he continued.

"I was out on the south deck with Mary and her friends Susan and Judith. I could tell he was looking at me. Part of me wants to go after him now. But, I don't want to spook him. It's only a matter of time before he tries something. Now, I know he definitely will tonight."

Nikodemus picked up the pictures of Officers McDade and Gage.

"I guarantee we'll see these guys tonight. They'll be used as a distraction. Secret Service. You need to have a minimum of four, and I would prefer eight men close to Mike at all times."

One of the police officers ventured a question.

"Who is Mike?"

Nikodemus shook his head.

"I'm sorry, Senator Mike Rollins. All officers of any entity stay in groups of three. I know that'll probably throw your ordinary procedures off, but we'll be looking for two officers together. Any pair of men need to be challenged."

Bone looked at Nikodemus with a new appraisal.

"That is an excellent strategy, sir. Groups of three it is. Like he said. Any pair gets challenged."

He then looked at Nikodemus.

"You said they'll be a distraction. What do you think the main action will be?"

"My guess is Markmor will go for the Senator. His amulet will make that difficult which means that he must think that it will be disabled somehow. I'll talk to Morgaine about that. In the meantime, stay alert. Remember groups of three."

Morgaine walked into the briefing room as Nikodemus finished. She looked stunning yet professional in her business woman's suit. Purple, though.

"I was just telling these gentlemen here that Yvette is going to stick close to Elizabeth. Yvonne is going to stick close to Mary. I was planning on roaming with you. How does that sound?"

"Bill will be with us too. We're running in groups of three. Trying to flush out the pair or missing police officers. Any pair gets challenged."

He went over and whispered in Morgaine's ear.

"I need to talk to you."

They both went into the hall. Nikodemus considered for a moment then looked at her.

"Is Myron protected?"

"Of course, his German guards. They've been with him forever."

"I ask because the glamoured policemen are probably a distraction to give Markmor a chance to attack the Senator directly. He knows about the amulet which means…"

Morgaine's eyes widened.

"I hadn't considered that. Do you think Markmor?"

"I think it'll be Leviathan. What is Ethan's status?"

Morgaine was looking away. Nikodemus thought she wasn't really listening.

"Morgaine?"

"He's still a statue. Father says if he wakes him now he'll just finish dying. Why is this happening?"

She looked at him imploringly. Even though he thought it was a rhetorical question, Nikodemus gave her his theory as an answer.

"I think the grand scheme was hatched by Aspekt. Leviathan was his apprentice. Somehow, Leviathan recruited or corrupted your brother. Lydia always did whatever he said anyway. Aspekt saw potential he didn't like with Senator Rollins."

"He's putting out a lot of effort if you're right. It must have been more than potential."

"Regardless, what do we do about protecting Myron?"

"I'll contact Hans. He can bring more of his brothers."

"I don't know anything about them except they're German. Is there anything special about them?"

Morgaine was texting. She looked up after she sent the text.

"They can't be glamoured. They aren't afraid of anything. And, they're loyal.'

"Works for me."

In Myron's castle, Hans looked at the text and addressed Myron.

"We should move. Our keep will be safer."

Myron looked at him. He didn't ask about the text. He was concentrating on the three amulets that were all at Senator Rollins' house. He nodded. Hans dialled a number and waited for a reply.

"Dieter."

"We're moving to the keep."

"I want you and four more to come to Myron's and wait to see if anyone shows up. Kill them if they do."

"Ethan's statue needs to remain untouched."

"Good."

He hung up and, with Gunther, went up to Myron and each put a hand on one shoulder; they went between and the werelight on the torches died. The brightly lit feasting hall turned into a dark shadowy abandoned castle in the mountains.

Dieter was a Level 9 Sentinel. His family had been Sentinels for Myron's family for generations. He chose four apprentices to take with him. Johann, Wilhelm, Norbert, and Hans Jr. They were all formidable in their own right. Armed with a combination of swords, guns, and cell phones. They went between to the recently vacated castle feasting hall. Dieter lit the torches with werelight, and the group settled in to wait. They stood in a ring protecting Ethan's statue.

Chapter 56

It was time. Guests had been arriving for almost an hour. The Texas sky was full of clouds that were turning gold, then pink, then purple as the sun slipped towards dusk. The streetlights came on. Leviathan had just finished disposing of the Latina woman's body. She had been truly delicious. Her fear had been sweeter than anything he had consumed lately. He would look for Latinas exclusively in the future. He sounded the clarion that could be heard by the policemen only.

From his vantage point next to the Laundromat, he watched through the telescope as the sheriff's car parked down the block from the Senator's house. They were in front of the lot where the gangbangers were supposed to be hiding. He saw the lights turn off. The interior light turned on and then off. They were out. Walking towards the gate. Leviathan panned over until he was looking at the gate. Three pairs of men stood there. Three in uniform. Three in suits. His text alert sounded. Looking down he saw Markmor's text.

"In position."

It wasn't three pairs waiting at the gate. It was two groups of three. One of the FBI agents saw the pair sauntering up. He raised his microphone to his mouth.

"Got a pair of uniforms walking towards the gate."

Agent Bone replied over the earpiece.

"Tasers out now. It's probably them. As soon as you can, either read the name on their uniform, or if they go for their weapon, tase them both."

Agent Williams, the senior at the gate, nodded to two of the policemen.

"Get your tasers out and stand behind me and Henderson. You see the edge of the pool of light thereby the mailbox."

"Yeah"

"When they reach that I'll either say stand down or I'll get out of your way. If we're wrong, they're police anyway. They won't sue us. Light them up. If you tase them. Everybody draw your weapon."

Leviathan was sending a signal to the four gangbangers. They were crouched in the bushes in the vacant lot. The mosquitoes had been feasting on them. The glamour Leviathan had placed on them made them ignore the bites. They had all been sweating profusely during the hike to get to their position. Close to six hours in 100+ degrees had taken its toll. Their jeans and Dallas Cowboy jerseys were soaked with sweat. They didn't speak. They were mechanisms. Leviathan had made sure their weapons were loaded. He didn't expect them to last long enough to need more ammo. They wouldn't have been able to reload anyway. The compulsion affected their dexterity. Their eyes were blank and lifeless. Their misery near its end.

At Leviathan's urging, they crept out of the bushes and crouched behind the sheriff's car. They carried one 12-gauge pistol grip pump, one .357 magnum, and two Glock 9-mm automatics. All stolen. Each held his weapon carefully. Waiting for the signal. Car headlights came down the drive to the laundromat. Leviathan looked for a moment and then focused on the coming exchange. They were probably lost or looking for a place to do drugs. He was thirty yards into the foliage from the back. They were nobody. He'd deal with them later.

Susan Simpson was one of several media personalities at the Senator's fundraiser. At strict orders from Gene Terrell, she had stopped working the Nikodemus story. She'd been so busy that she'd all but forgotten Greg Connor. Then she saw both of them talking. Here of all places. She walked up and swatted Greg on the rear end.

"Do I know you?"

Greg turned around and smiled. She looked at him then at Nikodemus.

"Who's your friend?"

"I'm Nick Demus, FBI ma'am. It's a pleasure to make your acquaintance. You're Susan Simpson. I've seen you on TV. You're much better looking in person, though. If you don't mind me saying."

Susan smiled and shook the offered hand. She looked at Greg.

"FBI?"

Greg looked at Nikodemus.

"Uh, she's seen the video from the Stockyards."

Nikodemus smiled unaffected.

"Well, I'm so glad. I'd like you to meet a friend of mine."

He looked over at Morgaine. She was being fawned over by a couple of guests that Nikodemus hadn't bothered to notice.

"Morgaine! Come over here and meet Susan Simpson. She's with Channel 4."

Morgaine smiled as she walked over. Susan was staring at her, mesmerised. She was beautiful beyond belief.

"Well, hello, Susan. So you know Greg here?"

Morgaine smiled at Greg then back at Susan. Susan smiled at her and then looked at Greg.

"What are you two doing here? Why here?"

She noticed that they had identical earpieces.

"You're working together?"

Her reporter mind started going overtime. She was supposed to cover the Senator's speech at the end of the night. She'd been bored to tears until now. She turned away and took out her phone. She turned on the video record function and slipped it into a pocket on the front of her purse. When she turned around, she was alone. She was looking for them when she heard gunfire at the front gate.

Nikodemus and Greg had been trying to act nonchalant with Susan while the news on their earpiece got hotter and hotter.

"Bone, it's definitely them."

Then louder as he yelled to the officers with him.

"Light 'em up!"

Tazers snaked out pinning two darts each into the officers. They were trying to draw their weapons but ended up dropping them as they shook uncontrollably to the electricity running through their bodies. Nikodemus advised on the earpiece.

"The shock will lift the glamour at least temporarily. If either one looks at you like he's awake. Ask him who did this. You won't have long before the glamour clamps back down on them!"

Agent Williams along with the other five personnel were focused on the downed police officers. They didn't notice the four men coming from the shadows until the lead discharged his 12 gauge from less than ten feet away.

BOOM!

The blast knocked one police officer and two FBI agents down. The policemen were killed instantly. Williams was missing one arm at the elbow and went into shock. He barely registered the sound of the three handguns. The other two police officers were still holding their tasers and went down. Taking rounds to the vests didn't kill you but it hurt like hell. The one FBI agent, a rookie named

Robert Rincon, drew his Smith & Wesson .40 calibre automatic and killed all four assailants. He emptied his magazine at the four shadowy forms, and all four went down. He looked back at McDade and Gage. Gage was dead. A stray round had taken him in the chest. McDade wasn't, He had the blank look in his eyes as he raised his service revolver. Rincon dropped to the ground, rolled, and came up with the 12 gauge that had killed his friends. McDade fired once and missed as Rincon worked the pump, chambering a round. McDade didn't get another chance to fire.

BOOM!

Leviathan hadn't been paying attention to what had been going on behind him. He heard a man's voice. Sounding angry.

"I'm telling you. Her phone is showing to be here!"

Another voice answered him.

"Call it then. I don't see anybody."

Leviathan had her phone in his pocket. They were standing behind the laundromat at the edge of the woods. Barely fifteen feet from Leviathan. The phone rang in his pocket, and both men started towards him. He waited till they got close and then glamoured them hard. A Necromancer can kill you by doing it hard enough. It was hard to kill two at once, though. It wasn't working. They were looking at him. He released one and concentrated on the other. The problem was that the one he released was armed. His pistol was in his hand. He raised it to fire, and Leviathan released the other and dropped to the ground. He cursed and went between. His fall-back place in emergencies like that was his house in the mountains in Yugoslavia.

To go where he needed to go, he had to go back to Fort Worth. His reference to Myron's castle was anchored there. But, both of them would be waiting. He knew he wouldn't be able to glamour them both in time. He cursed and sat down in one of his chairs. Markmor was on his own.

During the chaos of the gunfight at the main gate, Markmor had gone between and landed in a dark part of the yard. He was sure no one had heard the pop of his arrival over the gunfire. He was wrong.

Yvette and Yvonne both flinched like they'd been stung. They were with Mary and Elizabeth in the kitchen. Mary was overseeing an appetiser emergency. Elizabeth and Yvette were there to cool off in the air conditioning.

"Yvette, are you okay? You looked like you got stung by a bee?"

Yvette looked at Elizabeth panicked. Then at Yvonne. Two Secret Service agents were running through to go outside. Yvette yelled out the code for alarm.

"Firefly!"

They both stopped and looked at them.

"What is it?"

"Somebody just arrived from between. Outside."

One agent raised his mic.

"Firefly. I say again Firefly. Yvette says somebody arrived between. This is Sanchez and Hinkman. We got Mary and Elizabeth. Heading to safe room now."

"Acknowledged. Porcupine. On the Senator. Nikodemus, you are weapons-free."

Bone's voice reached every agent simultaneously. Four near the Senator were already shielding him at the sound of gunfire. Four more joined and started a moving cordon towards the house and the safe room. Greg Connor was with Susan Simpson. Shielding her from possible bullets. Her eyes got wide as she saw Nikodemus reach into his shirt and pull out a stick. It was barely a foot long. The tip started glowing yellow, brighter than the lights strung in the trees. His face in its light was emotionless and focused. He walked past them without looking at them.

Nikodemus hadn't needed the announcement. He could feel Markmor arrive. He went towards him. Realising he had the same problem as in the Stockyards. Anything he threw at him could be deflected into somebody. He spotted Markmor. He was watching the cordon of men marching the Senator towards the house. He put out his hand. He was getting ready to do something. Nikodemus sent a .00 buckshot blast into the tree five feet from Markmor. The rounds passed right in front of him and ripped the bark off the huge tree. It startled Markmor, and he turned his attention away from Senator Rollins. He saw Nikodemus and grinned. Then he noticed the wand, and his face blanched. He started looking around like he was expecting help.

"Who you looking for Markmor?"

Nikodemus had amplified his voice in a way he didn't know he could with the wand. He heard it echo off the hills behind the house. Again Markmor looked around.

"I'm right here. Come on Markmor. Dance with me."

Morgaine's voice in his earpiece.

"I know where he's going when he bolts Nikodemus. Goad him."

Nikodemus made the tip turn red. Then he started speaking demonic. It was gibberish, but it shook the ground. Markmor got a panicked look. He looked around again. At this point, Nikodemus wondered why Leviathan hadn't shown up. Then he went between. Popping purposefully hard like he had done in the Stockyards. He was near the kitchen window, and it cracked. It would have shattered except it was bulletproof. Glasses on tables near him shattered. Then a quieter pop as Morgaine went after him. Nikodemus raised his mic.

"It's over."

Chapter 57

The bright morning sun revealed the biggest bloodstain any of the police, FBI agents, Secret Service agents, and coroners had ever seen at the end of the driveway. Eleven men had been shot there last night. Nine of them were dead. Nobody had realised they were tracking blood all over the place in the dark. Senator Rollins came out of his back door and noticed red shoe prints on every sidewalk and virtually every flat surface that wasn't grass.

"Smith!"

Bone's voice startled everyone. Senator Rollins included. It was a parade ground bellow if there ever was one.

"Get some goddamn water hoses! Look at this shit!"

Agent Smith and Nikodemus were walking out together. They noticed the footprints at the same time.

"On it, sir!"

One of the groundskeepers was already unrolling a hose. Smith walked up to take it from him. The man glared at him.

"You keep your gun fed boy. I'll keep my hose if you don't mind."

He looked over at Agent Bone.

"I and Willy will take care of this up here, sir. You can get the fire department to do the street, though. I've never seen so much blood."

He looked at the Senator.

"You okay, Mr Rollins?"

"Yeah, Bill. I am. Thanks."

Bill nodded and turned on his hose. He started with the porch and soon had red rivulets running down the driveway. Nikodemus was standing next to Agent Bone watching the blood run down the drive when Melissa's voice came over the earpiece.

"Morgaine just arrived. She's waiting in your room."

Bone looked at Nikodemus.

"I'll be in the briefing room."

"Nonsense."

Nikodemus took his arm and pulled him towards the stairs.

"You're the agent in charge. We're debriefing her together."

Bone said nothing as Nikodemus opened the door, and they both walked in. Morgaine is lying fully clothed on the bed between Yvette and Yvonne. Who as usual are wearing only thongs. Yvette and Yvonne are holding her. She appears to be crying. Nikodemus gestures to a chair for Bone. As Bone sits in a chair, Nikodemus sits on the corner of the bed. He reaches out and starts absently running his hand over Yvette's exposed leg.

"Morgaine. What happened?"

She doesn't answer. Nikodemus pulls harder on Yvette dislodging her from Morgaine. He looks at Bone and then at Morgaine. His indication is clear.

"Morgaine. We need to know what happened. Is Markmor neutralised?"

At the sound of Bone's voice. Morgaine sits up. She sniffs once. Looks up at him. Then stands up and undresses as she walks to the bathroom. To his credit, Bone is remaining deadpan. From the bathroom, her voice echoes a little off the tile.

"No, he isn't. I had discovered where his house in the Alps was. I had it dialled in. When I got there, it was dark and smelled like death. I could see the bodies of two women he had taken from I don't know where. It looked like he had left in a hurry."

She came back in totally nude. She jumped over Yvette and in one move pulled the sheets up to cover her and turned so she was facing Bone.

"I looked around for hours. Flies were buzzing on the bodies. I found a lot of...well, let's just say evidence that Markmor and Lydia have been working either with or for Leviathan and Aspekt for a long time."

Nikodemus looked at her keenly at the mention of Aspekt.

"Aspekt? Hmmm."

"Before you killed him. There's no evidence that they've been trying to commune with the dead or anything. It looks like Leviathan took up the mantle Aspekt started."

Nikodemus was looking at Bone now. Bone didn't know what the significance of what she was saying was. But Nikodemus obviously did.

"Okay,"

Nikodemus got up. Bone stood up also.

"We're going to the briefing room. By the way Yvette and Yvonne. Great job last night. Mary and Elizabeth love you two to death."

Yvonne giggled and covered her head in the sheets. Yvette looked up innocently. Something about their demeanour was making him wonder.

"You didn't."

Then Yvette covered her head.

"Shit. Let's go downstairs."

He led Bone out of the room shaking his head. In the hall Bone finally asked.

"What was that about?"

"Nothing. I can't believe how far we tracked blood up to the house last night. That was kind of freaky at first sight."

"Are you changing the subject?"

"Most definitely."

They had reached the briefing room. They went in to find it packed with virtually every Agent plus Greg and his crew. Bone looked around.

"Who's on Rollins?"

Smith was sitting down with coffee.

"Secret Service second shift. They're logged in and verified by Rollins and Mary and Agent Spencer."

Smith indicated the senior Secret Service agent they had been dealing with. Smith looked at Nikodemus.

"Well, did Morgaine get him?"

Nikodemus shook his head in the negative and got a cup of coffee. Spencer and two other Secret Service agents smirked at Nikodemus.

"Mary is asking for you. She and Elizabeth and two of Mary's friends are wondering if you'll go with them to North Park Mall. Have fun."

Nikodemus smiled at them instead of sitting down he threw the coffee in the sink.

"Yeah. Mary and Susan were talking about buying me some clothes. Apparently, they want to see what I look like in a suit."

Without another word, he walked out. Spencer and Smith snorted in unison. Spencer said what they were both thinking.

"Shit. I thought he was going to have to follow them around buying dresses and shit. Carrying their purses. He's probably going to come back with a $10,000 wardrobe."

One of the staff at the Rollins. A Latino man in his late twenties. Obviously gay, rolled his eyes at them.

"Try again boys. That'll be how much they spend on shoes. I'm going with them."

He grinned and walked out the door.

Smith looked up at Bone.

"So you went into the room? Talked to Morgaine? Yvette? Yvonne?"

All the agents got quiet to hear. Greg smiled at him.

"Yes, I went in. Yes, they were naked. Yes. Yes. Now, drop it. What's the usual protocol on Mary and Elizabeth shopping?"

Spencer looked at his companions.

"They have a driver. We usually follow. Four in our car. Two detach and follow. We park near their car. We got that. So…are we out of immediate danger of attack or what?"

Everyone looked at Bone again.

"I believe so yes. Nikodemus seems unconcerned for the moment. We have Morgaine, Yvette, and Yvonne here. Nikodemus will be with Mary and Elizabeth. I'm going home. All my personnel are free to do so."

Then Agent Bone walked out the door. Straight into Morgaine, Yvette, and Yvonne. Yvette took his hand, and they started upstairs. When they got to the room, he hesitated.

"Uh. I was going home you know. Nikodemus is going shopping."

Yvonne opened the door, and they pulled him inside.

"We know. We also know that you're separated from your wife and living in a studio apartment while she is living it up with her boyfriend in your house."

They started pulling his jacket off him. At the mention of his wife, whatever resistance he had melted. They removed his shoulder holster and ankle holster with startling ease. Before he knew it, he was nude. He thought they were taking him to bed but they were pulling him to the bathroom.

"Uh Uh. We're going to bathe you first. Every nook and cranny."

Morgaine's voice was playful. She was down to a bra and panties. Soon Yvette and Yvonne were nude, and Bone was lowering himself into the huge bathtub that was already full. Yvette was already in, and Yvonne was right behind him. Morgaine was still wearing her bra and panties as she sat down at the vanity. She looked in the mirror and addressed Bone as Yvette started soaping up her hands and grinning.

"Hope you don't mind finishing our debriefing while they work Agent Bone. There are some things you need to know."

Chapter 58

Susan Simpson woke up lying on the couch in Gene Terrell's office. She looked at her watch. 7:07 a.m. There was a lot of noise coming through the door. She got up and opened the door. Gene saw her and started towards her.

"Okay, she's awake. Set up the booth."

Gene ushered Susan back into his office. He sat her down on the couch and went behind his desk. He punched the intercom.

"Coffee for Susan and me. Just bring cream and sugar."

Gene smiled and sat down. He waited a moment.

"So this Nikodemus story won't let you alone."

Susan panicked for a second.

"I dropped it, Gene. Just like you told me."

"Relax, I know you did. But, last night. Other stations saw him. That video of yours might end up being the gold you thought it was to begin with."

Susan sat up straighter. Finally.

"First, we're going to have you recount everything you can remember from last night. While it's still fresh. We'll pick it apart for info later. Then."

Gene paused and smiled at her.

"You start putting something together for me. We'll let other stations start it. See what the FBI does. They won't be happy. Then. Well, we'll blow them away."

The coffee arrived. Gene's cup was already sweetened. Susan took hers and put in two sugars and some cream. She sipped it and noticed Gene was looking at her expectantly.

"Right. I'll go to the booth. We'll talk later."

"I'm getting legal involved now. I'll want to talk to you when you're done."

Susan nodded as she went out the door. Everyone was looking at her and making way for her to the booth. She could get used to this.

Chapter 59

Markmor was pushing his luck. The only place he could think to go between to that he could reference was his hotel room at Hotel W. There was a cleaning woman in his room when he stepped between right in front of her. He glamoured her and, because she wasn't very bad looking, used her. Then he blanked her memory and sent her out the door.

Anita was her name. She went downstairs and, when asked, didn't know if she had cleaned room 1808. This was unlike her. The housekeeping manager called the room. Markmor answered. He handled it and hung up. Then he remembered he had stolen a car from the valet right in front of the cameras. He was contemplating this when someone knocked on his door.

Hoping it wasn't the police, he looked out and was relieved to see it was Leviathan. He let him in.

"So, was the plan to have me die last night?"

Leviathan sighed and sat down.

"I was concentrating on the gate attack and didn't notice that two men looking for one of the ladies was almost on me."

"How did they know where she was?"

"One of them said, "Her phone says she's here" I had the damn thing in my pocket, and they called it. It rang. I was glamouring one, and the other pulled a gun, and I barely went between in time. My emergency drop is in Yugoslavia. I couldn't go to Myron's without going back to Fort Worth where two armed men were waiting."

Leviathan got up and went to the little minibar. He rummaged around and got a small bottle of Johnnie Walker Red. He opened it and drank it from the little bottle.

"We're going to need a bigger bottle."

Markmor was irritated.

"That's the least of our problems. I stole a car from downstairs because I wasn't going to come back here. I'm on camera. It's only a matter of time before they send security or the police up here looking for me."

Markmor picked up the remote and turned on the TV. The news was starting, and the lead story was the gunfight at the Senator's fundraiser. Markmor and Leviathan both sat down and listened avidly.

"There was a shootout in the street in south Fort Worth last night. It occurred at 8 p.m. in front of Senator Mike Rollins' house on Maple. He was having his annual fundraiser dinner. Eleven men were shot, and nine men died. One of the victims was a sixteen-year veteran of the Fort Worth Police Department. Two others were FBI agents. All the assailants were killed at the scene. We have few details from the law enforcement agencies involved. However, this doesn't set a good tone for Senator Rollins' campaign. The Senator's office could not be reached for comment."

Leviathan grinned.

"Well, we accomplished something. That wasn't exactly good publicity. Not a good tone at all."

Markmor sat back.

"Nikodemus saw me."

"He knew you were involved anyway. It's nothing new. We'll figure out something."

Chapter 60

Agent Smith, Nikodemus, and Agent Bone rolled up to the vacant laundromat at the same time. There were two police cruisers plus a couple of unmarked police vehicles. Closer to the laundromat was a red Jeep Wrangler with a light bar and just about every off-road modification available.

One of the detectives met them at the yellow tape.

"We think this is related to the Rollins' incident. The owner of the Jeep a…"

The detective looked at his pad.

"Mr Danny Lopez came here the night of the incident because his wife wasn't answering her phone. Apparently, they have the location feature enabled so they can tell where each other is."

He paused. Looked at the three agents. Then continued.

"When he got here with his friend, Mr Joe Martinez, they saw nobody and no vehicles. He called the phone, and it rang in the underbrush. Now, here is where it gets weird. They went towards it and saw a man. Then the next thing they knew he was gone. Mr Lopez had discharged his .357 magnum apparently. However, he had no memory of doing so."

"How did he know he discharged his weapon?"

Bone started towards the group of men behind the building as he asked this.

"The gun was in his hand. The barrel was hot. It smelled like cordite, and one spent casing was in the cylinder."

The four men turned the corner to see one Hispanic man on his knees sobbing. Another was kneeling beside him trying to console him. The bay door to the laundromat was up, and the coroner team was wheeling out a gurney. The coroner van was behind the building. Smith and Nikodemus looked at each other. Then Nikodemus went to stop the coroners.

"Would you mind if I had a look at the body?"

He said this quietly to one of the men. He nodded and started to unzip the body bag. Nikodemus stopped him.

"Just pull down the street. I'll come to look."

The men acknowledged this and proceeded to load the gurney up and drove off. Nikodemus walked around the building as they left. Leaving Bone and Smith with the original group. Smith walked up to the two Hispanic men. As he approached, the one kneeling got up and stopped him.

"Hey, can we give him a minute? He just lost his wife."

"Of course. You were there last night too right?"

The man nodded.

"Do either one of these men look like the guy you saw?"

Bill pulled out his phone and showed the man Markmor and then Leviathan. The man jumped when he saw Leviathan's photo.

"Holy shit! That's him. That's the motherfucker we saw!"

Danny Lopez leapt up with fury in his eyes. He grabbed Agent Smith's phone out of his hand. When he saw the picture, he screamed.

"Yes! Goddammit yes! That's him. Who is he?"

Smith put his phone away and placed his hand on the man's shoulder. Trying to calm him down. It wasn't working. He started pacing like a caged tiger.

"He is a person of interest in another murder in Dallas. We're looking for him now."

"Well, put his goddamn face on TV then! Catch this motha…"

He broke down in sobs. He barely choked out his next sentence.

"Catch the man who took my Anna."

Just then Nikodemus drove back up and came around the building. His barely perceptible nod told Bone all he needed to know. Bone walked into the brush where a telescope was on a tripod. It was being dusted for fingerprints. He walked up and looked through it. It showed the back door of Rollins house. He could see Bill sweeping up leaves on the back patio. It was the door he, Smith, and everybody had gone in and out of repeatedly. Bone indicated to Smith to look through it.

"Son of a bitch. He was right here. Watching us get ready. Watching it all."

Bill panned around.

"He could see the gate too. Shit."

Bill stood up. Nikodemus was looking at Lopez. Lopez was staring like he was in a trance at Nikodemus. Martinez and all the police had stopped and been watching spellbound. Nikodemus voice was soft and neutral as he talked.

"Okay, Danny, you pulled up because you knew her phone was here right?"

"Yes."

Danny's voice was quiet and slow. Danny's friend was walking up to them. Bill stopped him.

"Let him. He'll find out what happened. Don't you want to know?"

"What is he doing? Danny looks like a zombie."

"It's hypnosis. Agent Demus is an expert."

Bone's explanation seemed to satisfy everyone. They watched in amazement as Nikodemus drew information out of the glamoured man.

"Then you called the phone?"

"Yes."

"Where were you? When you called it?"

"Over there. By that tree."

He indicated a spot barely fifteen feet from the telescope.

"What happened?"

"We heard shots from down there."

He indicated towards the Senator's house.

Then I called her phone. It rang. The screen lit up, and I could tell it was in someone's pocket. I could barely see the glow.

"Then what happened?"

Danny squinted. Like he was in pain.

"Then this guy. He looked at me. I started getting the worst headache I'd ever had. I had my pistol in my hand because it was dark and kind of spooky."

"Was he looking at you?"

"Yes. Yes. His eyes seemed too big. Then...all of a sudden the pain stopped. He wasn't looking at me anymore. He was looking at Joe. I raised my gun and fired. But he dropped to the ground."

Nikodemus was looking over near the telescope. You could see the spot when you knew where to look for it.

"What did you see next?"

"There was this pop. I thought he had shot back at first. With a silencer maybe. We ducked behind the tree. Then I realised he wasn't there. We beat the bushes looking for him. Joe thought maybe he had doubled back. You could tell the bay door had been opened recently. He opened it. Nothing. I kept calling her phone."

Danny fell silent. Joe took up the narrative.

"Then we heard crazy-sounding shit down there at the house. Sounded like a riot. We freaked out and booked. After seeing the news, we called the cops and met them down here. They found Anna."

At the mention of her name, Danny burst into tears again. Nikodemus went to the spot where Leviathan had dropped to the ground. Bill came up to see what he was doing. Nikodemus lay down in the spot.

"What are you doing?"

"Anyone who can go between has a panic place locked in. A place they go in emergency. Like when someone is trying to shoot you while you glamour his buddy. Myron could lay here and tell you where he went."

"You're wearing a $3,000 suit that Mary just bought you, and you're lying on the ground in it."

Nikodemus smiled at him and got up.

"He won't be there now, but it would be useful information to have. Relax. They got me like fifteen suits. I don't even like this one that much."

He wiggled his toes in the Italian loafers that exactly matched the colour of the pants. He raised his pant leg to show the socks that blended in so well they looked like they were part of the pants. Bone was observing them.

"Could Morgaine tell?"

Nikodemus walked over to him and raised an eyebrow.

"I don't know Agent Bone. I guess you could ask her or Yvette or Yvonne?"

Bone smiled and walked to his car. Smith looked confused.

"What do you mean?"

Bone smiled again as he closed the door to his car and drove away. Smith looked at Nikodemus.

"Are you telling me…?"

"I'm telling you nothing of the kind. I'm hungry. Let's eat."

They pulled out onto the road just as Bone's car disappeared around a bend in the road. Nikodemus pulled out his phone. He dialled and put it to his ear.

"Hey, we need to talk. How about you, Bill and I go to lunch? Really? Fine, we'll meet at the Senator's house. I need to change anyway."

"You're trying to get me to go to lunch with the boss? Why?"

"Just go to the Senator's house."

Bill snorted in derision and stayed off the freeway. Following Bone under and to the left into the Senator's neighbourhood. He parked next to Bone just as Bone got out and went into the house without looking at them. Inside Bone was disappearing up the stairs. Nikodemus picked up the pace and caught him outside the door to the room Nikodemus stayed in.

"Why here Bone?"

"She needs to tell you."

Without another word, he entered followed by Nikodemus and Bill. Morgaine was alone in the room. Sitting at the small table. Apparently, waiting for them. Bone said nothing as he sat down. Morgaine was looking at Nikodemus her tone was serious.

"I want you to look at this picture of Leviathan."

She took Bone's phone from him that the picture was loaded on. Nikodemus looked at it.

"Yeah. And…?"

"He doesn't look familiar at all?"

Nikodemus concentrated on it.

"No, should it?"

Bone took up the narrative.

"Nikodemus, we have an imaging app that will remove facial hair to show what someone might look like shaven if they have a beard."

Bone swiped a couple of times on his phone and brought up another picture. It showed Leviathan with no facial hair. Nikodemus looked at it. Bill saw it too.

"Shit, Nikodemus. That looks like you."

Nikodemus' suddenly inhaled and started to almost hyperventilate.

"Oh my god. Oh my god."

He looked at Morgaine. She said nothing. Only nodded. Nikodemus stood up and went to the window.

"That's my brother's body. That sack of shit is still wearing it. How did you find out?"

"When I was at Markmor's abandoned house, I found some items that I didn't understand. They were scrolls. Written in that cryptic whatever it is that Necromancer's use for spells and stuff. I took it to my father. He told me. He said he'd known for a while. He didn't know how to broach the subject with you."

"Does this mean my brother is dead? Or is he in some other body?"

"He doesn't know for sure. The only one who would know is Leviathan or Aspekt."

"I'm going to talk to Myron. I'm guessing he would have known that before I decided."

"But…"

She was interrupted as Nikodemus went between and was gone.

Bill sighed and went through the bathroom into his room.

"This isn't going to be good."

Nobody replied to his comment.

Chapter 61

"Why didn't you tell me about Leviathan?"

Myron was sitting in his chair near Ethan's statue when Nikodemus stepped between into his castle. Nikodemus question, uttered as soon as he stepped onto the dais, wasn't unexpected. Indeed is anything unexpected to a Prescient? Myron said nothing for a moment. Then just as Nikodemus was about to repeat his question.

"What purpose would it have served, hmm?"

Myron turned until he was looking at Nikodemus. All his pent-up emotion drained out of him as he saw the weariness in Myron's eyes. He was sitting next to his brother's form. Which was as unreachable as his own brother at the moment.

"Is Roger dead? Is he in another body somewhere?"

"I'm not a Necromancer, Seeker. I don't know. Right now, I'm just trying to keep Leviathan and my son from destroying the world as we know it."

Nikodemus pulled a chair from the table and sat down near Myron.

"What exactly is the Senator going to do that is so life-changing?"

Myron scowled a moment. Then turned a gaze on Nikodemus that made him remember why so many people were afraid of the Mage.

"It's what he isn't going to do. He won't be easily baited by criticisms and insults. A hothead in the oval office can destroy the world with a button. Every possible future without him involves nuclear destruction of this plane. You and I and others with our abilities can escape this, but billions cannot."

Myron looked at his brother's statue again.

"I had hoped to make Markmor see the consequences of his actions. Now, after the debacle at the Senator's house. I realise I cannot."

Myron sighed and closed his eyes.

"Kill him, Seeker. Before you ask, Leviathan's refuge is in the mountains of Yugoslavia."

Myron handed Nikodemus a stone. It was small, but Nikodemus felt a jolt as he touched it.

"Now you know where. Here is Markmor's."

Another stone, another jolt.

"I am releasing Agent Bone's amulet. Morgaine will guard him now."

Myron looked relaxed a little as he said this. Reducing a load by one third obviously making his duties easier.

"Markmor and Leviathan are at the Hotel W in Dallas. Markmor stole an automobile there yesterday. They'll find it near the Senator's house. Get your friends on that legal aspect as a reason to find him. Leviathan is not your brother. He is wearing your brother's body. Like a stolen uniform. Don't let him convince you otherwise. Kill him on sight."

Then Myron went between, and the werelight in the torches died. Nikodemus was sitting in an abandoned castle. He got up and stepped between back to the Senator's house. Yvette and Yvonne were waiting for him. Morgaine and Bone were nowhere to be found.

"I guess Agent Bone and Morgaine are an item now."

"Yeah."

Their voices were so similar that Nikodemus couldn't tell who said what.

"So. I don't care."

Yvette and Yvonne came over and started running their hands over him. He soon forgot what he was going to say.

Chapter 62

Billy Rainwater had been head of security for Hotel W in Dallas for nine years. He was an ex-Marine, ex-Cop, and had two ex-wives. He had Donny Martinez in front of his desk. Donny was a parking attendant. He had no memory or excuse for that matter, as to why he turned over the white Lexus to some red-haired skinny guy. Watching it on camera didn't jog his memory.

"Mr Rainwater, I don't know what to say. I don't know that dude. I'm not getting money from a chop shop or whatever."

Danny stopped for a minute, looking at the video. It was on a loop.

"Hey, I did see that dude walking to the elevator. He's a guest."

"You're sure."

"I'm not sure of anything except I swear I didn't give that guy's car away on purpose. The skinny dude looks familiar, though."

"Okay. Go back to work. Don't give any more cars away."

Billy was debating on how to handle the situation when his intercom buzzed.

"Mr Rainwater, Dallas Police Department on line two. They're asking about a stolen car. Asking if we have video."

Well, that's how he'd handle it.

"Rainwater here. Yes, sir. I have a video of a man taking a white 2017 Lexus from one of our valets."

He paused listening.

"I'd be happy to give you a copy. Give me an email address."

Billy wrote it down.

"It'll be on the way in five minutes. Always a pleasure to help."

Billy hung up. He turned around and looked at the monitors that showed every entrance, parking garage, and a few other locations on a changing slide show over fifteen monitors. He was about to look away when he saw the guy in the video getting in elevator four with a bearded man. He picked up his radio.

"Nick."

"This is Nick, go."

"I need personnel on elevator four ground level ASAP. I'll meet you there."

"I'm there now. Me and Mikey."

"Looking for a skinny red-haired guy. Hold him till I get there."

"Will do."

Billy ran out of his office. He slowed to a walk once he reached the hallway. He nodded to guests as he headed to the elevators. He picked up his radio.

"Nick, talk to me."

Nothing. No answer.

"Nick, status."

Nothing. Billy was worried now. He ran the last fifty feet to the south bank of elevators. He saw Nick and Mikey standing against the wall staring straight ahead. The red-haired guy was saying something, and he was grinning like he was having fun. The dark-haired bearded guy was watching. He noticed Billy and nudged the red-haired guy. Then Billy felt something he hadn't felt since he lived on the reservation in Oklahoma. He was a full-blood Comanche, and their medicine man had once, in a ritual, called him to dance. It felt like that. He brushed it off and kept coming at them. He looked at Nick, and he looked like he was a zombie. Staring straight ahead, drooling.

Markmor didn't know what was wrong, but the huge guy that was almost on him had ignored the glamour. It had never happened ever except on Nikodemus. Leviathan stepped back as he got to him. Then the man's fist was so big in his vision he couldn't see anything else. Then everything went dark.

Billy walked up and punched the red-haired guy in the forehead with everything he had. The guy's eyes crossed, and he fell hard enough that he bounced. At the same time, Nick and Mikey came out of whatever was wrong with them. But Billy knew what was wrong. He looked at the bearded guy.

"Who are you?"

The guy stared at him a minute. Billy felt it again. He got up in the guy's face.

"You try that again, and I'll bounce your head off of shit until you stop."

The guy paled.

"I'm sure I don't know what you're referring to, sir. I'll just be on my way."

He darted left and out the exit door. Billy started to go after him and then stopped. Nick and Mikey were holding their heads and groaning.

"Shit Billy, I got the worst headache I've ever had."

"Me too."

Mikey was leaning against the wall. Billy looked at him, and his left ear was bleeding. Two more security guys showed up.

"Scott, take these two to the infirmary. Franklin, help me get this sack of shit to my office."

They ended up putting Markmor on a bellhop cart and wheeled him to Billy's office. Billy went around his desk and found the cop's number that had called him.

"Hey, this is Rainwater with the Hotel W. I've got your car thief in my office."

Billy paused listening.

"He resisted and I knocked him out. He's unconscious."

Agent Smith and Nikodemus were sitting at Sergeant Wilson's desk when he took the call. Smith notified Bone while Nikodemus got them hooked in with the officers going to Hotel W.

Fifteen minutes later a squad car, an unmarked detective car, and the FBI Challenger pulled in front of Hotel W. They were expected, and the valet had set an area by the front door that they could leave the cars. A guy was in the lobby waiting for them.

"Hello, I'm Tony Franklin. Mr Rainwater said to take you directly to his office."

Smith showed his FBI badge; Nikodemus had his hung in the jacket pocket of yet another expensive-looking greyish blue suit. He never wore ties, but the shirt was obviously purchased to be worn with it. Several women they walked by smiled at him admiringly. They entered Rainwater's office. Markmor was still unconscious. Slumped in a chair. One wrist was handcuffed to it. Smith went over to look at him closely. Until now he'd only seen glimpses of him. Rainwater's eyes got wide as he focused on Nikodemus' badge.

"Holy shit. FBI? Ya'll are here about a stolen car?"

Nikodemus was looking at Billy closely.

"No, we're here for him. How did you subdue him?"

Billy looked at Markmor and then back at Nikodemus.

"I came up on him, and he had two of my guys kind of... I don't know. In a trance against the wall. He saw me, and he tried... Well, anyway, I punched him out. The guy with him..."

Nikodemus finished for him.

"He tried to glamour you too, didn't he?"

Billy looked at him.

201

"Glamour?"

"The guy there is named Markmor. One word. You said two of your guys were in a trance. He tried to do it to you, didn't he? And you... Wait a minute. Rainwater. You're American Indian, aren't you?"

Billy stiffened.

"Yeah, you got a problem with that?"

Nikodemus laughed.

"Hell no. I don't have a problem with that! Bill!"

Bill turned back to Nikodemus who looked back over to Billy, smiling.

"You'd felt that before, hadn't you? When you were a kid maybe? From a medicine man."

Billy stood up dumbfounded.

"How the fuck would you know that? Who are you?"

Nikodemus didn't answer him. He turned to Bill.

"Bill, a full-blood American Indian can't be glamoured. If they went through an "ordeal," they can't. I can't believe I didn't think of this before. You."

He turned to Rainwater.

"Are a priceless asset at this point. You said the other guy. Did he have long hair and a beard?"

"Yeah. He tried to glamour me too. I told him if he tried it again I'd bounce his head off of shit until he stopped. He ran out the exit door."

"Bill, we need to make sure that Markmor stays unconscious. Mr Rainwater, what's your first name?"

"Billy."

"Billy. Bill"

He turned to Agent Smith.

"We need this guy. I need this guy."

Nikodemus looked at Billy and smiled.

"That guy who got away. He's killed two women that we know of by glamouring them to death. I want him."

Smith was on the phone. He hung up.

"Medic is on the way with something to keep him under. What do we do if he wakes up?"

Nikodemus looked at Markmor and then at Bill.

"Shoot him in the head."

Billy said nothing. He just stared at Markmor. Smith drew his weapon and sat where he was facing Markmor.

"Okay. So…in the meantime?"

"In the meantime, I'm taking Rainwater here to FBI and get him credentialed. I didn't actually hear you say you'd come but…"

Rainwater was dialling a number.

"Henry, I've got an emergency, and I've got to leave now. I don't know when I'll get back. You're head of security until further notice."

He hung up. They went out the door where the policemen and detectives were waiting.

"There's a medic from FBI headed here. Get them in there as soon as possible."

Nikodemus went up to the detective and pulled him aside. Quietly in his ear, he whispered.

"Agent Smith has orders to shoot that guy in there in the head if he wakes up before the medic gets here to put him under."

The detective looked at Nikodemus. Then nodded. He'd been on this since the Stockyards.

"Understood."

"Let's hope they get here before that happens."

Nikodemus turned to Billy.

"You got a car here?"

"Yep."

"What is it?"

One of the bellboys heard the question and answered for him.

"It's the baddest black-on-black 85 Ford Bronco on the road that's what he's got. Lifted, headers, dual exhaust…"

He obviously could have gone on for longer.

"It's a Bronco. Come on."

Billy handed a key ring to the bellboy. Then his radio.

"Henry's taking over security for a while. Give him these. I'll get back to you when I can. Thanks, Jimmy. Oh…have him check on Nick and Mikey. They're in the infirmary."

"You're getting arrested, Mr Rainwater?"

"Shit no; he just got drafted."

Billy waved over his shoulder as they went out the door to the Security Chief parking place barely thirty feet away. The Bronco was gleaming black. If black can be gleaming. Headlight covers light bar covers, everything was black. Billy pushed the unlock button and blue halos flashed around the headlights. Step rails lowered on hydraulics and then lifted the two men up to get in.

"Fuck yeah. Billy. So I'm Nikodemus. I can do that magic shit too. In fact, let me start by giving you one of these."

Nikodemus produced a Colt Peacemaker from his cabinet. Billy's eyes got wide as he took the gun. He looked it over.

"This is…it is. An original Peacemaker. I can't fire this. It's priceless."

Nikodemus pulled another one out and laid it on the console.

"Check the serial numbers."

Billy did.

"They're the same. How can they be the same?"

"Like I said I can do that magic shit. I can't give you any ammo, but I can hand you another loaded one over and over. You need to get a gun belt or something. You know where the Fort Worth FBI office is?"

Billy nodded.

"Get us there. We got work to do."

The engine purred to life. Nikodemus nodded.

"On second thought, go to Maple Street off 35. Senator Rollins' house. He's the centre of this thing. I'll get the agent in charge to meet us there."

The Bronco accelerated smoothly up the entrance ramp and merged into the early evening traffic seamlessly. Neither noticed Leviathan watching them from the shadows of an office building across the street. He didn't look happy. He looked back at the hotel. Then he started walking back towards it.

Chapter 63

Myron's amulets were almost like an appendage. Morgaine now had possession (if that's the right word) of Agent Bone's. Cutting the load by one third had greatly eased Myron's efforts. The amulet that Agent Smith was carrying pulsed. Letting Myron know that something was happening, Myron concentrated on it. Something was getting nearer to the amulet. Something bad. Myron wasn't sure what it was, but Smith needed alerting. Myron still hadn't got a cell phone. Even though Morgaine and Ethan had been trying to get him to start. So he used the only method available. He sent a warning pulse to Smith's amulet.

Agent Smith was sitting with his gun in his hand watching Markmor. He'd just hung up with the medic. At least ten more minutes, maybe more. Then he felt a vibration. Like a phone on silent. But he had his phone in his hand. Then he realised it was the amulet.

"Shit! Shit!"

Unsure of what to do, he called Nikodemus. He answered on the first ring.

"Did you shoot him?"

"No, but the amulet. It's vibrating."

In the Bronco, travelling at almost eighty miles an hour Nikodemus was almost to the Senator's house.

"Okay, it's warning you. Somebody's coming. It's probably Leviathan."

Nikodemus paused for a minute. Billy was slowing down.

"You want me to go back?"

"No, we're too far to get there in time. Bill."

"Yes."

"Shoot him, now. Then get the hell out of there. It's the only thing I can think of for you to do."

Bill sat there a minute. Markmor wasn't moving.

"Look, I think Markmor is in a coma or something. He might never wake up."

Nikodemus voice was slower and more precise.

"Bill, I know that shooting an unconscious man in the head goes against everything you know. But, this is different. You know it is. He's an active threat to the United States Senator we're guarding. Kill that son of a bitch now!"

Leviathan tried the door he had exited the hotel from and found it only opened from the inside. As he went around to the front, an FBI Challenger came screeching into the circular drive with strobes on. He reached the car just as the two men got out. They looked at him, and their eyes glazed over. Leviathan smiled.

"Lead the way gentlemen"

The two men started walking into the hotel with Leviathan in tow.

Myron could feel the threat getting closer to the amulet. Having no way to communicate with the carrier, he opted to shield the carrier. This meant no defensive striking back. Just an impenetrable shield. Since he didn't know exactly what the situation was, it seemed the prudent choice.

Bill was agonising over whether or not to shoot Markmor when the door opened. Bill could tell the men were glamoured by the look in their eyes. Then he felt the shield go up. He could see it. Like he was in a bubble. Sounds were distorted. The two FBI agents drew their weapons and fired at Bill. Spurred by Leviathan. The rounds bounced off the shield upwards. Bill still had his gun but was unsure if he fired inside the bubble if it would bounce around in it.

Both men emptied their guns at Bill. To no effect. Leviathan pushed them aside and glared at Bill. He was obviously furious. He shook his head and then walked over to Markmor. He put his hand on him, and they both went between. As soon as they were gone, the two FBI agents in the room snapped out of their glamour. They both seemed surprised they had their weapons in their hands. They could smell cordite. The actions were both locked open from when they fired the last round in their magazine.

The shield went down as Myron detected that the threat was no longer in proximity to the amulet. Bill then noticed he was still holding his phone. Nikodemus was still on the line. He put it to his ear.

"Jeez Bill, you didn't have to empty your gun into him."

Bill looked at the empty chair that Markmor had been sitting in.

"I didn't. Leviathan walked in with two glamoured agents. A shield went up around me. Their bullets bounced off it. I didn't know if I could fire from inside the thing. Leviathan took him. They went between."

In the Bronco, Nikodemus ended the call. He tried to open the window on his side, but it was locked.

"Billy, can you unlock the window?"

Billy unlocked it, and Nikodemus rolled it down.

"Goddammit!"

Nikodemus screamed out the window. Then he rolled it back up.

"Thanks. Turn into that driveway. There's an intercom by the gate; just pull up to it."

Billy pulled in.

"So what happened?"

"Bill let him get away. That's what happened. We should have killed him before we left."

Billy had pushed the call button. Nikodemus recognised Steve Spencer's voice.

"May I help you?"

"Steve, it's Nikodemus. I've got some help. Log this vehicle in as staff."

The gate opened without a reply. The grounds around the house showed clean walkways with beautifully trimmed hedges. All lit from recessed spotlights in the ground. Hard to tell that bloody footprints had covered most of the walkways a day ago.

"Pull up and to the left. Then park next to…there, to the right of that Crown Vic."

Billy pulled in and killed the engine. Three Secret Service agents came out and were admiring the vehicle. Billy and Nikodemus got out and were lowered by the hydraulic step rails. Steve grinned at Nikodemus, then addressed Billy.

"What is it, an '87?"

"'85."

"Cool as hell. So what's up, Nick?"

Nikodemus walked up to Steve and presented Billy.

"This is Billy Rainwater. He is head of security for Hotel W. They had a run-in with Markmor and Leviathan. And I had forgotten something important. Full-blood American Indians can't be glamoured. Markmor tried, and he punched his lights out."

Steve whistled.

"No, shit. You got him?"

Nikodemus sighed and shook his head.

"Long story, but no. We need to set Billy up next to me in the house."

Then something occurred to Nikodemus.

"Billy, I never asked you if you're married. Girlfriend? Obligations? You just stepped up when I needed you. What's your situation?"

It was Billy's turn to sigh.

"Well, the divorce was final from my second marriage two months ago. She put my stuff in storage. I've been staying at the hotel for a little over a month."

Mary Rollins had come out along with Elizabeth. She heard Billy's statement. She walked up and slipped an arm through Nikodemus' arm.

"Well, Billy, is it?"

"Yes, ma'am."

"I'm Mary Rollins, and this is my daughter Elizabeth."

Billy smiled at Elizabeth and then returned his attention to Mary.

"I want you to make yourself at home with us."

Billy was embarrassed.

"Ma'am, thank you, but my problems aren't your res…"

Mary interrupted him, "Nonsense! Nikodemus says he needs you; then you're staying here. We've only got fourteen bedrooms I think we can squeeze you in… Rosa!"

Mary raised her voice and turned towards the house. A Mexican woman came out the kitchen door.

"Yes?"

"Have Mr Rainwater set up in the bedroom next to Nikodemus. We'll move Agent Smith across the hall."

Rosa was staring at Billy, and he was staring back. Mary and Nikodemus noticed it before Rosa spoke.

"Billy? Billy Rainwater? Oh my god!"

She ran over to Billy who welcomed her into his arms.

"My God Rosa, you look fantastic."

She pulled back. Tears were in her eyes. Billy was tearing up too. Everyone else was dumbfounded.

"Rosa and I went to school together. Her father didn't approve of me. They were military. One day, she was gone. I was seventeen. I never stopped loving you, Rosa."

Rosa burst into tears again. Mary and Elizabeth were starting to tear up just watching.

208

Nikodemus nudged Mary.

"Careful, I think ole Steve is gonna cry."

Steve laughed.

"Whatever. Well, I guess… We're going to go back inside."

Then everyone walked in one door or another, leaving Billy and Rosa to talk alone. Nikodemus went into the kitchen with Mary and Elizabeth. Elizabeth ran over and watched them through the window.

"Mom, that's the most romantic thing I've ever seen in my life. Did you see the way Rosa lit up?"

Elizabeth turned back to look at her mother. Tears were still running down her face.

"Mom?"

Then Elizabeth ran out and up the stairs towards her room. Mary sat down at the table and beckoned Nikodemus to sit with her.

"Rosa's mother died last year. She was the only family Rosa had. She's been listless. Elizabeth is right. She lit up. Mr Rainwater certainly is a big strapping man. Can't have enough of those around here."

She looked at him seriously.

"I heard you say something like 'he can't be glamoured'."

"Yes, a full-blood American Indian can't be. I'd forgotten that because I never encounter any."

Nikodemus leaned forward.

"Markmor tried to glamour him, and he punched his lights out. Leviathan tried to glamour him, and he got in his face and told him he'd bounce his head off of shit if he tried that again. Leviathan ran away in terror."

Mary nodded knowingly.

"Handy guy to have around."

"Yes, he is. Mary, to be honest, I didn't have any real strategy until now. We've been reacting. Now, I do. Billy and I are going to take down Leviathan. He's the real threat. Markmor's been kind of working for him."

Just then Rosa and Billy came in. They were holding hands. Rosa was smiling so big she seemed like another person.

"Mary, I'm going to show Billy around. If it's okay, I'm going to let Lucy finish dinner."

Mary's eyes were smiling as she answered.

"Are you going to show him your room?"

Rosa blushed. Billy started looking away.

"Uh no. Uh…"

Mary got up and hugged Rosa. Then she hugged Billy.

"Rosa, you can take him anywhere you want. He can stay in your room with you if you want. I'm just so glad to see you smile again. Billy, you are a godsend, even if you don't know it."

She looked over towards the cooking area.

"Lucy? When's dinner?"

She turned back to Rosa, but they were already gone.

Chapter 64

Having two forty-calibre automatics empty their magazines in the security office didn't go unnoticed by the occupants of the hotel. Leviathan had gotten them past the detectives and two patrolmen with a momentary glamour. Then it sounded like World War III when the door to the office closed.

Detective Larry Allogio drew his weapon and entered the office. He found Markmor's chair vacant. The two agents were looking at their guns like they didn't know what they were. Agent Smith was on the phone for a moment and then hung up. He sat down.

"Shit."

Allogio went back out into the hall and closed the door.

"Clear! It's over! You!"

He looked at the closest uniformed officer.

"Tape this off. I'm calling it in."

An hour later, all the shell casings had been collected. The shots had all ricocheted up into, thankfully, a concrete stairwell brace. Smith was still sitting where he had when he hung up. He was looking at the chair with a handcuff still attached to the arm. Agent Bone was in there with him.

"To tell you the truth, I couldn't have shot an unconscious man in the head either. You didn't do anything wrong."

"Tell that to Nikodemus. He hung up on me when I told him."

Bone sat down on the edge of the desk.

"He's not your superior. If anything he's like a junior agent. I'm your superior, and I'm telling you that you did what you were supposed to do. What you were trained to do. We're not even going to file it as a shooting incident. I don't want to start a glamoured shooting file."

Bone got up.

"Come on. Let's go."

Leviathan had first taken him to his emergency place in Yugoslavia. He felt that Myron might be able to find it, though. So he took them to Aspekt's house. It was in Romania. The servants had been dismissed a month before. Residual fear of Aspekt kept looters away. It was an old estate on almost one hundred acres. The woods covering virtually all of it came up to within forty feet of the two-storey house. Aspekt had installed modern conveniences including a generator. Leviathan had it liveable in less than an hour.

Markmor hadn't so much as stirred throughout all of this. Leviathan dug around and found a first aid kit. He took out one of the tubes of smelling salts. He cracked one and put it under Markmor's nose. Not even a twitch.

"Markmor! Wake up!"

Leviathan's yell echoed through the empty house. Leviathan began to wonder exactly how hard the Indian had hit him. He could recall vividly the big man getting right up in his face with no fear whatsoever. It had been Leviathan who was afraid. Not a situation that he was used to. Not at all. Leviathan sat in Aspekt's old chair and cleared his mind. He prepared to commune with Aspekt.

He looked on darkness. Swirls of smoke and then Aspekt's silhouette drew near him. Leviathan spoke the traditional greeting.

"Master."

Aspekt's silhouette moved closer to him than it had ever been. Leviathan felt a momentary twinge of fear.

"You failed."

Leviathan had expected this.

"Markmor failed us."

Aspekt's silhouette was so close Leviathan was looking through it. Aspekt's voice was vibrating through his bones.

"You failed. You were not paying attention to details. Cell phone in your pocket. Two ordinary men? How could they best you?"

Leviathan realised his mistake. Why was he trying to lie to his Mentor?

"You are right as always, Master. It was my fault. Their timing couldn't have been worse for the situation, though. They pulled up just as…"

"I know what happened!"

Aspekt interrupted him with a bellow that was almost painful. Even in his ethereal form, Leviathan winced. Leviathan said nothing for a minute. Aspekt whirled around first right next to him then so far he thought that he had departed. Finally, Aspekt drew to the customary distance for their conversations.

"Master, I fear Markmor will never awaken. Can you tell me anything about his condition?"

"He hasn't crossed over. He sleeps the sleep of what the doctors call a coma. He may awaken soon. In a year. Or never. His body must be cared for if he is to live. A nurse is needed. Maybe even a doctor. In my study amongst the scrolls, you will find an address book. Find Doctor Gary Ozier. He can be trusted. Pay whatever he asks, and it will be taken care of."

Aspekt started to depart.

"Master! What of the Senator?"

"You must wait. He is now guarded by a seeker, Mages, and an Untouchable. If you can awaken Markmor, then we will discuss further moves regarding the Senator. You were right to leave your house. Myron knows of it. He doesn't know that Ethan is dead. Lydia is poised to enter his body if Myron decides to awaken him."

Aspekt's form started getting farther away. Right before he disappeared he spoke once more.

"You must wait."

Chapter 65

At Nikodemus' urging, Billy parked his Bronco in the loading zone in front of the entrance to the Fort Worth FBI building. They waited inside it until Bill came out the front door. Nikodemus rolled his window down.

"Hey, Bill. Where should he park this thing?"

Bill was admiring the vehicle. He looked up.

"Beat's me. It looks too tall to get in the parking garage. I guess just leave it there for a minute."

"Hang on a minute. There's a parking place over there."

Billy was pointing across the street half a block down. Without waiting for a reply, he pulled out, made a U-turn, and parked. He and Nikodemus walked into the FBI building to find Bill waiting inside.

"Hello again, Billy."

Bill stuck out his hand.

"Follow me."

He led them to the elevators. They went up to the conference room floor. They walked into Conference Room 1.

"Bill, I'm getting tired of this room. Think about it. My first…uh…interview The meeting with Greg and Charlie. Plus the whole table incident."

Billy looked at Nikodemus quizzically.

"Don't ask."

Nikodemus smiled as he said this.

"Just kidding. I guess it's my room, huh?"

The door opened and Agent Bone along with Deputy Director Glenn walked in. Bone stuck out his hand. He had a folder in the other.

"Mr Rainwater, I'm Agent Charles Bone. This is Deputy Director John Glenn. We've been going over your background. Given your previous law enforcement and military experience and your unique 'abilities,' we'd like you to assist us."

Bone and Glenn had sat down. Bill gestured for Nikodemus and Billy to do the same.

"Nikodemus, Bill mentioned Billy's 'immune' to glamouring. Would you care to elaborate on that?"

Nikodemus leaned back and seemed to be trying to recall something. He was looking at the ceiling; then he looked at Bone.

"I can't exactly remember when this happened, but." He paused.

"I guess it doesn't matter when. Anyway. I was involved in finding an abducted woman. We were in Montana I think. I ended up on an Indian Reservation. I think they were Cheyenne. Then we ended up on the Crow Reservation. I was with a Mage. I was his Protector."

Billy was listening intently. He looked like he was going to say something. Then he didn't. Nikodemus, noticed.

"You wanted to say something Billy?"

"Cheyenne hate the Crow. In case you didn't know. Everybody hates the Crow. Go on."

"Hmmm. I didn't realise that. Anyway we get to where she's being held. They shoot at us. I shield us. The Mage wouldn't let me shoot back. Then he tried to glamour the guy in charge of the squad in front of us. The guy tossed it off and laughed. They all laughed. Then he said, 'Every one of us learned from a medicine man when we were kids how to keep you out of our heads, Shaman'."

Nikodemus looked at Billy.

"Old Maximillian didn't like it when they called him a shaman. I could tell he was pissed. I had just kind of perfected speaking kind of half-assed demonic. It shook the ground when I did it. So I did this, and it scared the shit out of them. Then I projected out of phase and got right in their faces before I flipped back. The guy freaked out and gave her to us."

Bone looked over at Nikodemus.

"Is that what you did that time that it felt like a bomb going off in here?"

Nikodemus grinned sheepishly.

"Yeah, but in my defence, Glenn was really pissing me off."

Glenn chuckled at this. He had come to look back on the days before he knew about all this magic stuff with nostalgia.

"You know, Bone, gone are the days when I could just have four guys haul anybody I liked into a cell. Thanks, Nick."

He was grinning and everybody laughed.

"I asked Maximillian later why the glamour didn't hold and he said that American Indians that are full blood are immune to glamour. He said, 'The great spirit protects them.'"

Billy was nodding.

"When I was a boy. Our medicine man performed a ritual. All boys that were twelve years old went through it. It's called 'ordeal.' He gets in your head. He introduces you to the great spirit. You earn your spirit name."

He stopped. Everybody was waiting to hear his spirit name.

"He won't tell you his spirit name, by the way. Keeping it secret is what protects him."

Billy looked at Nikodemus.

"Right, you seem to know a lot."

"Well, I have a little Indian blood in me. Nowhere near enough to be like you. After that incident, I did some research."

Nikodemus then addressed Bone and Glenn.

"In case you're thinking this. To be immune, the person must be full blooded. Mother and father both full blooded. Plus, he had to grow up on a reservation. If a medicine man didn't put him through "ordeal" at twelve years old, he isn't immune."

Bone then addressed Billy.

"Mr Rainwater."

"Please call me Billy."

"Very well, Billy. Could you tell us, with as much detail as you can remember, about your encounter at the hotel with Markmor and Leviathan?"

"Of course. You know about the stolen car. I had just looked at his picture on camera when I saw him on security feed in an elevator with a bearded guy. This guy Leviathan. I send two guys to meet the elevator, and I head towards it. Shortly after I dispatch them, my guys aren't answering the radio."

Billy paused and stretched out his legs.

"So I start running. I find my guys standing against the wall, in a daze. One has blood running out his ear. Then I feel it. The little guy. It's kind of like somebody is groping you. Inside. It pissed me off, along with my guy bleeding. I punched him hard, right in the forehead."

Billy made a fist. He was a big guy. His fist looked like a brick. Smith nodded smiling.

"I've hit guys bigger than him like that, and they were out for a day and a night. He might be dead or in a coma. Then the other guy Leviathan tried it. I got in his face and told him I'd bounce his head off of shit until he stopped if he tried it again. He ran out the door. I was going to go after him, but my guys were on the ground holding their heads. I was concerned about them. I didn't realise what that dude was, or I'd have clocked his sorry ass too."

Bill took up the narrative.

"I'm guessing he ran to somewhere nearby and watched you two drive away. Then he came back. He glamoured the medic and the Agent with him. If I hadn't had Myron's amulet, they would have smoked me. Leviathan was pissed off looking at me. He didn't try to test it, though. He took Markmor. He was still unconscious."

Nobody said anything for a minute while they digested this. Glenn was looking at Nikodemus.

"So, now what Nick?"

Nikodemus looked over at Billy. Then back at Glenn.

"Myron gave me the location of Leviathan's house and Markmor's. Morgaine already went to Markmor's so I don't see any reason to go there. I don't know if I ever mentioned it, but going between has a cost associated with it. I need to get more…well, let's just call them credits in my account. I'm going to leave Billy here with you while I do it. I'll be back probably tomorrow. Billy is set up at Rollins' house."

He grinned at Billy.

"More than set up. His long-lost love is working there. They love him already. Anyway…"

He stood up and went between. Billy jumped a little.

"Holy crap! What the hell was that?"

Bill smiled at him.

"That's how you're going to be travelling buddy. Let's get you processed. Shall we?"

Chapter 66

Myron was seated in his chair looking at his brother's statue. Funny how he didn't even think of him as Ethan anymore. It was Ethan's statue. If the world only knew, how many of the ancient statues in museums and castles were real people that had been turned to stone. Creatures too. Myron sighed and looked towards the dais.

Nikodemus stepped between to find Myron looking right at him.

"You need energy, eh Seeker?"

"Well, yes. I can go mine it. Or, since most of it has been expended at your behest..."

Myron smiled.

"You're right. It has. Tell me, Seeker. When you mine your energy. Do you feel guilty about how you take it?"

Nikodemus looked away. He walked over, gazing at Ethan.

"No. I don't. It is what it is. It's not like I'm doing it and going on vacations or something. I don't make for entertainment. I'm a Protector. Protecting this plane. So..."

Myron reached out. Filling his cabinet. Nikodemus could feel it as it swelled.

"Leviathan has moved. I can't tell where. I think Markmor is still unconscious."

"Really? It's been over a day. Is he dying? How can you tell all this but not be able to tell where he is?"

Myron smiled and went to get a drink. He rummaged around and found the old dusty bottle that isn't always there. He pulled it out and poured two tumblers half full of the sparkling liquid. He offered one to Nikodemus who looked at it curiously. It sparkled and moved of its own volition.

"Is this stuff alive? What is it?"

Myron looked at his drink. His eyes lit up as he watched the sparkles dance within it. He smiled and took a sip. Nikodemus did the same. It tasted like cold fire. Nikodemus could feel it permeate his body. It wasn't unpleasant. He finished his at the same time Myron did.

"That stuff is incredible. Can I have another?"

Myron looked in the cabinet and shook his head.

"Seeker, this is an ancient bottle of Elixir. My great-great-grandfather traded a live dragon for it. I'd give you another drink, but sometimes the bottle isn't there."

"What do you mean?"

Nikodemus looked around in the liquor cabinet. Then back at Myron. Myron was looking at Ethan's statue.

"I mean, sometimes, it isn't there."

Chapter 67

Dr Ozier had thought he was done with being summoned to the creepy old house in the woods. Nobody had heard from Mr Pekt in a while. Then the phone calls out of the blue. Mr Athan had turned out to be almost as creepy as Mr Pekt. Mr Athan had paid in cash for an ambulance to take Mr Moore to the hospital for imaging. Mr Athan had tried to avoid this, but some things can't be done at home.

"There is some swelling of the brain around the point of trauma."

Dr Ozier was reading from the radiologist report.

"We've admitted him. You have no identification for him? Insurance?"

Leviathan was uncomfortable being in the hospital. It was easier since it was in Romania. Nobody was looking for them here.

"No, but I can leave a $20,000 prepayment if that will help."

Dr Ozier's eyebrows raised. He nodded.

"That will probably work. We've started an IV to keep his body hydrated and nourished."

"How long do you expect him to be unconscious?"

Dr Ozier always dreaded that question in coma cases. Who knew?

"I've seen people in his condition wake up in a few hours. I've heard of people going months or even years and then waking up. Some never wake up. I can't give you a definitive answer."

Leviathan stood up.

"You have my number. I'll be staying at Mr Pekt's house until he returns. Here is $20,000. I'll be in touch."

Leviathan dropped the money on his desk and departed. In front of the hospital, he looked around wondering if cabs came to this area often. Probably never. He went around the hospital towards the parking lot. People were everywhere. He finally had to walk into the woods. Then he went between.

He arrived at Aspekt's house. Something was wrong. He could smell incense. He cautiously walked towards the living room. There were two immense men.

Almost seven feet tall each. Three hundred plus pounds each. Leviathan had never seen men of their size. Their dark skin gleamed with oil. They wore sandals. A kind of loincloth. No shirts. Gold bands around their biceps. Egyptian headdresses like the pharaoh's wore. He realised who it was before he saw her sitting in a huge chair that Leviathan didn't remember seeing before he left for the hospital.

"Nefernefernefer, it is always a pleasure to see you. To what do I owe the honour of this visit?"

Nefernefernefer was the oldest Necromancer that had ever lived. Nobody knew for sure how old she was. She looked like she was barely into her forties. Her beauty hadn't faded even one iota. She batted her eyelashes at Leviathan and smiled.

"Well, I just wanted to make sure that our plans were proceeding. Aspekt was worried."

Her gaze went from playful to frightening so quickly that Leviathan felt a shudder go through his body. Her guards were glaring at him. His mouth went dry.

"Madam, I am doing everything according to Aspekt's instructions."

He paused. Collected himself and continued with more confidence.

"Markmor is in the hospital under Dr Ozier's care as per Aspekt's orders. I was going to contact him once I settled in. With you here, however, I guess that won't be necessary."

She wasn't looking at him like a spider anymore. Her guards were emotionless in their gaze.

"Please consider me your servant Nefernefernefer. If there is anything you want or desire, I will do it."

This statement mollified her. She looked at him smiling. Almost with respect.

"Aspekt said you were smart. I thank you for your offer. We'll be leaving now. Keep Aspekt informed."

Then with a pop that rattled the windows, the living room was empty. Leviathan let out a long breath and sat down on the sofa. He could still smell the incense. To his right, he could see an imprint of the huge feet of one of her guards in the carpet.

"Markmor, wake the hell up. Soon."

Then he got up in search of something to drink.

Nefernefernefer could dwell in the plane of the dead for hours on end. She was with Aspekt. They were conditioning Lydia. A normal soul would cross over without looking back. Not so Lydia. She looked for the Necromancer that had gotten her killed. Necromancers by definition communed with the dead. A dead Necromancer was more powerful in that plane than a living one.

A dead Mage, however, found that their powers in Plane 1 didn't cross over with them. She knew to look and not follow the stream of souls passing through. When she found Aspekt, she wished she had gone with the others. Now, she couldn't. He had anchored her. Ethan's body hadn't died yet. Ethan had crossed over anyway. His body was a shell waiting to be filled. Lydia had no desire to inhabit it. But, like it or not, Aspekt along with Nefernefernefer had chained her to it.

Hidden behind his closed eyelids, Lydia waited for Myron to rouse his brother. She pleaded with Nefernefernefer one last time.

"Please release me. I don't want to do this. Isn't it enough that I died trying to fulfil your plans?"

Nefernefernefer's ethereal body swirled around her like a swarm of insects. Then it appeared in front of her. Whole, beautiful. Her eyes were the most terrifying thing Lydia had ever seen. Nefernefernefer's form moved closer.

"Why would failing me be enough?"

Chapter 68

Morgaine was lying in bed thinking about the way Nikodemus smelled. Agent Charles Bone was wrapped around her little finger. The FBI was on board. She was bored. She was in his studio apartment in south Fort Worth. It was small. It was clean and neat at least. The man did have that going for him. He seemed content but on edge.

"You know, you don't have to stay with me."

She hadn't noticed that he was standing in the doorway. Watching her. She looked at him curiously.

"What do you mean? Don't you want me here?"

Bone came into the room and sat down on his bureau. He was smiling.

"You are beautiful beyond belief, woman. You are also out of my league. That day with you and Yvette and Yvonne…"

Bone closed his eyes and sighed contentedly.

"I was in a rut. The shit with my ex. You knew. All of you knew. You helped me back to where I feel alive again."

He got up and sat down next to her.

"I also know that you aren't going to be mine exclusively. Or maybe I've fulfilled my purpose."

Morgaine knitted her brows together.

"Now wait a minute buster…"

Bone interrupted her.

"That came out wrong. Anyway I enjoy your company immensely. I can also tell you are bored out of your mind."

Morgaine smiled at that. This guy really seemed to care what she was thinking.

"Look, you call me. I'll move heaven and earth for you. I'll kill for you. Period. You are your own woman, though. You can go wherever you want, with whoever you want."

He leaned over and kissed her gently.

"But I won't be mad if you need to leave. I'm going to the gym in an hour or two. You know where to find me."

Morgaine stood up.

"Charles, you are the first man who ever seemed to care what I was thinking. You're right. But, I think you're something special. You've got my amulet. I do need to take care of some things. Be careful, sugar."

She kissed him lightly on the lips and went between. Bone could still smell her hair. He smiled and went into the kitchen.

Chapter 69

"There's been weird, unexplained things going on lately, William. Social media is blowing up with videos. Something happened in the Stockyards that had the FBI barricade all of it off for almost ten hours."

Martin McBride owned TV stations. Plural. He thought of himself as kind of an information broker to the masses. News organisations that broadcast on stations he owned were all clamouring to tell the world something crazy. Magic is real. Magicians do battle on the streets of the Stockyards.

"Videos from 'Trees' on two different occasions show impossible things."

"Don't forget Marty, there are two dead skinheads in the morgue to back up the second incident…"

William McBride was Martin's nephew. The son of his favourite sister Stella. He was a personal assistant/driver/hatchet man. Martin wanted somebody hired or fired. Call William. If he wanted a burger or a gun or anything, he called William. Martin pursed his lips and looked at William.

"Are you saying you believe this stuff?"

William smiled at him.

"Doesn't matter what I believe. What do you believe? Videos from five or six different people from different perspectives all show the same thing. Some of your sources regarding the Stockyards thing are cops. They can't all be lying. Telling the same exact lie? Can they?"

"No, I suppose not. Wayne Elliot knocked out by a fifty-something guy who just touched him? Have you talked to Wayne yet?"

William pulled out his phone. He pulled up something and then put it back in his pocket.

"Not yet. Supposed to buy him dinner tomorrow night. You, of course, are welcome to join us."

Martin shook his head in the negative. William knew his answer before he offered the invitation. But there were formalities to follow.

"We're eating at Nina's if you change your mind. Eight o'clock. I'm getting ready to go to Channel 4 and get some footage Susan Simpson came up with. Gene Terrell says you'll want to see it."

Martin looked up at William.

"He did, did he? Bring it out to the house then. I guess its movie night."

William nodded and went out the door. Martin listened to the outside door close. A car door close. Engine start up. He looked out the window and saw the back of William's green Maserati as it went out the gates of the Country Club. He looked around the cabana before he went to the bedroom.

Martin was sixty years old. Five feet nine, two hundred eighty pounds and losing his hair. The two twenty-something brunettes on his bed saw past all that. He looked green to them. They smiled. He smiled wider. Then he closed the door behind him.

Chapter 70

"So you're telling me that you found him. Then lost him. Oh, and that you can't do anything else at the moment."

Curtis Vieth was in Nelson Draft's office. He wasn't happy. Greg Connor was sitting to the side of Nelson's desk. Curtis looked at him.

"Greg, what gives? I thought you were going to catch him with the honeypot. Wayne Elliot was in on it. And, I fucking used up my last FBI favour for you!"

Curtis' screamed the last sentence in case Greg didn't hear him.

"That, my friend, was more valuable than the quarter mil I've paid your firm so far. I want my pound of flesh. I want that fuck, Markmor."

Greg interrupted Nelson as he was about to speak.

"Curtis, do you ever go on social media?"

His calmness made Curtis lose the wild-eyed look a little.

"No."

"Well, you have a computer I know. I'd say have your daughter help, but she'll recognise him. That might not be for the best. Anyway get on Facebook and enter 'Stockyards Magic Show.' You'll see Markmor. Then you'll understand what our problem is."

Lori had come in. She had heard Curtis scream. She sat next to him and patted his knee. Curtis got all dreamy-eyed looking at her.

"Curtis."

Her voice was like liquid honey. No man could resist the tone she was using. Nelson and Greg grinned, but Curtis didn't even notice. He was acutely aware of how far up his thigh her hand was resting, though.

"Come on with me, and I'll show you the videos. There's some with me and Charlie trying to get that son of a bitch."

"Darlin, I'd follow you to hell."

He looked at Nelson.

"This isn't over."

Then back to Lori. All bedroom eyes.

"Lead the way beautiful."

Lori and Curtis got up and left Nelson's office. Greg shook his head.

"Nelson, he's not going to be satisfied until he buries Markmor behind his house. You know that."

"Yeah, I know. Who knows, maybe he'll get to."

Chapter 71

DHS Officer Mark Dudley entered Agent Bone's office and handed him a folder.

"We didn't shoot a 105-mm sabot round at him. We shot it for him to copy. Specifically for that purpose."

Dudley paused until Bone looked up at him.

"Two years ago."

"So you're saying US Military knew about this stuff two years ago and didn't tell anyone?"

Dudley said nothing.

"If they fired it specifically for him to copy, then, what happened?"

Dudley leaned back and looked at Bone's commendations on the wall.

"That report is so redacted that the grammar and punctuation look like a fourth grader wrote it."

"Well, do you know anything about the details? How did you find out what you did?"

Dudley looked back at Bone and shook his head.

"That's the weird part. They hand me this report that reads like a mad lib without the answers drawn in."

Bone chuckles at this.

"Then, remember I'm sitting in the classified records perusal room at the pentagon, this woman walks in and sits down next to me."

Bone smirked.

"Let me guess, she had long flowing red hair."

Dudley was astonished. You could see it in his face and hear it in his voice.

"How the hell would you know that?"

"Let's just call it a lucky guess. Please continue."

Dudley was still staring at Bone strangely, but he continued.

"So she tells me that the information I'm looking for has been redacted from every official report. Then she says, 'You're asking about the 105-mm sabot round, right?'"

Dudley gets up and is walking around the office getting a little worked up as he tells the story.

"So I say, 'Well yes.' So she says, 'Nikodemus needed a large round to copy and use on…well, whoever he needed it for.' So a C-130 with rack-mounted howitzers fired a round on coordinates supplied to them. They fired; there was no visible impact. End of story."

Dudley stopped pacing and sit back down.

"Then she walks out without another word. I get up to follow her and almost run over the clerk who got me the file I had. The redhead was gone."

Bone was thinking about how to handle this. He had after all sent Dudley to find out. But, now…

"Are you aware that Nikodemus is now an FBI agent?"

"What?"

"So you know his real identity?"

"We do."

"Who is he?"

"Nick Demus, FBI. Agent Bill Smith is his partner."

Dudley was looking at Bone wondering what had changed. Bone didn't seem too hot to pursue the subject anymore.

"So the matter is closed?"

"Indeed it is Agent Dudley. Thank you for your efforts."

Epilogue

Nikodemus had an emergency bolthole. It had been a submarine refuel and repair pen at the end of World War II. It was in the South Pacific. Only he knew where. Well, he, Yvette, Yvonne, and Morgaine. He had shipped a generator there and eventually photovoltaic solar panels. The generator rarely ran now. The solar panels took care of most of their needs. The submarine pen was accessible by water at low tide only. Inside he had a large pontoon cabin sailboat. He also had an old Chris-Craft that didn't run.

No matter. When he left Myron, he found all three women sunning themselves topless on his little beach. They turned at the sound of his arrival and ran to him. Markmor, Aspekt, and Leviathan. The sound of the waves pushed thoughts of them further back into his mind. The sun was touching the horizon, turning the world orange and gold. Yvette and Yvonne watched as Nikodemus took off his clothes and ran into the breakers.

CPSIA information can be obtained
at www.ICGtesting.com
Printed in the USA
BVHW041117131221
623919BV00007B/177